PRESUMED
DEAD

HUGH HOLTON

PRESUMED DEAD

A TOM DOHERTY ASSOCIATES BOOK
NEW YORK

PRESUMED DEAD

This book is printed on acid-free paper.

A Forge Book
Published by Tom Doherty Associates, Inc.
175 Fifth Avenue
New York, N.Y. 10010

Library of Congress Cataloging-in-Publication Data
Holton, Hugh.
     Presumed dead / Hugh Holton.
        p. cm.
     "A Tom Doherty Associates book."
     ISBN 0-312-85710-1
     1. Police—Illinois—Chicago—Fiction. 2. Chicago (Ill.)—
Fiction. I. Title.
     PS3558.O4373P73   1994
     813'.54—dc20   94-2174
                                           CIP

First edition: July 1994

Printed in the United States of America

0 9 8 7 6 5 4 3 2 1

This book is dedicated to my mother, Mrs. Frances Holton, my father, Commander Hubert Holton, Sr., retired, and all the men and women of the Chicago Police Department, which is the best police department in the world.

ACKNOWLEDGMENTS

There are so many people I would like to thank that it would probably take as many pages as are contained in the PRESUMED DEAD manuscript to do so. However, there are a few who must be mentioned. Foremost among these is Barbara D'Amato, whose patient instruction and encouragement kept me writing. Then there is my agent, Susan Gleason, who took on a new client during a very tough time for the publishing industry. Finally, a very special thanks to Robert Gleason and all the great people at Tor.

Hugh Holton
Chicago, Illinois
September 1993

Cast of Characters

THE POLICE
Commander Larry Cole
Sergeant Manny Sherlock
Acting Detective Edna Gray
Lieutenant Blackie Silvestri
Detective Judy Daniels
Chief of Detectives Jack Govich
First Deputy Superintendent Terry Kennedy

CITY OFFICIALS AND CORPORATE TYPES
Seymour Winbush —
Chairman of the Board,
the DeWitt Corporation

Harry McElroy —
former President of the
McElroy Lakefront Development Company

Bill McElroy —
current President of the
McElroy Lakefront Development Company

Edward Graham Luckett —
City of Chicago
Director of Public Safety

THE NATIONAL SCIENCE AND SPACE MUSEUM
Eurydice Vaughn — Curator
Winston Fleisher — Chairman
Homer
The Mistress

PROLOGUE

July 1, 1901

Katherine Rotheimer studied her embryo lab specimens through the small, German-made microscope her father had given her for Christmas. A frown twisted her features. Each of them was dying: the butterflies, the mice, even the worms. And she didn't understand why. Breeding livestock was a common practice, as was the cross-fertilization of certain grains and plants. Why had her experiments failed?

Katherine straightened up from her labors. Her back was stiff and she was developing a headache from squinting into the microscope's lens. Someone needed to make a magnifier, she mused, that would enable one to see specimens with the same ease as opening a book. It was something she would mention to Jim.

She thought of him as she walked across the wooden boards of the first floor of the lab. The two-story, red-brick structure was located on the south side of Chicago, behind the building left over from the Colombian Exposition that now housed the horrid History Museum. The land behind the Museum belonged to her father, Ezra Rotheimer. Someday he would be the richest man in all of Chicago. The thought made her smile.

She pumped water into the porcelain bowl under the mirror against the lakeside wall of the laboratory. Unfastening the neck and sleeves of her blouse, she used a rose-scented bar of soap to wash her face, arms and neck. The frustration of her failed experiments receded.

She recrossed the laboratory, with all of its slides, bunsen burners, surgical equipment, and even a large icebox for storing small cadavers. She could hear Jim's footsteps upstairs. He was testing another experimental weapon for her father. Some type of security device.

Katherine stared at the ceiling. She could feel him moving around up there, so very intent on his work. He could work nonstop for hours, sometimes for days, without sleeping or even eating, and never show any ill effects.

She decided to join him.

Jim Cross had designed and set up the catapults to operate on the island behind the lab. At the signal, they would launch their projectiles toward the moving targets and strike at any location he designated.

He heard Kathy coming up the steps. He smiled. He could test the device later. In fact, after the sun went down.

He heard Kathy reach the top step. He turned from his work and folded massive forearms across his large chest. "You lost, little lady? The only people up here are us warmongering opportunists."

She stared back at him. In the afternoon heat, he had been working without his shirt. Now his bare upper body glistened with sweat, making every sinew stand out with startling definition. His pectoral muscles were the size of dinner plates.

"My experiments were a failure, Jim," she said in a soft voice. She turned to the window that faced north behind her. Through the glass she could see the back of the History Museum. She pulled the shade.

"I'm sorry, Kathy," he said sincerely. He knew how hard she'd tried, even though what she had been attempting was unnatural.

She walked toward him. Unlike her lab downstairs, his was more of a mechanic's or blacksmith's workshop, and Jim Cross had the body for either occupation. A body made to satisfy a young woman.

"Are the doors downstairs locked?" he asked as she stepped to within arm's length of him.

"Yessir."

"We'd better dim the lights."

"I like it better with them on."

He dozed off. When he awoke, the summer sun was low in the west and he was alone on the pallet they had assembled for their secret lovemaking. He sat up and looked around the second floor. Kathy was nowhere in sight.

He could still feel her with him. Her scent was in his nostrils, her taste in his mouth. He dropped back on the starched sheets she'd stolen from the mansion to construct their love nest with. The sheets had been here only a day or two, but she was so clean. She had probably gone down to the pond to wash before—

Jim Cross leaped to his feet, feeling his heart race to a jackhammer pace with fear. To reach the pond, she would cross the bridge onto the island. She could trip the wire signal that caused the weapon to launch.

He snatched on his pants, ignoring his shoes, socks and shirt. He ran as fast as he could to the back door. He leaped from the balcony to the ground, twenty-five feet below, rolled over on the grass, came up on his feet and raced off toward the island behind the laboratory. There was no one else in sight.

Katherine Rotheimer wore only her skirt and a blouse as she trod barefoot toward the bridge leading across the small stream onto the island. The pond was down the second path to the right. She carried a towel with her. At the pond's edge, she planned to strip naked and bathe. The water would be delightfully cold and after the steam of their passion back at the lab, she needed cooling off. She wondered if this was a bad, unladylike thought. Mrs. Fitzwalters, her governess and tutor, had always taught her that sex was strictly for procreation, not for enjoyment. Once she'd said that righteous, God-fearing women didn't enjoy sex at all. That they engaged in such loathsome acts only to please their husbands.

As Kathy bounced across the wooden bridge, she laughed. She wondered what Mrs. Fitzwalters would have said if she'd seen her and Jim about thirty minutes ago. Would have probably given the old spinster a seizure.

Again Kathy laughed. This time louder. Then she stopped. Her laughter died among the tall trees shrouding the island like the naves of a huge cathedral. Generally, she never felt this apprehensive when coming out here. Even alone at dusk. But something was different than the way she remembered it before. Something about this place had changed.

She took a couple of steps and listened. There were sounds out there. Crickets, birds and even the hum of flying insects could be heard. Everything at least sounded the same. She started forward again, at first slowly and then faster, until she had once again resumed her former jaunty pace.

The island belonged to her. Well, at least it belonged to her father. He also owned the woodland behind the History Museum, all the way to the cemetery wall, nearly two miles away. It was private land, but lately trespassers had been sneaking out here. Kids to play, men to fish, and men and women to do the same thing that she and Jim Cross had just done in the privacy of the lab. Jim had been working on something to keep the place secure. She hadn't given him a chance to tell her what it was. Well, he could tell her after she got back from her bath.

Suddenly she stopped again. She had advanced about an eighth of a mile onto the island. Supposing one of the trespassers was out here now? she asked herself. Maybe one of those men Daddy told her to watch out for.

As thoughts of skinny-dipping evaporated from her mind, she heard her name called. It came from the direction of the lab. Someone was calling to her.

"Kathy! Kathy, wait! Stop!"

She smiled. It was Jim. With him accompanying her, she'd skinny-dip at the public beach over on the lakeshore. She'd wait right here for him. She spread her towel on the grass beside the path and was just about to sit down on it when she heard the whistling noise. She'd never heard anything like it before. And it was coming closer.

If nothing is heard from the missing
person for over seven years . . . they are listed
as "Missing: Presumed Dead."

—E. Gray

1

SEPTEMBER 16, 1997
8:00 P.M.

Carl "the Razor" Robinson sat in his South Lake Shore Drive apartment and stared at the wall. The surface was painted a flat, off-white shade, but the Razor was not aware of it. In the last hour he had snorted two ounces of cocaine and was now so high that his brain was as blank as the off-white wall.

He didn't hear the phone ring even though the instrument was less than five feet away from him. Melva, his lady, unwound herself from the couch where she had been watching *Tales of the Strange and Unexpected* on a cable television channel. She was a tall girl with good features and a stunning body. In the apartment, when they were alone, she wore little in the way of clothing. Now she was clad in only a see-through black nightgown. The display was wasted on the Razor.

Before she picked up the phone, she looked at him. He was skinny, but he dressed nice, wore lots of expensive jewelry, drove expensive cars and had money to burn. She knew that he ran the Black Gangster Disciples street gang and sold drugs for a living, but she didn't care. At the age of twenty-three, Melva had many times before been with men who made their money on the wrong side of the law. In fact, she liked it. Gave spice to life. Even danger. They had what she needed and she gave them what they wanted in return. A fair arrangement. But of one thing she was certain: She wasn't going to end up in a stinking public-housing project with a bunch of kids and a welfare check like her mother had. She'd rather die first.

The Razor still hadn't moved to pick up the phone. The ringing was getting on Melva's nerves, reminding her that it would soon be time for her to shoot up again. But she didn't do cocaine like the

Razor did. She rode the white horse. Heroin. Her habit cost a hundred and fifty dollars a day, another reason she needed rich men.

She lifted the receiver. "Hello?"

"*Lemme speak to the Razor*," the male, Spanish-accented voice said.

"Who wants him?"

"*None of your business, bitch! Now put the goddamned Razor on right now!*"

Melva was about to slam the receiver down when the Razor came out of his drug trance. His hand snaked toward her, palm up. He didn't turn to look at her. She handed him the telephone.

"Yeah." His voice was low and husky when he spoke.

"*My main man! What's happening? We gonna meet and talk business tonight or what?*"

The Razor nodded his head. "Tonight's good."

"*Like they used to say in them old gangster movies, pick some-place nice and neutral, Bro.*"

The Razor looked around his apartment. His red-rimmed, half-mast eyes took in the barren, but expensive furnishings Melva had let some mouthy Michigan Avenue salesman foist off on her for fifty grand. The floor-to-ceiling windows displayed a breathtaking view to the north of Lake Shore Drive and the skyscrapers of the Loop seven miles away. But the view was wasted on the Razor. He was trying to get his drugged brain cells to come up with a place to meet with the Hispanic. Someplace neutral.

"*Hey, Razor, my man, you there?*"

The wide-screen television Melva had been watching was still on. The Razor's eyes flicked over it in his initial scan of the room, but he hadn't noticed what was on. Now he swung back to it.

There was a picture of a wooden bridge across a small stream. On the other side of the bridge was a dirt path leading through a stand of trees.

"*This is Seagull Island in Chicago,*" an off-screen announcer said. "*It is a short distance from the National Science and Space Museum, which is visited every year by millions of tourists. But few people ever visit Seagull Island during the day, and especially not at night, because the island is rumored to be haunted.*"

The Hispanic was talking again, but the Razor had his entire attention focused on the television set.

"For nearly a century, Seagull Island, or as some call it, Haunted Island, has been the location of a number of strange and inexplicable disappearances. A few of these disappearances have reportedly occurred in broad daylight; many after dark."

"A beautiful, almost idyllic setting—" the commentator, a portly, balding man in a business suit, appeared on the screen walking at the middle of the island *"—at the center of one of the largest cities in America, now few venture out here at any time and no one ever comes here at night. At least no one in recent memory who has returned to tell the tale."*

The Hispanic was fast reaching the end of his patience. He screamed obscenities across the phone line so loud that Melva, still standing near the Razor, could hear them. For his part, the Razor, the receiver flush against his ear, seemed totally unaffected.

"You know where the National Science Museum is?" the Razor asked.

"Yeah, man, I even been there," the Hispanic spat over the phone.

"Well, you ever been behind the Museum? Place called Seagull Island? Maybe you heard it called by a different name, like Haunted Island."

There was silence from the other end.

"You still there, Bro?" The Razor put a sarcastic lilt on the "Bro."

"Yeah, I'm here, man." The phony machismo dripped off every word. *"Fuck you and this Haunted Island, Razor, but we gonna be there, man. You can bet your ass, we gonna be there!"*

"I'll be there too, my friend. At midnight. And one more thing. Just you and me going out onto that island, Pancho. After all, this is supposed to be a peace conference, right? We won't need any muscle to just talk. But if there is something out there that shouldn't be, you can count on the Razor to protect his little spic buddy."

The Razor hung up on the obscenity the Hispanic screamed over the phone.

2

The National Science and Space Museum was located on twenty acres of parkland south of Fifty-seventh Street on Chicago's lakefront. Constructed of limestone and marble blocks in a Modern Greek architectural style, the Museum buildings took up nearly a million square feet. There were over a hundred exhibit halls and five thousand exhibits demonstrating the most advanced scientific and technological advances achieved by man on Planet Earth from the dawn of time to the eve of the birth of the twenty-first century. Over a third of the Museum's displays were devoted to aeronautics and space technology. A domed theater, on the ceiling of which a projection of the Milky Way could be shown, along with space shuttle, jet fighter and commercial airline in-flight simulations, had been constructed at the western end of the Museum and was connected internally to the main buildings.

Attempts were made to obtain the actual items used to make history or to achieve the milestones in human development being heralded. As such, the Museum possessed one of the Explorer shuttle crafts donated by NASA; a fighter jet used in the 1991 Desert Storm War in the Persian Gulf; a British light cruiser that had seen action in the North Atlantic during World War II; and numerous space suits, military uniforms, timepieces, weapons and other memorabilia—all of which had had some impact on the advancement of science or space exploration.

The Museum charged a nominal fee for entry and was financially self-sufficient, resting on parkland bequeathed by its famed founder, Ezra Rotheimer, in 1906. A picture of the heavily sideburned, bushy-mustached Rotheimer graced the main portico of the central building.

A black-and-white 8½-by-11-inch photo, it was secured in an alarmed plastic case. Only the founder's name and dates of birth and death were written on the small card beneath the picture. During the earlier days of the Museum's existence, larger portraits of Rotheimer, one of them an oil painting, had been displayed. Inexplicably, each had vanished, forcing the curators to adopt the smaller, easier-to-secure display.

The National Science and Space Museum was one of the gems of the city. It was mentioned prominently in every guidebook on Chicago printed since the end of the First World War.

A twenty-four-hour-a-day, seven-day-a-week police detail of six officers from the Chicago Police Department was provided by the city for the Museum buildings and parking lots. The area of the park directly behind the Museum was another story. The police seldom ventured into the woods there unless there was a call for them to do so. There were rarely any calls during the day. There were never any at night.

The patrol car assigned to cover the exterior of the Museum and its parking lots had gone on duty at 11:00 P.M., or 2300 hours military time. Two officers, Peggy Warren and Dane McGuire, were assigned to the beat, designated as 331Adam, or 331A. Warren, with five years on the force, had nine semester hours to go before obtaining her bachelor's degree in accounting. Then she planned to use her education and police experience to apply for the FBI. McGuire was a sixteen-year veteran and a recovering alcoholic. He hadn't had a drink in three years. He was afraid that if he went back to normal patrol work, the stresses and strains of the job, along with the camaraderie of his fellow cops, would force him off the wagon. He was certain that if this occurred, it would kill him. He was fortunate to have an understanding commander.

Warren usually drove for the first four hours of their midnight tour, McGuire for the last four. The work was tedious, routine and often boring. No one had attempted to break into the Museum in over twelve years. There was a strange story going around about that too. Possibly no more than a legend.

As Warren and McGuire pulled their squad car from in front of the darkened Theater of the Future, it was 2327 hours.

"I think we should have a look back there tonight, Dane," Peggy, a Sandy Duncan twin, said.

Dane was a middle-aged black man with an easy smile and a shy manner. That is, when he wasn't drinking. Alcohol to him was like Dr. Jekyll's formula for turning into Mr. Hyde. "Why?" he asked her flatly. "There was nothing back there. No one ever goes back there at night. The island's supposed to be haunted."

She shot him a sideways glance. "So you saw *Tales of the Strange and Unexpected* too? What did you think?"

"I didn't think nothing, Peggy, except that some TV exec has latched onto a surefire way to sell more high-priced advertising to a lot of gullible people."

"So now I'm gullible."

He turned to look at her profile. Her cheeks were flushed, but he didn't argue. He'd had more than his share of arguments during his drinking years.

"What's the matter with you, Peg? You that anxious to see a ghost?"

"I don't believe in ghosts any more than you do. I just think I saw something . . . I mean, uh, somebody walking across that bridge last night. It looked like a woman, but we were too far away to tell."

"I didn't see anything."

"You were half-asleep, Dane. You wouldn't have seen the superintendent if he'd knocked on the window."

"Yeah," Dane agreed, "but, Officer Warren, if you plan to investigate your spectral figure on the island tonight, you can take me back to the command post first. I've seen enough ghosts in my time to last me to the grave."

"I thought partners were supposed to do everything together."

"Not dumb shit like ghost-hunting. Haven't you heard the stories some of the old-timers tell?"

"Oh, c'mon now, Dane! You don't really believe all that crap's been said about this place?"

He was quiet for a moment. "I been around this district since I was a rookie. I've seen things that aren't covered in General Orders or at roll calls. Chalk them up to 'weird shit' and I never chase after anything I'm not dead certain of."

"You mean like whether it's human or not?"

"Let's make our first check and forget things that go bump in the night."

"Killjoy," she said, heading for the floodlit space shuttle parked on the northeast side of the Museum.

"331Adam." The dispatcher's voice crackled over their portable radios.

Dane acknowledged.

"Return to the command post a.s.a.p."

"10-4," Dane acknowledged.

Without comment, Peggy made a U turn in a vacant parking lot in front of the Museum and started back along the route they had just traveled.

Lieutenant Strickland, their station watch commander, and Sergeant Johnson, their sector supervisor, were waiting for them in the security office inside the west wing of the Museum. The other four officers assigned to the first watch detail were also there. Having a watch commander, especially Strickland, on the scene was an unprecedented event.

Strickland was an overweight, humorless man with a pissed-off-at-the-world expression. His temper was at the meltdown point. "Organized Crime has an operation going down near the Museum tonight, so all of you people are restricted to inside duty until it's over."

"What kind of operation, sir?" Edna Gray, the other female on the detail, asked him.

His frown deepened. He didn't like questions, especially from female cops. "It doesn't concern you or us whatever goes down, Gray. But I heard a couple of big-time dope dealers are involved. Show's being run by Commander Cole from Organized Crime."

The cops exchanged glances. Everyone had heard of Larry Cole.

"You said 'around the Museum,' Lieutenant." Peggy chanced a question. "Do you have any idea where?"

"Yeah, Seagull Island, out back. The one on the television show earlier. The one they call Haunted Island."

"What's Cole looking to bag, Boss?" a sarcastic cop named Anderson asked. "A ghost?"

"I don't know and neither will you," Strickland barked. "Make me happy and stay out of Organized Crime's way."

Peggy Warren started to say something about what she'd seen crossing the bridge onto the island last night, but a look from Dane McGuire stopped her. Later, she would regret the omission.

3

SEPTEMBER 16, 1997
11:35 P.M.

The Leamington Hotel, located on Fifty-sixth Street, overlooked the National Science and Space Museum and the surrounding park. Built in 1930 in the style of other grand hotels in the city, such as the Palmer House and the Stevenson downtown, the Leamington was known for its stately elegance and outstanding service. A number of the aging, wealthy members of Hyde Park and South Shore families now used the Leamington as a retirement home.

The accommodations for the most part consisted of spacious suites, each with a living room, a dining room and bedrooms. To cater to the modern jet set, individual rooms on the lower floors, originally reserved for the personal servants of guests, were made available to the public. Of course, in order to stay even a single night at the Leamington, a prospective guest had to have either a recommendation from a recognized and respected former patron or make application directly to the Leamington by filling out a lengthy questionnaire. After all, the independently owned and operated hotel did not want to be considered a glorified Holiday Inn.

At eleven-thirty on the sixteenth of September, Commander Larry Cole of the Organized Crime Division was in Suite 903 of the ten-story building staring through a pair of high-powered military binoculars at the floodlit Museum. The space shuttle, the Theater of the Future and all the other external exhibits were in full view. The wooded area behind the Museum, where the so-called Haunted Island was located, was dark.

Cole was uninterested in the island, at this point anyway. He instead concentrated on the access routes to the area. From his vantage point, he could see eighty percent of them: the inner drives around the Museum, the parkways and the city streets leading into the park from the north and west. The area beyond his field of vision was being monitored by Lieutenant Blackie Silvestri and his crew in a mobile surveillance van.

For this operation, Cole had pulled out all the stops and had called in every officer assigned to his section of the Organized Crime Division. Fifty-five cops ringed the Museum, the park and the so-called Haunted Island, waiting for the mouse—or rather, the mice— to spring the trap.

Cole, a tall, muscular black man with well-defined features, stepped away from the binoculars and looked out through the window at the scene below. The ninth-floor suite had been turned into a command post. Sergeant Manny Sherlock, whose glasses and scholarly manner made him look more like a college professor than a cop, was coordinating communications between the CP and the field units. Everthing was ready. Ready for Carl "the Razor" Robinson and Matteo "Pancho" Martinez to show up. The cops had learned of the impending peace conference between the two notorious dope dealers by way of a court-ordered wire tap on Martinez's phone.

Cole watched Sherlock dart around the room. His excitement was obvious. Cole had not seen Manny like this in months. In fact, the commander felt a bit anxious himself. He took a moment to check the Organized Crime people in the room with him. Unlike Manny, Blackie and Judy, whom he had brought with him from the Detective Division, he had inherited the five cops in the suite with him now. Pretty good people all in all, Cole figured, but a couple of them looked nervous. They were not used to Larry Cole as their commander. A year ago, he hadn't been assigned to Organized Crime. He had been doing something different. A year ago, he had been a completely different person.

Cole turned back to the view of the Museum below. His mind drifted back to the past. A lot had happened to him since then.

It was the beginning of his third year as a deputy chief assigned to the Detective Division under Chief of Detectives Jack Govich. There were three deputy chiefs in the division and Cole was the administrator of the CPD's investigative arm.

It had also been a year ago that the Iron Maiden resigned, leaving the post of superintendent open. Cole didn't even think about applying for the job until he received a call in late September from Edward Graham Luckett, the rotund director of Public Safety.

Judy Daniels took the call and buzzed Cole on the intercom. *"Boss, the secretary of the director of Public Safety is on line three for you."*

Cole had been reviewing the revision in the Gang Intimidation and Anti-Stalking Statutes prior to preparing a directive for the Detective Division. He'd never had any personal dealings with Luckett, whose authority extended over the Police, Fire, and Streets and Sanitation departments, but he knew of him. Cole picked up the phone and punched the button over line three.

"Deputy Chief Cole," a woman's voice said, *"please hold for the director."*

A moment later a deep voice, with breathing containing a noticeable wheeze, came over the line. *"Deputy Chief Cole, this is E. G. Luckett. I wonder if you have time this afternoon to come by my office?"*

Cole didn't ask why. Luckett was one of his superiors.

"What time would you like me there, Director?"

They settled on three o'clock. Cole arrived ten minutes early.

Luckett's inner office was an antique monument to the past, with lots of wood paneling, old desks and even a couple of coat trees. Cole sat across from the four-hundred-pound Luckett, who, despite some obvious breathing difficulties, was smoking a cigarette.

"I'm glad you could stop by, Deputy Chief Cole," Luckett said. "I've heard so much about you that it's a real honor to finally meet you in the flesh."

Cole smiled his thanks, but said nothing. He waited for Luckett to get to the point.

"I've been talking to the mayor and he feels the same way I do. We think it's about time the department had someone in charge whom the rank and file can look up to. A hero cop, so to speak."

Cole maintained his silence.

"I think you'll be an excellent choice for superintendent," Luckett concluded, "once you meet the right people."

At that moment, the world stopped for Cole. Things seemed brighter, colors more vivid, and sound possessed greater clarity. It was as if he was sitting on top of the world. He didn't yet know that the entire thing was a setup.

Back on the ninth floor of the Leamington Hotel, overlooking the National Science and Space Museum, Cole continued his surveillance of the Museum below.

"Boss!" Sherlock said. "Blackie reports activity on Sixty-third Street off of Lake Shore Drive."

Cole left the window and walked over to Sherlock, who was listening intently to a small, powerful Saber portable radio. Blackie Silvestri's voice purred softly over the speaker. *"We've got a tan Mercedes with tinted windows. A black Buick's following it. Both cars just turned off LSD into the park at Sixty-third. They've stopped at the service road. A guy's getting out of the Buick and trotting up to the Mercedes."*

"Let me talk to him," Cole said to Sherlock. The sergeant handed over the radio. "Can you get a plate number on the Mercedes, Blackie?"

"Negative, Boss. The Buick's got our view blocked. I was able to run the tail car's plate though. Comes back to 'Chicago U-Drive.' "

Cole released the key and looked at Sherlock. "Our narcotics peddlers are really turning into corporate giants. Rental cars, no less." Depressing the transmit button again, Cole asked, "What kind of make you got on the guy who got out of the Buick?"

Judy Daniels took over for Blackie. *"It's Mo Escobar, Boss. Pancho's enforcer. At least half of them are here."*

One of the Organized Crime dicks in the suite waved to Cole. "We got movement downstairs, Commander."

Still carrying the radio, Cole turned back to the binoculars. Two black vans were traveling along the Drive in front of the Museum. They slowed to make a right turn on Lake Shore Drive and passed the space shuttle, the British cruiser and the Fighter jet. The exhibits were surrounded by a twelve-foot-high cyclone fence. At the edge of the fence, the two vans bumped over the six-inch curb. Both scraped their undercarriages as they pulled into the shadows of the darkened park. They drove fifty feet across a grassy incline to a stand of trees that stretched to the stream on the north end of Seagull Island. Here they were forced to stop. Going any farther would have to be on foot.

Cole raised the radio. "What are the occupants of the Mercedes and Buick doing at your end, Blackie?"

Judy Daniels again answered for Silvestri. *"They just made a turn onto the side drive heading north. They're as illegal as hell, but we're letting them go."*

Sherlock stepped up beside Cole. Aware of the sergeant's presence, Cole said, "The Razor's going in from our end of the island, Pancho from the other end. Let's give them five minutes out there before we roll up their escorts."

Sherlock raised another walkie-talkie and began transmitting instructions to the other units on the surveillance. Cole kept his eyes glued to the binoculars.

4

Razor Robinson's nerves were in a state of hibernation from the cocaine. Melva was in the back of the second black van with him. Despite the coolness of the fall evening, she had on a dress with a split that exposed her thighs all the way up to the curvature of her buttocks. However, the Razor had carefully chosen the two Disciples seated in the rear of the van. They were, in the parlance of the gangbanging, dope-pushing trade of the Chicago streets, "Stone Killers." That is, they would kill anyone, anytime, anywhere, for anything. Razor knew they would probably rather kill Melva than make love to her. The thought would have made him laugh, but he was beyond humor. The narcotic had taken care of his emotions on the way up. On the way down, it would be a much different story.

Razor wore dark glasses and a wide-brimmed black hat with a genuine eagle feather in the band. His shirt was open to the navel, and a large gold medallion with the signs of the zodiac engraved on it was anchored around his neck. A long, black trench coat was draped around his shoulders like a cape. He raised an ebony hand from beneath the coat.

"Give me a MAC 10 and one of the nines."

The Disciple closest to him complied, retrieving the two black matte-finish weapons from a suitcase on the floor of the van.

"Don't you want no body armor, baby?" Melva asked with concern.

"Ain't goin' to no war, woman," Razor rasped. "Supposed to be a peace conference with the spic, so we can stop killing each other and start making money again."

Despite herself, Melva looked worried.

"Open the door," the Razor ordered.

The other Disciple complied.

Razor stepped to the ground. With his back to them, he said, "You D's stay cool unless you hear me open up with the MAC 10. Pancho's crazy, but he's supposed to be a man of his word."

The two gangbangers in back of the black van flashed their leader a gang salute he didn't see. Then Razor headed for the dark, wooded area behind the National Science and Space Museum. A chill went through him when he recognized the old, but still sturdy, bridge spanning the pond. A bridge Katherine Rotheimer had crossed on a summer day nearly a hundred years before.

At the opposite side of the island, Pancho Martinez started for the bridge connecting the south end of the park with the island. He experienced the same odd chill as did the man he was going to meet at the center of Haunted Island.

5

The Constellation space shuttle was on display at the northeast section of the exterior grounds of the National Science and Space Museum. The huge craft, its blunt nose aimed skyward, was illuminated by ten spotlights. It could easily be seen from not only the traffic on Lake Shore Drive, but also from the beach across the Drive. From the police command post in the Leamington Hotel, Larry Cole had observed it any number of times during his surveillance of the Museum grounds below. Every time Cole looked through the binocular lenses, the shuttle was just at the periphery of his vision. The huge bird was so obvious that Cole and all the other cops on the surveillance had taken it for granted. That is, until it moved.

Cole had been taking one final look through the binoculars before leaving the command post in Sherlock's hands. The commander was planning to go down on the street in order to be close by when they sprang the trap on the Razor, Pancho and their combined entourage. His attention was focused on the dark area on the east side of the Museum, where Razor Robinson's two black vans full of Disciples were parked. As nothing was happening there, he had just started to turn away when the shuttle emitted a flash.

Cole's head snapped back to the binoculars. The scene below was the same as before, with no unusual movement. He trained the binoculars to focus on the Constellation. The exhibit sat in silent, white-glaring splendor above the lights. Nothing around it was stirring. Except . . . Cole thought he detected movement in the moonless sky high above the shuttle. But by the time he readjusted his glasses, that area of the sky was empty. Probably, he mused, it had been that way all the time.

Cole stood up and looked over the top of the binoculars down at the shuttle. Without the magnification, it appeared no bigger than a toy airplane.

"Something wrong, Boss?" Sherlock asked, stepping up beside Cole.

Cole started to say nothing was, but as he replayed the last few seconds in his mind, he was certain that he had indeed seen something. Like a flash bulb going off. "There was a light or something out there a moment ago," he said in response to Manny's question.

The sergeant's brow furrowed. "One of our units said they saw something too. Over around the space shuttle. Said it was a strange light. They didn't say anything after the others started in on them."

"Started in on them about what?"

Manny swallowed noisily before saying, "Seeing ghosts."

Cole smiled, then turned away from his observation post. "I'm going downstairs. Alert everyone to get ready to move on the escorts."

"Ten-four, Boss," Manny said. He was about to key his mike to alert the units below when he looked down at the shuttle. An eerie feeling gripped him. Then he quickly began transmitting Cole's message.

6

SEPTEMBER 17, 1997
12:11 A.M.

Kind of spooky at night ain't it, Sarge?" Officer John Anderson, a potbellied cop with a bald cranium, asked. Anderson and his partner, Officer Edna Gray, were being accompanied on their rounds inside the Museum by their sector sergeant, Woodrow Johnson.

Night-lights were on in most of the galleries, and many of the exhibits were never completely dark, so there was ample illumination. However, there were a great many shadows. This, combined with the immense size of the place, made being alone there something most people avoided.

But Woody Johnson, a Vietnam vet, who had been involved in three shoot-outs since becoming a cop, was not the type of man who frightened easily. Broad-shouldered and with a narrow waist at the age of fifty, Johnson wore his uniform with pride and usually had an unlit cigar stuck in one corner of his mouth. His nickname around the Third District station was "the D.I.," for drill instructor. He enjoyed cultivating the image.

The sergeant had been mulling over Anderson's question. Now he replied, "I wouldn't call it spooky, Andy. Just empty."

Edna Gray giggled. Anderson liked to get unsuspecting people in the empty galleries on the midnights. Then he'd start on them with the same type of crack he'd made to Sergeant Johnson about the place being spooky. If the mark fell for it, he'd really give it to him. Start with the stories about the bizarre accidents that had delayed completion of the Museum for years; then go on to the deaths of the first four Museum curators, which occurred on the same date, each exactly five years apart; and finally, the vanishing people.

This thought drove all the humor out of her. She had been very close to the disappearance of a child in this place. So close that she'd lived with it every day of her life for the past twenty-five years.

Edna Gray was an attactive, thirty-two-year-old black woman with a light complexion and dark eyes that gave her an intriguing, exotic look. She had a good figure that she maintained religiously by a daily, hour-long aerobics routine. She was intelligent and sensitive, which, along with her looks, drew men to her like moths to a flame. But no relationship ever seemed to work long for her, which had led to two divorces and the breaking of three engagements.

She realized that the problem was not with those she became involved with, but with herself. A problem she was powerless to do anything about.

They completed the rounds and arrived back at the command post. Edna turned to Sergeant Johnson. "Do you mind if I take my lunch now, sir?"

Johnson was surprised at the request. Generally, midnight officers waited until very late in the tour to eat. Of course Gray's stomach was her business.

"All right by me, Gray," he responded. "Just pay attention to your radio in case we need you."

The shadow of a smile crossed her face as she patted her hip-holstered walkie-talkie. Crossing the CP office to her locker, she removed a paper sack and a thermos bottle. Carrying them with her, she exited the command post and headed back into the dimly lit Museum.

When they were alone, Johnson asked, "Where in hell is she going?"

Anderson was sitting behind one of the desks. Leaning back, he had his feet propped up on an open drawer. "To sit out there in the dark by herself. She's a fucking nut case, if you ask me."

Sergeant Woody Johnson turned to stare at the smart-mouthed older cop. He had never really liked Anderson, but had tolerated him. Now the sergeant's tolerance level had been exceeded. "Nobody asked you, Andy, and take your feet off the goddamned desk!"

At the sergeant's bark, Anderson jerked into an upright position. His cheeks flushed as his face froze in a self-pitying "What-in-hell-did-I-do?" look.

*   *   *

Edna Gray walked through the cavernous Museum, passing the tele-
communications and petroleum exhibits in the main gallery. She
knew the Museum so well that starting at any reference point inside,
she could have found her way around blindfolded.

After leaving the main gallery, she entered one of the smaller
exhibit areas that was honeycombed with darkened corridors and
small demonstration rooms shrouded in deep shadow. Many would
have called this place eerie. To Edna, it was like an old, familiar
house she had spent many years in. The stories about the Museum
didn't bother her. Even the things they said about the island out back.
She understood haunted places and things. She felt that she was
haunted herself.

She entered the *Glassware from Around the World* Hall. Here
every form of glass, from crystal goblets to the finest hand-painted
china, was displayed. The Museum's collection was priceless, with
items of such age and artistic delicacy that no amount of money
would ever be sufficient to either purchase or replace them.

A stone bench, purchased by Ezra Rotheimer himself from a
monastery he had visited in the Himalayan Mountains shortly before
his death, was situated at the center of the gallery. This was an exhibit
that had a practical use. It was permissible for visitors viewing the
glass displays to sit on the rough stone, which was reportedly carved
out of the side of one of the mysterious mountains over a thousand
years ago.

Edna removed her cap and nylon jacket. She carefully placed
them on the bench before sitting down and opening her lunch bag.
Inside was half a ham-and-cheese sandwich with lettuce and mayo,
a small pear and two diminutive, low-cal chocolate-chip cookies. She
unwrapped her lunch before unscrewing the thermos and pouring
iced tea into the cup. She began nibbling at the sandwich between
taking short sips of tea.

She looked around at the glass. Some of it, particularly a glass
platter with a mirrorlike surface, reflected her image back at her. The
distortion made her appear even more sad than she normally did. A
sadness that surrounded her like a burial cloth. That choked and
destroyed anyone who tried to get close to her. A malaise of melan-

cholia that infested anyone who was around her for any prolonged length of time.

This condition had been with her since she was seven years old. Before that, she had been a happy, smiling child, as photographs of her from that period revealed. But that had been before the incident with her baby sister, Josie. An incident that had occurred right in this Museum. In fact, in the very same room where she was now seated.

Edna looked over at the last place she had seen the then four-year-old. It was right in front of the case with the platter reflecting her mirrorlike image. Edna's mind took her back to that day.

Their mother had brought them to the Museum, which was an unusual thing for her to do. Mother had always been a sickly person, seldom healthy enough to do anything, and never satisfied with anyone in her life. She blamed Edna and Josie's father for everything, until finally he began seeking solace away from their small southside apartment. Solace that he found in the arms of other women and in excessive drinking.

As Edna recalled, before the incident, her mother had shown some affection for her. She would comb Edna's hair, fix her meals and make sure she had clean clothes for school. But there was little else. From what Edna was able to find out later, her mother had wanted to be a professional dancer, but could never afford the lessons she was certain would provide her with that big break. A break she knew would have propelled her to Broadway or Hollywood. When the dream did not come true, Edna's mother became bitter and turned against everyone in her world. At least until Josie came along.

Even as a baby, Josie loved to dance. When she could barely walk, she would stumble around in circles, her diaper hanging off, as she tried to keep awkward infant-time to a song playing on the radio. This had delighted their mother. Perhaps the mother now saw the possibility of fulfilling her own dreams through the child. At that point, Edna was forgotten, but she really didn't care that much, because she loved Josie too. Possibly even more than her mother did. And it was not because the baby liked to dance.

Edna placed the remains of her sandwich back in the wax paper and deposited it in the bag. She looked at the glass case again. Josie had been standing right there, wearing a little pink dress with white lace trim, a white hat and white patent-leather shoes. Edna could see her so clearly in her memories. The same exhibits that had been displayed back on that day were on display now. Everything was—

The policewoman stiffened in shock. A face was staring at her from the glass platter inside the case. A woman's face! Edna stood up and took a tentative step toward the case. Suddenly, the face vanished.

She felt her knees go weak. There had been someone there. She was certain of it. Instinct forced her hand to wrap around the grip of her revolver. But then, she rationalized, what was she going to shoot?

Cautiously, she crossed the twenty-odd feet to the display case. She didn't take her eyes off the plate for an instant. With her nose less than an inch from the glass, she stared in at the shiny platter. Her own image was reflected with startling clarity back to her. Could that be what she had seen? Her own reflection? She turned to look back at the stone bench. There was no way that what she saw could have been her reflection from way over there. But then, the face had looked like hers.

"You're cracking up, Officer Gray," she said, listening to the echo of her voice reverberate through the empty hall.

But the echo even sounded wrong. As the "Gray" softly echoed back to her, she thought she heard a voice say, "Now, Homer!" But it had been as faintly uttered as the dying echo and there was no way she could tell from which direction the sound came. That is, if she had heard it at all.

What was happening to her? Could she finally be cracking up? Her first husband, a heavy drinker just like her father, had frequently called her crazy. Maybe he was right. Maybe she just hadn't realized it herself until now.

The sound of her walkie-talkie crackling to life made her jump. It was Sergeant Johnson.

She snatched the radio out of its holster. "331David. Go ahead, Sarge."

"Get back to the CP, 331D. The Organized Crime people made their move outside and we've got shots fired behind the Museum. I want everybody on the detail at the command post in case we're needed."

"Ten ninety-nine." She responded with the code designation for a one-person unit.

She rushed over to get her jacket, cap and the remains of her lunch. As she started from the hall, she took one last look at the shining platter. Then she headed for the CP at a dead run.

7

The black vans sat immobile behind the Museum at the northeast end of Haunted Island. There were eight armed Disciples in the two vehicles: six in the lead van and two in the one with Melva. The Razor's woman was also armed, with a stainless-steel .45 automatic. They were a deadly bunch, but not very concerned about external security. A sharp wind was blowing off the lake, so they sat comfortable and warm inside behind tinted windows. All attention was directed toward the darkened area surrounding Haunted Island, onto which the Razor had vanished a few moments before. They were tense, and ready for anything except what actually happened.

A fire department light wagon, the size of a beer truck, had been quietly driven to the edge of the Museum parking lot on the opposite side of the cyclone fence from the vans. When Cole gave the signal, four banks of floodlights were illuminated, filling the park area with a blinding glare. The Disciple vans were caught at the center of this glare.

Cole's voice carried over a loudspeaker from outside the circle of light. "This is the Chicago Police Department! You are all under arrest! You are to immediately get out of the vehicles with your hands in the air!"

There was a moment of brief hesitation during which nothing moved. Then staring, frightened faces appeared at the windows of the lead van. A moment later, the side door of this van slid open and the first of six Disciples, clad in silver-and-black gang colors, stepped into the glare of the floodlights.

"Okay, you in the second van!" Cole said. "Let's see some movement out of there, people!"

On cue, the second van's engine roared to life and its backup lights flashed on. It raced in reverse, throwing up dirt and tufts of grass.

"Stop!" Cole's voice roared through the bullhorn.

The van driver ignored him. The side door opened and a burst of automatic weapons fire split the night. The gunfire was returned from ten different locations. The van was pockmarked with bullet holes as it continued going backward, to ram into a tree. The gunfire from inside stopped. The police ceased firing as well.

Cole watched the damaged vehicle for signs of movement. He was directing operations from the cover of an unmarked police car. Lowering the bullhorn, he picked up the radio. "Everyone hold your fire! Get someone over to cuff the gangbangers in the other van! The rest of you cover me! I'm going to take a look at our runaway."

Cole tossed the radio on the front seat of the squad car just as Blackie screamed over the speaker, "*Larry, don't!*"

Cole motioned for the firemen to kill the floodlights as he trotted across the grass to the van. The engine had stalled on impact with the tree, and the side door stood gaping. Cole flattened himself against the rear panel and extended his 9-millimeter Beretta at the opening. With his other hand, he yanked open the door. The twisted, bullet-riddled bodies of the Razor's lady and his Stone Killers greeted him.

Cole reached in to pull the .45 from Melva's lifeless fingers, when the distant sound of gunfire came from the island. Without hesitating, Cole ran for the bridge.

Razor Robinson's cocaine high had been erased by terror. Now he stumbled aimlessly across the darkened island, firing at shadows. Minutes earlier he had watched as Pancho Martinez was decapitated right in front of him. Then Pancho's head and body had vanished. But there had been no one there. Nothing that the Razor had been able to see that could have caused his rival's head to be snapped off at the shoulders as clean as an ax going through a chicken's neck.

Razor backed against a tall tree. His eyes searched the dark. Something was moving out there! Something coming toward him! He fired a burst from the Mac 10. He couldn't tell if he hit anything.

There was no sound out there. Pancho hadn't even had a chance to scream before he died.

Razor forced his drug-seared brain to work. He had to get out of here. Off this island. He attempted to get his bearings. Remember which direction the bridge was. Left! No, right! He stepped away from the tree and took a couple of tentative steps. Then he heard the whistling noise.

Cole pulled a Kelite from the ring on his belt as he approached the bridge. Flicking it on, he ran over the wooden planks onto the island. The six-cell flashlight threw a beam hundreds of feet into the dark, only to be swallowed up by the shadows of tall trees and the density of overgrown bushes.

He advanced, realizing for the first time that he was alone and without communications. The weight of the automatic in his hand was comforting. He had fired only four shots at the black van. That left him with fifteen in the Ramline clip. He had enough ammo to start his own war out here.

Cole heard a noise behind him. He spun around. The flashlight beam and the Beretta's luminous night sights lined up on the same thing at once. Cole's mouth went dry as he stared at the image trapped in his beam. The figure was shrouded from head to toe in a black, gauzy material. It was moving parallel to his position, but making no attempt to approach or flee. It even seemed to be floating.

"Hold it!" he warned, but the figure kept moving at the same pace. Now Cole noticed the curvature of a woman's body beneath the wrappings.

"I said stop!"

Abruptly, it halted. Slowly, it turned toward him. Even with the intensity of the light, he could see nothing but the filmy black material. It moved toward him; first slowly, then more rapidly. Its arms flew out to the sides as if to embrace him. Cole's finger tightened on the trigger just as he heard the whistling noise approaching him.

8

Edward Graham Luckett, the director of Public Safety, squeezed out from behind the wheel of his Cadillac and waddled into the Municipal Administration Building at LaSalle and Lake. At this hour of the morning, the lobby was virtually deserted, as all the other city workers were already at their desks. A security officer, working the information station, said a cheery, "Good morning, Mr. Luckett," as the director passed. Luckett nodded, which caused his double chins to inflate like the bladder of a belching frog.

He boarded an elevator and rode to the eighteenth floor. He ignored the elevator's bounce when it was relieved of the burden of his weight and crossed the narrow hall to the double doors emblazoned with his name and title.

Inside, there was a reception desk manned by a severe-looking female with her hair done up in a spinsterish bun. "You're late, Edward!" The screech of her voice made him wince.

"I'm the boss, Nadine," he argued. "I can't be late."

"Well, if you ask me, that's the problem around here. Nobody does what they're supposed to and you're the one as should set the example, Edward."

He walked around her desk, fighting the urge to tell her that how he ran this office was none of her damn business.

"Mornin', Ed," said a sad-eyed man with the emaciated face and figure of the heavy drinker. He sat at the first desk.

In turn, the occupants of the remaining three desks greeted him with "Morning," "How's it going, Ed?" and a simple "Hi." Nobody called him "Mr. Luckett," or "Director Luckett." He would not have tolerated such disrespect from anyone else in or out of city government. He allowed these few this familiarity, because each of them was a member of his family.

From Aunt Nadine Luckett, the receptionist, who was his deceased mother's sister; to brother Donald Joseph Luckett, who served as the official auditor for the Department of Public Safety, but was seldom sober enough to audit anything more than bar tabs; to cousin Sally Luckett, a constantly husband-hunting, shrewish woman, whose approach to the age of forty had turned her into a terror; next, Zenobia Luckett Benson, a baby-maker of constantly spreading hips, whose parental responsibilities to her brood of eight never allowed her to stay in the office past two; to, finally, Eugene Thomas Luckett, the twenty-seven-year-old youngest of the group, who thought he was the greatest cocksman in history—each of them was the honest-to-goodness blood relation of Edward Graham Luckett himself.

As Luckett entered his office, he realized that as a staff, they weren't worth a Confederate two-dollar bill, but then, they were family and he could trust them. The type of games Ed Luckett played, he needed people around he could trust.

His office had been designed to resemble that of a LaSalle Street lawyer of the Depression Era. Wood paneling, old leather and frosted glass were everywhere. Doffing his black homburg and hanging it on an antique coatrack behind the door, he walked around his desk and lowered his rear end slowly into the desk chair. The seat had been customized to take his weight, but it still groaned with the pressure of the three hundred and seventy pounds it was expected to support throughout the day. For his part, Luckett was always careful of when and where he sat down. Over the years, he had found himself sprawled embarrassingly on many a floor due to a chair not up to the task of being a stationary forklift.

Besides his weight problem, Ed Luckett was a two-pack-a-day man who had asthma, bleeding hemorrhoids and fallen arches. He was balding and bloated, and due to his obesity, which caused excessive perspiration, he had a tendency to develop a pronounced body odor toward sundown. But it was a serious mistake for anyone to judge Luckett by his size, ailments or smell, because he had the most devious, cunning, short of outright criminal, political mind in Illinois. His fame had not spread beyond state boundaries because he had not tried his hand west of the Mississippi or east of Lake Michigan, but that day was coming and, Luckett hoped, soon.

From a plumber's apprentice living in a rented southwest-side apartment, Edward Graham Luckett had schemed and clawed his way to the post of city director of Public Safety, with a salary of a hundred thousand a year and oversight powers over the Police, Fire, and Streets and Sanitation Departments. Along the way, he had picked up night-school bachelor and law degrees, been elected to two aldermanic terms in his home ward and gained the post of chairman of the Cook County Democratic Committee. But he had his sights set on yet bigger and better things. He also knew how to get what he wanted.

There was a folder on Luckett's desk. Aunt Nadine had paper-clipped a note to it: "You're going to love this. N."

He slid the stack of pages out of the cardboard sleeve and began reading. As he did, his breathing became labored to the point that he was wheezing like an over-the-hill locomotive before he was halfway through.

Snatching open his center desk drawer, he took two healthy whiffs from an inhaler. Tossing it back in the drawer and clearing the mucous from his lungs with a loud, rattling cough, he shouted for Cousin Sally. By the time she extricated herself from studying a facial pimple in her compact mirror and walked into his office, he was lighting his first Newport of the day.

"Get me Seymour Winbush over at the DeWitt Corporation on the telephone."

Cousin Sally scowled. As she turned to go back to her desk, she mumbled, "Don't see why you can't dial your own numbers, Ed. Your fingers ain't broke."

Luckett ignored her as he scanned the report again. This could be his ticket to the big time. His passport right to the top. That is, if the stuffy chairman of the board of the DeWitt Corporation was able to understand exactly how much Luckett had been able to personally do for him.

Two minutes later, Cousin Sally buzzed to tell him that Winbush's secretary was on the line.

After Luckett made the connection with the DeWitt Corporation executive secretary to the chairman of the board, it took Winbush a full five minutes to answer. Luckett understood this. The esteemed chairman was demonstrating his superiority over a poor public servant, who made less than a tenth of the yearly salary the DeWitt Corporation paid him. This was no problem for Luckett. At least not now. However, someday it might become a problem for the chairman.

"*Winbush,*" the crisp, authoritarian voice proclaimed over the line.

"Good morning, Mr. Winbush, sir." Luckett made his tone subservient and respectful. He played this game well. "E. G. Luckett here."

"*What do you want, Luckett?*"

"I'm sorry to bother you. I know you must be busy, but—"

"*You're right, I am busy, so would you please get to the point?*"

"Certainly, sir. At about midnight last night, Commander Larry Cole led a force of some fifty-five officers in an attempt to arrest two notorious narcotics peddlers who are both wanted on local and federal felony warrants. Three Disciple gang members, two males and a female, were killed. Cole was seriously wounded. On top of that, the drug dealers escaped."

Luckett didn't wait for Winbush to comment. "Now, in line with what we talked about a few months ago, I'm certain this situation could be worked to our mutual advantage."

"*How?*"

Luckett frowned. There was a strangely sharp tone in Winbush's voice. As if what he'd just been told was irrelevant. Luckett forged on.

"We have all the elements here to pronounce Cole's career dead and buried, with no resurrection possible. Letting those drug dealers escape smacks of the most gross dereliction of duty. I'm sure a word or two to some of my friends in the media and—"

There was a muffled sound from Winbush's end. Luckett was unable to hear it clearly, but it sounded like the renowned DeWitt Corporation chairman had called him an idiot.

"Hello, Mr. Winbush, are you there?"

"*Yes, I'm here, Luckett.*"

"Well, I was just saying—"

"*I heard what you were saying, Luckett, and the idea is perhaps one of the most imbecilic I've heard in years. You don't discredit wounded cops in this town; you make heroes out of them! So I suggest you re-think your position in regard to Commander Cole. Now, good day, E. G!"*

Luckett sat staring at the dead phone in his hand. He was shocked, confused and more than a little outraged by Winbush's outburst. But then, he could always find a way to settle with him later. E. G. Luckett was a firm believer in the old saying that no matter how powerful a man may be, the day will always come when a lesser man will get the opportunity to destroy him. And Luckett didn't consider himself that much of a lesser man, simply one who moved in a different orbit from that of the high-flying Seymour Winbush. E. G. Luckett sat back to ponder his position. He did so for a long time.

9

SEPTEMBER 17, 1997
2:00 P.M.

B arbara Schurla Zorin and Jamal Garth presented themselves at the lobby information desk of St. Anne's Hospital and requested passes to visit Commander Cole.

"I'm sorry," the brown-uniformed security officer said. "There are two visitors already up there. Officers Kennedy and Govich."

Barbara and Jamal knew that Cole's visitors were First Deputy Superintendent Terry Kennedy and Chief of Detectives Jack Govich. Kennedy and Govich had survived what the new superintendent had called the "flattening out" of the command structure of the Chicago Police Department and the "decentralization" of police responsibilities from the headquarters building out to field units around the city. Cole had not survived these moves and was demoted along with fifty percent of the department's deputy chiefs back to the rank of commander. As the superintendent saw it, the deputy chiefs were "unnecessary."

Cole had been further speared with another administrative shaft when he was transferred from the Detective Division to the Organized Crime Division.

With no other options available to them, Barbara and Jamal retreated to the waiting room off the main lobby. There they joined single individuals, as well as couples, seated around a ceiling-mounted television broadcasting a daytime soap opera no one was paying any attention to. Each of the occupants of the lounge exuded pronounced degrees of anxiety. Some were either just over or on the verge of tears; others appeared numb to the point of shock. Each, whether alone or with a companion, kept his distance from the rest.

Barbara and Jamal found seats as far away from the mindless chatter of the television as possible, which took them to a sofa over by the far window. On an end table beside the couch was a stack of magazines. When they sat down, Barbara noticed that the second magazine from the top was a year-old edition of *Chicago*. As Garth sank down next to her, she picked it up and showed him the cover.

"Bring back memories?" she asked as cheerfully as she could.

He managed a weak smile and said in response, "Of better times." Then his face fell and he lapsed into a solemn silence.

Jamal Garth was a strong man. He had once been a fugitive from justice, forced to escape to Europe to elude capture and probable execution for killing a policeman in Chicago. Now he sat in a hospital waiting to see a wounded cop. A man who was like the son Jamal never had.

Barbara could sense that Jamal had a tenuous hold on his emotions. She started to comfort him with a word or gesture, but quickly decided against this. She would play it as if everything was normal. That would not only help him, but also herself.

She looked at the magazine cover again. Two stylishly dressed people stared imperiously back at her. They appeared to be either professional models or a well-to-do couple possessing that unfathomable, relaxed look that only the very wealthy can afford. The caption under the photograph read: "Neil and Margo DeWitt: killers without consciences. In this issue, Part I of an exerpt from the bestselling book, *The Strange Case of Neil and Margo DeWitt*, by B. S. Zorin and Jamal Garth."

Barbara flipped to page twelve of the magazine, where the book excerpt began. There were a number of pictures accompanying the piece. Pictures of her and Jamal; of Debbis Bass and Marty Wiemler, whom Margo DeWitt had murdered; and a picture of Cole with his wife Lisa and son Larry "Butch" Cole, Jr.

Barbara studied her picture critically. Not bad for fifty. But then, she'd always had an easy smile that made her look and feel years younger. She contrasted her appearance with that of Margo DeWitt on the opposite page. No contest, Barbara thought with a touch of vanity. Barbara was definitely better looking than the DeWitt woman and she didn't have Margo's billion dollars to play with.

Jamal's photo made him look exactly as he did right now. Perhaps this was a sign of agelessness. His hair was no more gray than it had been a year ago; his black skin had not wrinkled in the interim, which he had once explained to her could be because of the natural oils and melanin in his flesh; but the brown eyes were as sad and resigned to the ugliness of existence as they were now. A quarter of a century of running from the law could have done this to him. But then, he had been acquitted of all charges and was currently one of the top ten bestselling authors in the country, which should have been some compensation. But she realized that you had to walk the mile in the other person's shoes before you could really say you understood them completely.

Barbara looked back at the photograph of the Coles. *The Strange Case of Neil and Margo DeWitt* had been a tale of murder, arrogance and insanity. The DeWitts had been responsible for the wanton murders of over fifty people and had finally paid for their crimes with their lives. But after it was all over, their legacy of destruction continued. Continued on to destroy Larry Cole's family.

Although Barbara and Jamal lost their fellow writers, Debbie Bass and Marty Wiemler, they became fast friends with Cole, Blackie Silvestri, Manny Sherlock and—Barbara thought with a smile— Judy Daniels, the infamous Mistress of Disguise / High Priestess of Mayhem. As the deputy chief of administration for the Detective Division, Cole had authorized Barbara and Jamal to ride along with detectives on certain investigations, to review the actual reports of non-active cases, and to use his staff of Blackie, Manny and Judy as resource persons for the authors' fiction works. This last part had proved to be an invaluable asset to them.

The detectives and the writers talked on the telephone at least once a week and had dinner together at least once a month. So it was that they got to know each other. Know each other well enough to be aware of the fact that Larry and Lisa Cole's marriage was on the rocks.

Barbara tossed the magazine back on the end table. "You want a soda or a cup of coffee, Jamal?"

"No. Nothing," he said tightly.

She noticed his jaw muscles rippling under the flesh of his cheeks.

"How about a Coke?"

"I said nothing."

She stood up. "Maybe a Dr Pepper?"

"Barb—" He caught himself.

"You look like a Sprite person. Be right back."

She left the waiting room and entered the gift shop.

It was something that happened to her every time there was a book rack nearby. She was drawn to it like a moth to a flame. She smiled when she saw one row of Clancy Blackburn books—Clancy Blackburn was one of her pen names—and another row of B. S. Zorin titles. There was even a Jamal Garth row. *The Strange Case of Neil and Margo DeWitt* was not displayed.

Barbara surveyed the rest of the rack quickly, finding nothing that interested her. She was crossing to the counter to purchase a couple of sodas when she looked through the glass wall out at the lobby and spied a familiar face. It was Eurydice Vaughn, curator at the National Science and Space Museum. She had helped Barbara with some scientific research for a book a few years ago.

As she paid for her sodas, Barbara recalled that the papers and newscasts said that Cole had been injured behind the Science and Space Museum. She wondered if Miss Vaughn was here because of Cole.

Barbara left the gift shop, but by the time she reached the center of the lobby, the curator was gone. Barbara was starting back for the waiting room when she saw the tall Vaughn woman striding down a corridor adjacent to the lobby; it led toward the rear of the hospital. On a whim, Barbara turned to follow her.

She was too far away to call to the curator, so she increased her pace. But the curator's long-legged strides enabled her to reach the end of the corridor before Barbara was at the halfway point. Forced to nearly run, she watched Miss Vaughn go through a door marked "Stairs." By the time she reached the door, it had shut itself automatically.

Hesitating for a brief instant, Barbara looked back the way she had come. Off the corridor were closed doors with signs above them reading: "Nursing Payroll," "Nurse's Registry," and "Employee Benefits." Yet no one had been in the corridor for the past several minutes except herself and the Museum curator.

With her curiosity raging, Barbara opened the stairwell door. Inside was a dimly lit passageway with stairs going up and down. As she stepped across the threshold, she lost control of the door. It sighed shut behind her with an audible click. She tried the knob. The door was locked.

"Great!" she muttered. Then she heard a noise coming from somewhere below. Concentrating on the sound, she was able to pick up the steady clicking of a woman's high heels on a hard surface. Probably Miss Vaughn, Barbara hoped. The way the curator had moved around the hospital, it appeared that she knew where she was going. She could show Barbara the way out.

Barbara Zorin descended the stairs.

At the bottom of a single flight, the staircase ended. A corridor stretched off into a shadowy twilight that faded to total darkness some yards away. She could still hear the clicking of the heels, but the noise was growing fainter.

Enough of this cat-and-mouse nonsense, Barbara thought. "Hello!" she called into the darkness. "Miss Vaughn. Are you there?"

The faint clicking either stopped or was now too far away for Barbara to hear it. Either way, the silence was discomfiting to the point of terror.

"What are you doing here, B. S. Zorin?" she said out loud. Her fingers were starting to ache. She realized that she still held the two sodas she had bought at the gift shop for herself and Jamal. Right now she should be up there drinking them with him instead of being trapped in this stupid hospital basement.

Well, one thing she was certain of, it was time to vacate the premises. She considered going back upstairs and climbing to a higher floor, but all the doors on the upper floors were probably locked too. The Museum curator had come down here. At least Barbara had heard her, hadn't she? So there had to be a way out somewhere in the dark, or someone who could tell her how to get out. And if they asked what she was doing here, she would simply tell them she got lost. In fact, this was the truth.

She started down the corridor. She could see nothing in front of her. Looking back over her shoulder, she saw the light at the bottom of the staircase receding. Then she came to a brick wall. She could go no farther.

Turning her head to the right, she could see nothing but pitch blackness. Turning to the left presented her with the same sight.

Decision time! She turned right. With the stairwell light gone, she became immersed in total, impenetrable darkness.

This has got to end soon, her brain screamed. There has got to be a light or someone down here somewhere.

A noise directly to the rear startled her. She stopped and listened. It first sounded like no more than air hissing through a heating duct. But then it had a rhythm: A rhythm like someone inhaling and exhaling.

"Is anyone there?"

There was no response, but the breathing became heavier and closer. She began backing into the dark. She was being careful and moving slowly because she couldn't see. Whoever or whatever was out there didn't seem to have the same restrictions as it closed the distance between them.

She turned to run just as something touched her shoulder. She reached up to knock it away and felt an object her brain refused to accept as an accurate transmission recorded by her sense of touch. In that brief moment of contact, it possessed the configuration of a hand. A hand with rough skin, thick fingers and coarse hair on the back. A hand as big as a catcher's mitt!

Barbara screamed, dropped the sodas and ran headlong into the dark. She rammed into a metal door, felt the panic bar and slammed it down. She was suddenly outside and blinded by bright sunlight. Before her eyes could adjust, someone grabbed her and held her fast.

She opened her mouth to scream, but stopped when a familiar voice said, "Mrs. Zorin, what's wrong?"

Barbara looked into the dark brown eyes of Eurydice Vaughn,

curator of the National Science and Space Museum. Dark brown eyes set in a face framed by black curls.

Barbara looked back the way she had come. An emergency door leading into the hospital stood open. She was standing on a loading dock behind St. Anne's. She stared down the corridor she had just exited. It was empty.

10

OCTOBER 1, 1997
10:32 A.M.

Dr. Dean Drake, medical director of the Chicago Police Department, removed the bandage from Commander Cole's back. The knife wound was eighteen inches long and had been inflicted with a near surgical precision.

Drake began cleaning the incision with peroxide. The doctor looked like a middle-aged Huckleberry Finn, complete with freckles and cowlick. He approached the treatment of his patients, most of whom were cops, from a holistic perspective. He believed in treating the mind as well as the body. Cole had been in his office a number of times with injuries over the years. The one he had sustained now was nowhere near the worst, but Drake could tell that Cole needed more treatment than just a simple cleaning and redressing of the wound.

"This is healing very nicely, Commander. It needs to get more air, though. Maybe you could go topless when you're at home."

Cole grunted what passed for a laugh. "You're kidding about the topless part, aren't you, Doc?"

"Not at all," Drake said, applying a gauze dressing to the wound. "Exposure to the air will make it heal faster."

Drake walked around in front of Cole, studying his physique. There was good muscle tone there, but he had lost too much weight lately. On top of that, he looked exhausted.

"Let's take a look at that blood pressure. You know you have a tendency to run a bit high."

Listlessly, Cole submitted to the procedure. Drake found his blood pressure, heart and respiration normal. The wound was healing satisfactorily. But the doctor didn't feel that his patient was well. In fact, he was very concerned about his condition. His mental condition.

A few minutes later, Cole was seated across from Drake in the medical director's office. The doctor was making notes in Cole's file. "Have you been experiencing much pain from your wound?"

"When I first got out of the hospital, it bothered me from time to time."

"Take anything for it?"

"Aspirin. But no more than six a day."

Drake looked up from his notes. "Why?"

Cole shrugged. "I guess I don't want to become an aspirin junkie."

"I don't think you're in any danger of overdosing on aspirin, Larry. So, do you think you're ready to go back to work?"

"Ready, willing and able."

Drake looked down at his notes to mask the close examination he was giving his patient. Cops like Cole, no matter what their rank, were people who craved action. Go-getters, risk-takers and overall tough individuals who lived for the job, the streets and the danger they encountered every day. The type who would do police work even if they didn't get paid for it. Yes, Cole was such a cop, but something about him had changed.

The doctor had also seen police officers suffer burnout after witnessing too much or having too many near misses with death. They would fall into a deep depression or turn to excessive drinking to ease the pain. If not treated quickly and effectively, they would, in the parlance of the trade, "eat their guns," a locker-room euphemism for blowing one's brains out.

But Cole didn't fit the burnout mold, so it was something else. This left family problems or job-assignment woes. Dr. Drake wasn't a marriage counselor and didn't want to become one. However, his duties as medical director encompassed not only healing, but also pronouncing the officers under his care fit to return to duty. The extent of that duty was also up to the doctor.

He looked up from the file. Cole stared at him with a blank expression. "Suppose we send you back in a convalescent-duty status. Ease you back into the swing of things slowly. Give you a chance to catch your breath."

Cole looked like he was about to protest but thought better of it. Finally, he said a resigned, "Whatever you say, Doc."

When Cole was gone, Dr. Drake called his secretary on the intercom. "Sandy, get me Chief Govich. When I finish talking to him, I need to speak to the first deputy."

Drake might not be able to cure Cole's personal problems, but he could do something about his professional ones.

11

OCTOBER 1, 1997
11:11 A.M.

Larry Cole left the Medical Section, which was housed in the Police Academy at 1300 West Jackson Boulevard. It was a warm, balmy Indian-summer day, with a bright sun shining out of a cloudless sky. His squad car was parked in the back row of the Academy lot and as he crossed to it, two female recruits in smart blue uniforms passed him and said a snappy, "Good morning, sir!"

Cole managed a weak "Good morning" in reply. He had trouble finding his voice. He had trouble doing a number of things lately.

When he reached his car, he noticed that it needed washing. It hadn't been cleaned since his release from the hospital. But he didn't feel like having it done today. Maybe tomorrow.

Getting behind the wheel, he started the engine and put the car in gear. Then he just sat there. "Where are you going now?" he asked himself.

Finally, he eased his foot off the brake and pulled from the lot. On the street, he turned north. He lived south. Aimlessly, he rode the side streets, going nowhere and noting little of what was happening around him. He was just killing time. Getting through one more day alone.

He remembered coming home from work about a year ago. The headquarters building had still been buzzing about the *Police Case Book* television-show episode he had hosted on the Neil and Margo DeWitt case. He had done a good job as the real-life cop on the docudrama, even if he did say so himself.

When he walked in the door at about seven-thirty on that fall evening, he found his nine-year-old son Butch sitting on the living-room floor in front of the television set—a place Butch seemed to stake out lately on a continuing basis. The child looked up at his father and Cole noticed instantly the troubled expression on the boy's face.

Months ago, Cole had promised to spend more time with Butch, but the job was so demanding. He remembered that his father, who retired from the U.S. Post Office after spending thirty-four years sorting mail, always reserved weekends and took time off in the summer for him. Those times had been some of the best Cole could remember in his life. He'd had very few such times with his own son.

"What's going on, Slugger?" Cole asked, playfully rubbing Butch's head.

The boy managed to crack a slight smile that faded quickly. Then he looked across the living room at the entrance to the kitchen. Lisa Cole could be heard preparing dinner in there. Then Butch whispered, "Dad, can I talk to you later?"

"Why don't you talk to me now?"

"No!" Butch seemed actually terrified as he looked again in the direction of the kitchen. "I'll come to your study after dinner."

Lisa appeared at the kitchen door and stared at them. Cole noticed the chilly look on her face. If he hadn't known better, he would have sworn it was a look of hatred. He was to later discover that he had been right, and also wrong. The part about the look being one of hatred was correct; he was wrong about it being intended for both of them. The look was meant only for him.

Later, after they sat through a very silent dinner, Butch came secretly to the study and closed the door behind him.

"Dad," he said sitting down beside his father on the couch, "why won't Mom let me go out anymore?"

"What do you mean, Butch?"

"I can't stay out and play after school, she won't let me go to my friend's house and I can't go anywhere at all on weekends. I just sit home all day reading or looking at TV."

Cole smiled. "Sounds to me like you're on punishment."

"But I'm not!" he protested. "I've been real good. You know she would have told you if I'd done something wrong."

Cole knew Butch was right. But if the boy wasn't on punishment, why was Lisa keeping him in?

"I'll speak to her about it, son."

"Thanks, Dad."

And later in their bedroom, he did. And she reacted. Reacted like he had never seen her do before.

"Are you going with him when he's outside playing, Larry?" she screamed. "Maybe you could hire a bodyguard to make sure one of his father's enemies isn't lurking around some corner waiting to snatch the child and take him someplace so they can cut him up in little pieces!"

That previous summer, Margo DeWitt had kidnapped Butch with the intention of dismembering him in an abandoned church. Although the DeWitt woman's plan failed, it had left a mark on Lisa's soul. A scar Cole was only beginning to find out about.

That night he had managed to calm Lisa, and they had talked for a long time. She expressed a number of fears and insecurities he had been unaware of. Fears not only for their son, but for him and for any future children they might have. To Lisa, the department seemed to be Larry's whole life and she could no longer accept this.

Cole vowed to change, to spend more time with his son and Lisa. And as fall turned to winter, things around the Cole household improved. At least two nights a week he made it a point to get home before six, and he spent at least one full weekend day, and often both days, with his family.

Christmas had been almost normal. They opened presents, went to mass at Our Lady of Peace Catholic Church and afterward spent the day together. After Butch dozed off at about ten, Lisa donned the new nightgown he bought her for Christmas and dabbed herself with the Clinique perfume that was his favorite. These were unmistakable signals.

But their lovemaking had been strangely remote. A detachment existed between them, which had allowed the act to be physically satisfying, but then also to seem like something that had occurred between two strangers.

They had lain in the dark for a long time afterward, not touching or speaking. Finally, she said, "I need to get away for a while, Larry."

"How long is a while?"

"A week. I could take Butch to visit my folks in Michigan. They haven't seen him since he was five."

He started to protest. To tell her he needed her here in Chicago with him. But he said, "Maybe that would be a good idea. When do you plan to leave?"

"Tomorrow morning."

He nodded to himself in the dark. So, she had it planned in advance. But he'd had no way of knowing that she wasn't planning to come back.

12

Cole was back to work and it was almost as if nothing had changed for him. He was in the same office he had occupied when he was a deputy chief in the Detective Division a short year ago. Thanks to some fancy maneuvering by Terry Kennedy and Jack Govich, he even had his old staff back: Blackie, Judy and Manny. The only thing wrong was the work. In a lot of ways, Cole couldn't really call it work.

When he was a deputy chief, there had been cases to review, manpower allocations to examine and workload projections to anticipate—all of these on a nearly continuous basis. Now he had been relegated to examining Detective Division productivity from a retrospective standpoint. To see where they had been rather than where they were going. Not a very demanding job, but one that had left him time to do some investigative work on his own.

On top of that, he wasn't a full-duty, full-time employee, although he was paid as such. Dr. Drake had sent him back on convalescent duty, which was an active status with limitations: no more than six hours a day in the office, weekly checkups and daily rehabilitation exercises. And the good doctor was watching Cole like a hawk, having taken to dropping by Detective Division headquarters every day at varying times and explaining lamely that he just happened to be in the neighborhood.

But Cole wasn't complaining. He was actually feeling better than he had in months and even looking forward to returning to active duty in the Organized Crime Division. He was looking at the time he was spending now as a transition period. A transition period encompassing a number of phases of his life.

There was a knock on his office door. "Come."

The door opened and Chief of Detectives Jack Govich walked in.

"Quitting time, Larry," Govich said, perching on the edge of Cole's desk. "Doctor's orders."

"But it's only a couple of minutes after seven, Chief."

Govich feigned anger. "Don't get me in dutch with the medical director, Larry. He said six hours maximum as far as your duty hours go. So I let you talk me into this crazy one P.M. to seven P.M. schedule."

"That's so I can do my rehab in the morning, Boss."

"Yeah. I heard about your rehab. Running four miles, then lifting weights like you're in training to play tight end for the Bears. Didn't Drake explain to you that you're supposed to be recuperating? Taking it easy, for chrissakes!"

"Yes, sir," Cole said. But he didn't feel like "taking it easy." However, Govich and Drake were in charge and he knew that they, along with Kennedy, had stuck their necks out to have him reassigned to the Detective Division.

"I'll close it down right now, Chief," he said, starting to straighten up his desk. Govich nodded a curt okay and left.

Cole removed a black, string-tied portfolio from the bottom drawer of his desk. He added the two pages of research he'd completed to the twenty-odd pages already there. He would review everything when he got home tonight. He slipped the portfolio into his briefcase and went to the door. Taking one last look around the office, he extinguished the lights.

Judy Daniels was seated at her old desk outside in the main office bay. She'd been going through a thing with wigs since they'd been reassigned back to the Detective Division. Every day she'd worn a different artificial hairpiece. With a few basic changes in accessories, she'd come off looking like a completely different woman each day. But the effort had been wasted on Cole and the rest of the staff. Perhaps this was because they had seen Judy in so many different disguises over the years. In fact, a number of various bizarre disguises. So it hadn't been considered a big thing when she'd switched from a helmetlike Cleopatra wig, long black lashes, heavy makeup and large gold bracelets that Manny called baby hoola-hoops, to

Whoopie Goldberg dreadlocks and a complexion seemingly devoid of any make up, to today's Aphrodite look with the swept-up blonde ponytail and figure-enhancing tight sweater.

"I've been ordered to call it a night, Judy," he said, recalling how long it had taken to get used to her many appearances when she first came to work for him.

"You know you've got that seven-thirty dinner engagement with Mr. Garth and Mrs. Zorin at Houston's, Boss."

Cole frowned. "I thought that was tomorrow night."

Judy consulted her desk calendar. "No, sir. It's tonight."

Actually, Cole had nothing better to do. In fact, he was looking forward to seeing Jamal and Barbara again. The last time he'd seen them, he was lying flat on his back in the hospital.

"I'm on the way," he said.

"Boss," she called before he could turn around.

"Yes?"

She opened her desk drawer and removed two books. "Could you ask them to autograph these for me?"

Cole looked down at the books. They were Clancy (aka Barbara Zorin) Blackburn's *F.B.I. Confidential* and Garth's *Love Killer*, both of which had recently been published.

"Sure," Cole said, taking the books.

"I would ask them myself," Judy said sheepishly, "but . . ."

Cole stared at her. "But what?"

"I wouldn't want to invite myself someplace I wasn't welcome."

Cole smiled. "Would you like to come to dinner with us, Judy? I'm sure Barbara and Jamal won't mind."

"I'd love to, Boss," she responded. "And I'll even pay my own way."

"Gee, thanks," Cole said as they left the office. "You're a real sport."

When they entered Cole's car in the parking lot at Eleventh and State, the radios—both commercial and police band—blared an instant of deafening static.

"Wow!" Judy said, grabbing her ears. "You need to get that fixed, Boss."

"It's been doing that a lot lately," Cole said. The interference ceased and the radios played with crystal clarity.

"It's probably caused by sun spots," Judy said.

"The sun went down an hour ago."

"But we could have lingering radiation in the atmosphere because of the depleted ozone layer."

Cole thought about this for a moment before deciding not to pursue the issue with her. He drove from the lot and headed north for Houston's Restaurant.

In a darkened area under the elevated Chicago Transit Authority tracks on Fourteenth Street, three blocks south of headquarters, a panel truck bearing the National Science and Space Museum logo started up. Its lights were turned on as it traveled west to State Street and turned north to follow Cole and Judy. Inside the van, a receiver picked up the signal being transmitted from a magnetized device attached beneath the commander's back bumper. This transmitter had been in place for three days.

"You look very fit, Larry," Barbara Zorin said. "Going back to work agrees with you."

"I'm really not completely back yet," he explained. "But I have been getting lots of rest and exercise lately. They'd better give me some real work to do soon or I'll be too lazy to be of any use to them at all."

"That'll be the day," Judy said.

"What have you been doing so far?" Jamal asked.

Cole gave a brief description of his less-than-demanding duties.

"That wouldn't seem to be enough to occupy the hours you spend at headquarters," Barbara said.

Cole hesitated for a moment before saying, "I've been occupying my time with a special project of my own. It's managed to take up quite a few of the empty hours I would have spent going over old reports."

They were seated at a corner table. The restaurant was crowded and Barbara had called ahead to make reservations for them. A waiter had taken their dinner orders and served a round of cocktails.

"Is your project secret?" Barbara asked.

"No," Cole said, sipping slowly from a glass of draft beer. "In fact, it's really more of a historical research project than a police investigation. But I'm using police records to complete it."

"Let me guess," Barbara said, shooting a knowing glance at Jamal. "You've been looking into crimes connected with the National Science and Space Museum."

Cole smiled. "I guess I can't fool a couple of sharp sleuths like you two."

"We figured you'd be looking into the place," Barbara said, "so we decided to give you a hand from our end. There's been a lot written about its history over the years."

Garth added, "A strange and horrifying history."

"So," Barbara said. "Who goes first, Jamal?"

"The National Science Museum, as it was called—the 'Space' part was tacked on in nineteen sixty-six—was founded by multimillionaire financier Ezra Rotheimer in nineteen-six. Rotheimer was reportedly so impressed by a museum he had visited in Switzerland in nineteen-four that he vowed to build a similar one in America.

"The millionaire spared no expense in filling it with all types of scientific gadgets and priceless artifacts he collected from all over the world. The jewelry and glassware exhibits placed on display in nineteen-ten were appraised back then at a million dollars each. Now both are worth so much that they're virtually irreplaceable.

"He also turned it into the wealthiest institution of its kind in the world with a lavish bequest made prior to his death in nineteen-thirteen."

"What kind of guy was he?" Cole asked.

"There isn't a great deal known about his private life. There are indications that this was by design," Barbara said. "We know that he immigrated to the United States from Europe sometime after the Civil War, but no one knows from where. He settled in Chicago around eighteen-seventy and went into the retail sales business. He prospered and by eighteen-ninety had made a fortune. We know that when he arrived here, he was married and had two children. His first wife, Sarah, died during an influenza epidemic and he remarried. His second wife, Estelle, bore him five kids."

She opened the shoulder bag slung across the back of her chair and removed a leather folder from it. She extracted a stack of reprinted black-and-white photographs encased in plastic sleeves, which she handed to Cole.

The four pictures were very old and their grainy texture indicated that they had been enlarged to the current 8½-by-11-inch size. The first was a posed family picture. Cole counted eleven men, women and children present.

"Is this Rotheimer?" he asked, pointing to the sturdy-looking man with the bushy mustache and balding head seated bottom row center. A sad-faced woman sat beside him.

"That's him and his wife," Barbara said. "The rest are his children: three boys and four girls, ranging in age from five to twenty-five. The oldest girl's named Katherine. She was sixteen when this picture was taken. That's her at the far end of the first row."

"That's Jim Cross," Garth said, pointing to the next photo. "He worked for Rotheimer."

At first glance, Cole thought that Cross looked oddly familiar. It was as if the policeman had seen him somewhere before. Or perhaps a picture of him. Cole did recall having seen photos of heavyweight boxing champion Jack Johnson that were posed in a very similar fashion to the one of this Jim Cross. But Cross, who wore an ancient suit and carried a derby hat in his pose of mannequin-like rigidity, looked nothing like Johnson.

Judy had slid her chair over so she could look over Cole's shoulder. Now she said, "Boss, he looks like you."

"We call tossing insults at superiors insubordination, Detective Daniels," Cole said with a grin. "This guy doesn't look anything like me."

"But he does, Larry," Garth said. "Not your twin, but he could have been an ancestor."

"There are no people named Cross on my family tree."

But intrigued by their comments, Cole studied the photo more closely. He had to say one thing for this Jim Cross—he was one well-built sonofabitch. That's what had initially made Cole think of Jack Johnson. The upper bodies of both men seemed capable of bursting out of conventional clothing. They were better suited for short sleeves and open-neck collars. Of course this was before there were tall and big men's apparel stores.

But Cole had a more pressing question about Jim Cross. What was he, a black man at the turn of the century, doing in a white millionaire's family photo?

Sensing his puzzlement, Barbara said, "We know that Jim Cross worked for Rotheimer and did a number of different jobs. One of the Museum-authorized biographies of the millionaire listed Cross as the family chauffeur. There's nothing in any other documentation to support this contention. In fact, all the evidence would indicate that Mr. Cross was an inventor."

Cole looked up from the picture at Barbara and then looked again at Jim Cross. There was indeed something compelling about this man.

"How do you know he was an inventor?"

"I found his profession on a contract to purchase mechanical equipment from one of Rotheimer's manufacturing outlets downtown. The contract was a standard installment agreement of the period, executed between Mr. Cross and Rotheimer personally."

"We also found out," Garth added, "that Cross had studied under Booker T. Washington at Tuskegee Institute, in Alabama. All the records indicate that he majored in mechanical engineering before leaving Tuskegee to come North and work for Rotheimer some time around nineteen hundred."

Cole turned to the last photo. It was a picture of Jim Cross and Katherine Rotheimer together. They both appeared substantially older than they did in the other photos. As much as ten years older.

Puzzled, Cole and his over-the-shoulder co-viewer, Judy Daniels, looked across the table at the writers.

"That's where our mystery begins," Garth said.

13

OCTOBER 8, 1997
7:42 P.M.

Sam Sykes, DDS, was the self-proclaimed Casanova of the Magnificent Mile of North Michigan Avenue. With a lucrative dental practice he had inherited from his deceased father and uncle, and a plush suite of offices in the Wrigley Building, overlooking the Chicago River, Dr. Sam dressed in stylishly expensive ensembles that showed lots of chest hair and were tight across the shoulders. He was suave in a superficial way and would easily drop a hundred at the bar while romancing a prospective bed partner.

Dr. Sam roamed only the most exclusive bars from DeWitt Plaza back to the river and occasionally drifted over to Wabash Avenue, which he considered something of a backwater. Houston's Restaurant, which had a comparatively small, circular bar, was on Wabash.

Dr. Sam was looking for something new and exciting on this October evening. Since his last patient at five, he'd been wandering the watering holes of the near north side searching for the right prey to meet his stringent sex-partner requirements. During this nocturnal foray, he had been forced to rudely brush off a couple of his old flames, who had demanded to know why he hadn't called. Because it was possible he could have many such encounters before the evening was through, he abandoned Michigan Avenue for Wabash.

The bartender greeted him when he walked into Houston's. "Doctor Sykes, good to see you again, sir." The young man in the red-plaid jacket looked barely out of high school, which made the dentist painfully aware of his own forty-five years.

Sykes merely nodded by way of a return greeting and ordered a Perrier with a twist. The doctor never drank alcohol, but he did do cocaine and marijuana. As the bartender went off to get his drink,

Dr. Sam scanned the bar for potential female companionship. He had to do it only once.

When the boyish-looking bartender returned, Dr. Sam asked conspiratorially, "What's with the amazon in black down at the end of the bar?"

"Isn't she something?" The bartender cast an admiring glance in the direction of his beautiful customer.

"What's she looking at? She hasn't moved since I walked in the door."

The bartender shrugged. "Maybe somebody in the restaurant. You think she followed her husband here or something and he's in there with another woman?"

"Could be," Dr. Sam said. "Now that does present a challenge. I want to sit as close to her as I can without attracting attention to myself." He added "yet" with a wink.

A ten-dollar bill appeared between Dr. Sam's thumb and index finger. It disappeared into the bartender's palm. "Doc, I'll get you a seat on the wall right behind her. You'll even be able to see the same part of the restaurant she can't take her eyes away from."

"That's my boy."

14

K athy was Rotheimer's favorite child," Barbara was saying. "He gave her everything she wanted. That is, until she asked for his blessing so she could marry Jim Cross.

"There is no way for us to know exactly how Rotheimer reacted, but in September of nineteen-two, he fired Cross. A short time later, Cross was also arrested."

"What did they charge him with?" Cole asked.

"According to old county records, rape," Barbara said.

"Would the victim have been Katherine Rotheimer?" Judy asked, her cheeks coloring with emotion.

The writers nodded. "But there was never a trial," Garth explained. "On top of that, Kathy put up his bond."

"What happened then?" Cole asked, making no attempt to conceal his interest.

"That's one of our problems," Barbara said. "As far as the Rotheimers go, we hit a dead end."

"So the rest is just conjecture," Garth added. "But all the bizarre incidents connected to the Museum begin with the Rotheimer family. Since their deaths occurred so long ago and there were no surviving relatives—"

"They're all dead?" Judy interrupted.

It was Cole's turn to explain. "All of Ezra Rotheimer's offspring met with either violent or mysterious deaths, or they simply vanished. Of those in the family portrait, not one of them survived beyond nineteen-thirteen. There was no heir to the Rotheimer fortune. His entire estate went to the Museum."

"Do you believe in ghosts, Commander?" Judy asked skeptically.

"No, I don't. But I did see something strange on that island. Then there was this noise."

Before they could question him, the waiter came to their table with a fresh round of drinks.

"We didn't order anything," Garth protested.

"They are already paid for, sir," the waiter said, continuing to set glasses down in front of them. "A young woman at the bar. She said she's this gentleman's wife." He pointed to Cole.

Cole's head snapped around to stare off across the restaurant at the bar, in the far corner. There was no one in sight who looked even remotely like Lisa. He stood up.

"Where is this woman?" he asked.

The tall guest's aggressive manner frightened the waiter. "I didn't see her, sir. The barman took the order."

Cole spun away and started across the restaurant. Garth excused himself and followed. Judy and Barbara exchanged puzzled looks as they remained seated at the table.

15

D r. Sam was in a perfect position to see the results of his little prank. It was his idea to send the round of drinks to the table. A stroke of brilliance, aimed at flushing the philandering husband out in the open. Perhaps there would be a scene. If things went right, Dr. Sam would be around to pick up the pieces. If not, then it would be a decent night's entertainment.

He was seated on a stool against the wall directly behind the looker in black. Only once since he sat down behind her did she take her eyes off that table. On that singular occasion, she had turned to look at him. The glance had been noncommittal, not even mildly curious. Then she had gone back to her surveillance.

It wasn't easy for Dr. Sam to pick up exactly who it was she was watching, because the restaurant was crowded. But then the foursome at the far table began passing around the black-and-white photos. This had caused a reaction from the woman at the bar. A very intense reaction. Dr. Sam had watched her go through rigidly controlled alarm, fear or anger, to finally a lingering tension. He wondered what those pictures could be of. His exotic beauty in a compromising position with another man? The thought charged the playboy dentist with excitement. That was when he came up with his plan to buy the foursome at the table a round.

It had been pure guesswork to select the younger, broad-shouldered man as the wandering husband. It was possibly because the blonde chick seated with them got real close to him when they were examining the photos. Any woman who ever got that close to Dr. Sam would have been in deep trouble. Then he sat back to watch things start to pop.

The woman at the bar was drinking plain grapefruit juice. Dr.
Sam had gleaned this bit of intelligence from the bartender. She paid
by the drink, refusing to run a tab even though she could. When the
tall man jumped up and started across the room, she slipped off her
bar stool, dropping a five-dollar bill beside her still-full glass.

Then things happened very fast. The tall guy charged into the bar
and looked around frantically. Dr. Sam was certain that the guy had
seen the woman in black, who was on her way out the revolving door
leading to the street. But there hadn't been the slightest instant of
recognition on his face. Of course, her back had been to him.

There were not a lot of other people in the bar at the time, so it
hadn't taken long for the guy to see that his wife wasn't there. Then
he went for the bartender. He also flashed a badge, which was a cue
for Dr. Sam to make himself scarce. The ten he had dropped, plus
the cost of the drinks, wouldn't keep the boy bartender's mouth shut
for long.

At the revolving door, he glanced back at the confusion raging
inside. The tall guy was seriously pissed. The older guy from the
table was trying to calm him down. The kid bartender looked scared
spitless. Dr. Sam kept on going, out into the street.

Then, surprise of surprises, he saw the beauty in black standing
across the street, watching the restaurant entrance. Fingering the gold
Ankh he wore around his neck as a good-luck charm, Dr. Sam crossed
the street.

She gave him another nothing reaction as he approached. It was
as if she wasn't even aware he existed. She was standing beside a
panel truck with some writing and a scientific logo on the side. He
didn't pay it any attention.

"Quite a bit of excitement in there," he said, lighting a menthol
Tiparillo with a gold Dunhill lighter.

"What happened? Larry . . . I mean, that man seemed very upset
about something."

"So his name's Larry," Dr. Sam said with a leer.

She turned to look at him. Oh, she was indeed Level Ten, center-
fold material. He had never seen any woman quite so exquisite. Her
skin and hair were absolutely flawless. But she didn't speak. There

was no anger there, no emotion, no nothing. He began feeling like a nonperson again.

"You know," Dr. Sam said, puffing on his cigar, "he's really not worth it when there are so many more desirable chaps you could lavish your attentions on. Say, for instance—"

"You did something in there, didn't you?"

She seemed almost amused, which he took as a good sign. Maybe his little stunt had succeeded in cracking the ice. Chalk one up for the doctor. He clamped his cigar between his front teeth and uttered a very smug "uh-huh."

She reached out and struck the side of the van with her fist. She shouted, "Take him, Homer!"

Casually, Dr. Sam turned his head toward the truck's back door just as it flew open and a . . . thing came out! Before he could turn to run, or even shout, he was snatched into the back of the truck by . . . it. Struggling was useless. Dr. Sam would never see the light of day or play another practical joke again.

16

OCTOBER 9, 1997
12:15 P.M.

Dr. Winston Fleisher was entertaining Mr. Harry McElroy and his two associates, George Doyle and Kyle Peters, at the Museum. A buffet lunch was carted in from the kitchen and set up on tables at one end of the executive dining room, which could accommodate up to seven tables with ten settings each. Now an oval table with place settings for five was at the center of the room.

A plate-glass window on the wall opposite the buffet provided an excellent view of the Constellation shuttle on the grounds below. The only other furnishings in the room were two photographs: one of Ezra Rotheimer and the other an exterior shot of the Museum, circa 1958.

Winston Fleisher was a thin, sad-eyed man in his mid-sixties, who wore out-of-date suits and always looked to be brooding about something. He had obtained his Ph.D. in history from the University of Chicago and spent his entire professional career at the Museum. Over the years, he had held a number of Museum posts: curator, administrator, adviser to the chairman and, finally, chairman. It was remarked, among those who had been around the institution for a while, that although Winston Fleisher had been employed in the building that housed the National Science and Space Museum for many years, he had never actually done anything. That is, he had occupied offices, attended numerous meetings and held positions on one committee or another, but, in fact, he had done nothing of any merit or of lasting value for the Museum. He was one of those rare individuals who attach themselves to an institution or endeavor and spend so much time there that eventually few can remember when they weren't around. In flourishing places like the National Science and Space Museum, staff depletion due to cost-cutting had never been necessary, so Winston had survived in his do-nothing status and managed to prosper.

The chairman was an easy man to get along with and so, to some extent, was an easy mark for anyone who wanted something either from him or the Museum. It had been a simple matter for Harry McElroy, head of the McElroy Development Company of Chicago and Northern Indiana, to simply call and invite himself and his associates to lunch. Dr. Fleisher was too nice a guy to refuse.

Now McElroy sat directly across from Fleisher. He was sizing up the chairman. McElroy figured this was going to be easier than he thought. Maybe too easy, which worried him. Nothing in his entire life had ever been easy.

Harry McElroy was a bear of a man, weighing in at two hundred and fifty pounds. He had a bald head, brutal features and reptilian eyes, which some branded evil and others intriguing. He was the founder and principal stockholder in McElroy Development, which was a combination construction, building-site promotion company.

The two men with him, George Doyle and Kyle Peters, were respectively his attorney and his chief architect.

The main course of beef stroganoff and noodles was finished. As the dishes were removed by a white-jacketed waiter, Dr. Fleisher led his guests back to the buffet table for dessert. Each of them selected either pie, cake or a whipped-cream-topped chocolate pudding before returning to his seat. The waiter poured freshly made coffee for each of them and left the dining room.

"You got one helluva impressive setup here, Winston," McElroy said, polishing off a slice of cake with vanilla icing. He brushed crumbs off his suit jacket and reached into his inside coat pocket for a cigar. Kyle Peters jumped to light it for him.

Dr. Fleisher coughed nervously. "The Museum is smoke-free, Mr. McElroy."

"Nonsense!" McElroy boomed, puffing clouds of smoke to get the cigar going. "That 'no-smoking' crap is for the public areas.

This is a private dining room, isn't it, Winston? And I'm your guest. I heard somewhere that a good host always sees to his guests' needs."

Dr. Fleisher started to press the protest, but then perhaps McElroy was right. After all, as chairman of the board, he did have a responsibility to the Museum's guests.

"Winston," McElroy said, "how much money did the Museum clear last year after expenses? I mean, how far were you people in the black?"

Fleisher gave his guest a weak smile. "I have asked Miss Vaughn, our curator, to join us. She handles most of the business matters for the Museum. She should be—"

The door opened from the outer corridor and Eurydice Vaughn walked in. She proceeded straight to McElroy, removed his cigar and crushed it in his dessert dish. She took the vacant place setting next to Fleisher and said, "I'm sorry I'm late, but my duties leave little time for long lunches."

"Eurydice," Fleisher said, "Mr. McElroy was just asking how much in the black we were last year."

"Mr. McElroy," she said very formally, "the Museum is not a simple business venture. It is a public accommodation. We have no need to make more money. Mr. Rotheimer's bequest was invested wisely and we're financially sound."

Kyle Peters, the architect, intervened, "Excuse me, Mr. McElroy, perhaps I could show Miss Vaughn what we have in mind?"

McElroy nodded solemnly.

Peters picked up a string-tied portfolio from the floor and opened it to reveal a series of thirty-inch-square renderings inside. He propped the full-color drawings up on the table and began to explain what they were.

The centerpiece of each drawing was the Museum. But instead of being surrounded by parkland, it appeared as if it had been transplanted to Disneyworld.

The beach across the outer drive from the Museum had been turned into an amusement-park midway, with roller coasters, Ferris wheels and fast-food concessions. The park had disappeared under high-rise apartment buildings, with a glass monstrosity in the center that looked like a child's plastic block that had been caught beneath the wheel of a truck. The Museum was unchanged with the exception of the Constellation space shuttle. Eurydice focused her eyes on a ramp in the drawing that led into the shuttle. Stick figures representing people were on the ramp.

Peters explained, "The urban environment of the twenty-first century." He flipped through the remaining drawings. Each revealed a more detailed, close-up version of the additions to the Museum's surroundings. "The city on the lake in microcosm. Entertainment, residential living, history and the future, all combined within a few short blocks."

The last drawing was of the lopsided glass cube. Eurydice asked, "Could someone explain what that is?"

"My own design," McElroy said, pulling a fresh cigar from his pocket and fondling it slowly. "That will be the hub of the entire complex. Administrative offices, security and headquarters of the McElroy Lakefront Development Company." He snapped his fingers. This time Doyle leaped up to light his boss's cigar.

Fleisher looked at Eurydice. He was surprised to see her ignoring the crass businessman. Instead, she was idly fingering an antique, heart-shaped brooch with a ruby in the center, surrounded by a cluster of clear stones. She said, "You realize you'll be destroying not only one of nature's gifts, but also ruining the environment?"

"Who gives a shit?" McElroy sneered. "I can make a quarter of a billion dollars off this deal."

Eurydice stood up and walked around the table. She picked up the drawing of McElroy's "hub of the entire complex."

"This is the ugliest thing I've ever seen." She ripped it in half. "The whole scheme is a greedy swindle and, Harry, I'll never let you get your hands on any of the land around here. At least not in this life."

McElroy's eyes were closed and his face tightened in a grimace. He was panting like a winded dog.

Eurydice turned to Fleisher and said in a calm, businesslike voice,

"Doctor, I'm summoning medical help. Your guest is having a heart attack."

Winston Fleisher responded sleepily, "Of course, Eurydice. Whatever you say."

Doyle and Peters remained motionless.

17

October 10, 1997
11:03 a.m.

Officer Edna Gray exited the elevator on the fifth floor of police headquarters and checked the directory for the location of Detective Division offices. At the glass doors, she peeked inside at the frenetic activity.

"Edna, what are you doing here?" she muttered to herself.

A voice said from behind her, "May I help you?"

She turned around to find a tall black man standing about a foot away. She was obviously blocking his entrance into the office. He smiled, which relaxed her a notch. She was in foreign territory and she really needed a friend now.

"I'm supposed to see a Lieutenant Silvestri."

"Sure," he said, stepping around her and pushing the door open. "He's right this way."

After hesitating a moment, she stepped across the threshold.

"You'll find the lieutenant right over there." Her escort pointed across the office at a doorless cubicle.

Edna stopped at the cubicle. The lieutenant, seated behind the lone desk in the office, talked on the telephone while he smoked a cigar. The fumes drifted out to her.

With the phone still pressed against his ear, he looked up and motioned her inside. She came. He squinted to read the photo ID card clipped to her jacket. Having done so, he placed his hand over the mouthpiece and said, "Have a seat, Gray. I'll be with you in a minute."

She sat down in the chair next to his desk.

Edna had gotten the call to see her commander out in the Third

District at the end of her tour of duty two days ago. She had questioned
Sergeant Johnson as to why the commander wanted to see her.

"Don't know, Gray, but I wouldn't sweat it. Probably something
routine."

But she'd never been called into the "front office," as it was
called, before. With mounting apprehension, she went.

"Edna," the commander said, "the Detective Division's looking
for someone who knows the National Science and Space Museum. I
understand from Woody Johnson that you're something of an expert."

"I've worked the detail for a couple of years, sir, but I don't think
that qualifies me as an expert."

"Sergeant Johnson thinks so and that's good enough for me.
You'll be detailed to Detective Division headquarters. Soft clothes,
straight days. So what do you say?"

She'd been on midnights so long that she'd forgotten what it was
like not to be eating breakfast when everyone else was eating dinner.
"I'd be glad to help out the Detective Division, sir."

The lieutenant was still talking on the phone. She attempted to
distract herself by looking around. The cubicle appeared as if it had
been only recently inhabited. There were some photos on the desk,
but there wasn't much else. Finally, the lieutenant hung up.

"Blackie Silvestri," he said, extending a hairy, ham-sized hand
with a palm as rough as sandpaper. "Welcome aboard, Gray. Your
commander speaks very highly of you."

Edna found that she was beginning to like this man.

"Let me introduce you to the rest of the staff. Right now we're
all kind of low-key. We don't talk much about what we're up to. If
anybody asks, just tell them you're on special assignment for the
chief of detectives."

She nodded even though she didn't see what this had to do with
the National Science and Space Museum.

As they recrossed the office bay, she said, "Could I ask you a
favor, Lieutenant? Could you just call me Edna?"

"Edna it is."

At the first desk, Blackie introduced her to Sergeant Manny
Sherlock, who reminded Edna of a young Groucho Marx. At the next

desk, she was introduced to a conservatively dressed, spinsterish woman named Judy Daniels.

"Now we meet the boss," Blackie said, walking over to an office a short distance from Detective Daniels' desk. Edna followed the lieutenant inside.

"Edna," the commander said, "have a seat."

She looked around the office. The only chair was directly across from the commander. She took it.

"I'd like to talk to Officer Gray alone, Blackie," Cole said.

As the lieutenant turned to leave, she heard him say, "She'd rather be called just Edna, Boss. I've already introduced her to Manny and Judy."

The door shut and they were alone. He was smiling at her. There was no way she could smile back now. Not after what he had done.

"I could have saved the lieutenant the trouble if I had simply introduced myself outside. But then, you seemed very intent on finding him yourself."

She nodded and heard herself say, "Yes."

"Could I ask you a favor, Edna?"

She nodded again.

"Do you think you could lighten up a little?"

"I'll try."

"The Museum is beautiful and interesting, Edna," Cole said. "It also has a strange history."

"A lot of strange and interesting people have passed through its doors."

"That sounds like it came out of one of the Museum brochures."

He was smiling again. She really wished he wouldn't do that. She remembered how she'd liked it when she first saw him. However, that was before she knew he was a commander.

"It didn't," she said.

Then his smile was gone and he was all business. "The problem that I have with the National Science and Space Museum," he said, "is that a number of the people who either passed through its doors or went out onto that island behind it were never seen again."

"I know," she said. "At last count, since nineteen-ten, over a hundred eighty-three men, women and children have disappeared either inside the Museum or on Seagull Island. In fact, I was surprised you were found alive that night." She paused for a moment. "There's a classification the Chicago Police Department's Missing Persons Section sometimes uses. If nothing is heard from the missing person for over seven years, Commander, they are no longer dismissed as mere disappearances."

"Really?" Cole said, displaying a noticeable apprehension.

"Yes," Edna said solemnly. "They are listed as 'Missing: Presumed Dead.' "

18

OCTOBER 10, 1997
5:45 P.M.

Fifteen minutes before closing, the National Science and Space Museum loudspeaker system announced that it was time for guests to leave. After the visitors exited, members of the Chicago police detail made their rounds of the displays to ensure that no stragglers remained behind.

The most expensive displays were alarmed, but that wouldn't stop an enterprising thief. However, no burglary or theft had been attempted at the Museum in twelve years.

Standing at one of the windows of her office, Eurydice Vaughn looked down at the uniformed police officer patroling the corridor below the aircraft exhibit. She watched the blue-uniformed man walk doggedly to the end of the area, checking every exhibit and shadow in case someone had attempted to conceal himself. But she realized that no matter how diligent the policeman might be, there was no way he would be able to check every place where a human being could hide in the area he had been assigned to cover.

That was how professional cat burglar Tommy Bascomb had managed to hide in the Museum after closing back in the spring of 1985. He'd been fifty at the time, and something of a legend. After learning of the Museum's *Hall of Gems*, he'd decided to rob it. Eurydice had discovered the distinguished-looking Englishman sneaking toward the display and silently she had followed him. She remembered that he'd looked like a muscular version of George Saunders, who played "the Saint" in all those old movies on television. He had feigned wry amusement when she caught him disabling the alarm system wired to a case in which there were eight blue, full-carat diamonds arranged on black velvet.

Tommy Bascomb had not remained amused for long.

The lights dimming brought Eurydice back to the present. This signaled that the security personnel and the police had completed their sweep. Now she would make one of her own. One that would be far more thorough than that of any guard or police officer.

Entering her private washroom, which was as large as her secretary's entire office, she stripped off her two-piece suit and black heels. She unlocked a sliding-door closet, stepped inside and closed the door behind her.

Immersed in pitch blackness, she reached out for the items around her: a black Spandex body suit with a hood, lightweight, soft-soled boots, thin Isotoner gloves, and a utility belt to go around her waist. A number of items were attached to the utility belt, including a small tool kit, a sharp knife with a serrated edge, a flashlight and a coiled, twelve-foot bullwhip.

It took her less than a minute to dress. Then she moved again, this time traveling farther into the chilling darkness. Some twenty-five feet from where she started, she reached out her hand. She touched a lever that slid to the left.

A panel opened in front of her, revealing light on the other side. She stepped through the opening. The panel slid silently shut behind her.

She was in one of the small theaters of the Museum's enormous *Man in Space* display. When in use, the screen showed a movie detailing the relationship of Earth to the solar system, the Milky Way galaxy and, finally, to the other known galaxies. The projection, with accompanying narration, took twelve minutes. Now the screen was dark. Had spectators been sitting out in the theater, they would have seen a tall figure, dressed in black and shrouded in shadow, step from the area where the screen was supposed to be.

Now Eurydice began her rounds.

She traveled through the enormous space and aircraft exhibits, passing under and around rockets, lunar landers, jet aircraft, prop planes and hot-air balloons. She passed beneath the perpetually spinning model of Earth circling the sun and leaped over the barrier leading into the Theater of the Future. It took her a full ten minutes to cover the thousand-seat theater.

From the Theater of the Future she entered the *Fine Arts* Gallery, a full acre filled with paintings, drawings, etchings, prints, sculpture, jade and transplanted mosaics. Any one of the items would fetch a king's ransom.

From *Fine Arts* she covered the petroleum exhibit, the *Children Around the World* Hall, the *Heroes—Past and Present* Hall, which featured original costumes or replicas of costumes worn by the characters in the television and 1979 movie, *Superman.* Also, a costume and sword—purchased from the Walt Disney studios—worn by actor Guy Williams in the *Zorro* television series, the *Lone Ranger* television character's six guns, and a Darth Vader light saber, to name a few of the items that would fetch a hefty price from a collector. She covered the Carlsbad Cavern mockup, the gold mine, the Pullman train and the military exhibits. Twice she had to dodge police sentries on their rounds. She did so quickly and so silently they were unaware of anything moving in the darkness surrounding them.

Finally, she came to the *Glassware from Around the World* Hall. Here her run stopped, as her security rounds were concluded. Her path through the Museum had taken her on a course that had covered over five miles in actual distance, due to the circuitous route she had traveled. But her breathing was barely labored and only a slight sheen of perspiration covered her face.

Pulling her hood off and shaking her curly hair loose, she entered the hall.

She walked over to the stone bench and stopped. She had been back to this room to stare at this same thing every night since she had watched the policewoman through the special platter in the case against the far wall. There had been something about this spot and that woman. Something Eurydice was unable to put her finger on, because it was as intangible as a wisp of smoke or an experience in a dream.

She suddenly became aware that she was no longer alone. Slowly, she turned around.

He was standing over by the glass case with the shiny plate inside, which had startled Edna Gray the night Larry Cole had been wounded out on the island. The head hung below shoulder level, as if the neck grew horizontally instead of vertically from the torso. The shoulders measured nearly sixty inches. His five-foot arms hung to his knees. His large round eyes were a disarming cobalt blue.

Eurydice took him in and smiled. "You're getting better, Homer. I wasn't even aware you were there until the case moved." She walked over to him. "And what have you been doing all day?"

"I've been working with the Mistress, Eurydice. She wanted to look at that man you brought her."

"That *we* brought her, Homer." She reached down and removed a hand towel he always carried in the pocket of his bedsheet-sized shirt. She wiped the drool off his chin. She noticed something else about him. "No shower today, Homer?"

His head dropped in shame until it was at the level of her waist. "I wanted to wait for you to do it."

"I told you you're . . ." She stopped. There was no sense in scolding him. He was nearly twice her age. The fact that she could get him to bathe and feed himself at all was an accomplishment. Before her arrival, the Mistress had ignored him, like the bad experiment he had turned out to be.

"Eurydice, you're not going to argue with the Mistress, are you?" He was very sensitive to her moods. She wondered if such childlike sensitivity would have survived had he turned out to be the god in the flesh the Mistress had planned.

"No, Homer, I won't argue with her. I know it upsets you. C'mon, I'll help you wash."

The display case in which the two-way glass platter was located was thirty-five feet long and ten feet tall. Stepping forward, Eurydice pressed the toe of her foot against the base of the case. A soft click echoed through the room, but nothing visibly changed. As she marched to the end of the case, Homer followed. At the wooden panel enclosing that end, she used both thumbs and index fingers to tap out a code on the plain wooden surface beneath which were secreted sensor pads. When she concluded this code, the entire display rolled back ten feet, revealing a passageway leading down beneath the Museum.

As she walked through it, she asked Homer, "Was the Mistress satisfied with the man?" The panel closed behind them.

"No, Eurydice. She said he's too old and uses narcotics. She said you should have brought her the policeman. She said she wants you to get rid of the man. She said she wants the policeman. She said she wants you to check the Lullaby."

They had descended a hundred feet on a spiraling staircase cut through narrow stone walls. There was no light in the passage, but the two people had been up and down these stairs so many times that they knew every brick in the walls.

In the darkness, they stopped. With an uncanny instinct, he halted without running into her. The Lullaby of Death was the device Jim Cross had built out on Seagull Island ninety-six years ago. It had remained in place and operational since that day.

Eurydice turned to Homer, whom she couldn't see. "Why does she want the Lullaby checked?"

"She wants to use it tonight."

19

OCTOBER 10, 1997
10:57 P.M.

Dr. Sam Sykes had managed to escape from that horrible dungeon his hideous kidnappers had taken him to. His half-crazed-with-fear mind kept screaming "Beauty and the Beast!" There had been someone else there also. Someone as terrible as the monster that had grabbed him off the street downtown.

He spun around, attempting to find a landmark or street sign. There was nothing but tall trees everywhere. Then something moved nearby. His head jerked in that direction. He let out a choked cry of fear and began moving backward. He stumbled and fell on his behind. But he quickly got back up. He never took his eyes off what had looked like a black shadow initially, but that now moved toward him with a pronounced purpose. A shadow that had the substance of a vapor cloud. A black vapor cloud.

He turned to attempt headlong flight, but his wobbly knees would not support his weight. He collapsed to the ground again. He looked back frantically at the moving blackness. It was gone.

Dr. Sam struggled up on his knees. The area around him was empty and wet. This did not surprise him. It was fall and there was always a lot of autumn rain in Chicago. On top of that, his suit was filthy after his ordeal at the hands of Beauty and the Beast.

Unknowingly, Dr. Sam was kneeling on one of the pressure plates dotting Haunted Island like explosives in a mine field. Now a computerized message was transmitted to one of the launch sites. There were twelve of them on the half-mile-square wooded island. The system determined Dr. Sam's position. A millisecond later, a projectile was launched. The projectile was a spinning, whistling blade of tempered, L-shaped steel. Years ago, Jim Cross had named his terrifying creation the "Lullaby of Death," because of this distinctive sound.

Now Dr. Sam heard the sound. It reached him in seconds, severing his head at the shoulders and then continuing on to the launch site directly opposite its original position. The decapitated body and the head dropped through a hole in the ground where the pressure plate had been. There was no sign left of the violence that had just taken place at this spot.

When it was over, the shadow Dr. Sam had thought to be a vapor cloud or ghost moved toward the place where the decapitated body had vanished. The black veil was parted to reveal Eurydice's face beneath the ghost disguise. Homer came from the dense line of trees leading up to the Museum's south fence.

"Retrieve his remains from below, Homer," she said. "The Mistress will want to study them."

Homer nodded and turned away.

Eurydice wondered if Jim Cross had wanted his work to be used like this, wreaking destruction on everyone trapped in the Mistress's coils.

Well, she thought, not exactly everyone. One had gotten away— the cop, Larry Cole.

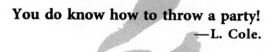

You do know how to throw a party!
—L. Cole.

20

Detective Edna Gray parked the unmarked police car she had been assigned in front of the Third District station. Getting out, she turned to admire the finish on the four-door, two-year-old Chevy with the whitewall tires and AM/FM radio. She had never driven a police car this nice. In fact, it was hard to believe that it was a police car at all, despite the two-way radio concealed in the glove compartment. She'd even had her choice of colors from the Detective Division motor pool. The car was midnight blue, one of her favorites.

She crossed the sidewalk to the station entrance. She wore a charcoal-gray business suit with a ruffled white blouse and black pumps. The outfit was a bit severe, but compared to the masculine police uniform, it was a Paris original.

Inside, she went to the desk. The uniformed female officer at the information station was filling out a form. She didn't look up although she was aware that someone was standing there.

"Be with you in a minute," she said.

Edna waited. A slight smile played at the corners of her mouth.

Finally, the policewoman completed the form and looked up. When she saw the acting detective, her eyes went as wide as saucers. "Edna, is that you?" The scream echoed through the quiet station.

Detective Gray smiled and did a little pirouette. "It's me, in the flesh, Jo-Jo."

A few heads turned and curious faces appeared in the doorways of the administrative offices.

"Hey, everybody! C'mere and look at Edna!" Jo-Jo yelled. "She's a real, live detective now!"

Suddenly, Edna was surrounded by a score of her former co-workers. Being the center of so much attention made her ill at ease. Maybe she could have visited her old assignment with a bit less fanfare.

The district commander called her into the front office. A short time ago, the place had seemed so forbidding. Now, after her exposure to the Ivory Tower, which the downtown headquarters building was called, the commander's office seemed kind of small.

"So, how's it going down there, Gray?" the commander asked.

"Very good, sir. It's an interesting experience."

"What are you working on?"

She looked away from him. In a way, he was still her boss, but Blackie had told her not to tell anyone. But then, the Third District commander wasn't just anyone.

He saved her the trouble of having to explain. "Don't sweat it, Edna. I understand how these things can be. I spent five years in Patrol Division headquarters. I'll wait until the next command meeting and ask Larry myself."

An overwhelming curiosity made her ask, "Do you know Commander Cole well, sir?"

"We made sergeant together a few years back. He was the youngest in the class. One heckuva guy and the best cop I ever met. What do you think of him?"

Her mind said, "I think he's just wonderful," but "He's a very nice man" came out of her mouth.

The look the commander gave her transmitted that he had detected something from either her reaction or her words, but he made no comment.

"So, what brings you out this way?" he asked.

"I want to talk to Mr. Eddings over in the cemetery."

"Old crazy Luke Eddings!" the commander said with a grin. "What could he have to do with your investigation?"

Again, Edna couldn't comment, but she did say, "He's been the caretaker of the Havenhurst Cemetery for about fifty years. Before that, his father and grandfather were caretakers."

The Havenhurst Cemetery was located right across the street from the Third District station. It had been there since before the Civil War.

Edna found that her day centered around the hours when she was at work, or more appropriately, the time when she was around Larry Cole. There were too few such times of painfully short duration for her taste. But when he was near her, she could almost feel his presence like a charge of electricity in the air.

And he felt something too. As a woman, she knew this. She could tell by the way he looked at her, the way he moved when he was close to her, the nervous energy he expended in her presence.

Once, at the end of her first week in the Detective Division, they were accidentally left alone in the office at quitting time. He was inside his private office, but the door was open. She was at her desk. She decided to see if he needed anything before she left. To have a chance to see him once more before she went home for the weekend. At the same time, he apparently decided to check the outer office before leaving. They collided in the doorway.

Their contact was fleeting, but it had a lingering effect. They were mutually embarrassed and spent a couple of moments stepping all over each other's apologies. Then there had come a deafening silence.

"Are you working late tonight, Commander?" she'd asked with a mouth so dry that detaching her tongue from the roof inside was like pulling taffy off a wall.

"No. I was just going. Would you like me to leave the lights on for you?"

"No. I was leaving also. I just wanted to see if you needed anything before I left."

"No. Nothing. But I can walk you out."

"You don't have to."

"Well, we are leaving together."

"Yes, sir. We are. I'll get my things."

He seemed to concentrate particularly hard on locking the office and making sure everything was secure. The hallway outside the elevators was also deserted. It was as if they were the only two people in the building.

"How do you like the Detective Division so far, Edna?"

She had turned to face him. Somehow being alone like this gave her courage. "I think being assigned to your office is the best thing that has ever . . . happened in my career, Commander," she finished lamely.

The elevator came and they boarded.

"You've been quite an asset to us."

"Thank you, sir," she said. "Your staff is almost like family. You must have been together for a long time."

"Not that long."

The elevator arrived in the lobby and they walked out of the building together. At the entrance to the parking lot, Cole hesitated a moment before saying, "Well, have a nice weekend, Edna. I'll see you on Monday."

"You have a nice weekend too, Commander."

For just a brief instant, the two of them stood there together. Finally, Cole turned and walked to his car, parked along "Commanders' Row."

And each day she found their orbits circling closer, and a week later, he asked her to come to his office. The chief of detectives, whom she found to be a very amusing and pleasant man, had been in there for a half-hour. They came into the outer office together.

Govich said, "Larry, I'm sure you can handle Luckett."

"Don't worry, Chief. I don't think he'll have too much to say to me anyway."

After Govich walked away, Cole turned to her. "Edna, would you get your car and meet me in front of the building?"

When Cole got in the car, he asked, "Do you know where the Municipal Administration Building is?"

"Yes, sir. It's on LaSalle."

"Okay, let's go."

She drove quickly through Loop traffic. He seemed preoccupied. He left her outside while he went into the building. He was gone forty-five minutes.

"What time is it?" he asked when he returned.

She checked her watch. "Eleven-thirty."

"How about an early lunch over in Greektown?"

"That would be nice, Commander." They had large Greek salads with freshly baked bread. Because they were on duty, they had no wine or cocktails.

21

Edna pulled up in front of the Havenhurst Cemetery administration building. A young, curious cemetery manager gave her directions to Symphony Shores Meadow, where Luke Eddings was working. She found the Civil War monument flanked by a wrought iron cannon and a stack of welded-together cannonballs at the center of a grassy area dotted with small, white tombstones. She parked the car and got out.

Walking around to the front of the monument, she came to a stone pillar she originally thought to be a tombstone. She stopped to read the inscription on it: "IN HONOR OF ALL THOSE BRAVE AMERICANS OF THE SOUTH, WHO REFUSED TO FOLLOW THE CONFEDERACY INTO THE TREASONOUS ACT OF SECESSION THAT LED TO THIS GREAT NATION'S MOST BLOODY CONFLICT."

She was still reading when she became aware of someone standing behind her. He was standing too close to her. She turned around and took a step back without removing her hand from the butt of her gun. He looked like a derelict, with unshaven cheeks, red-rimmed eyes and an odor that even the stiff wind couldn't completely dissipate.

"Who are you?" she asked.

"Luke Eddings. I'm the caretaker here. Plant the flowers, look after the graves and the like. You a cop?"

She relaxed her grip on the gun and straightened up. She still eyed him suspiciously. "Why did you sneak up on me like that?"

"I didn't know I did," he said, shrugging shoulders that seemed to come to points under the ratty T-shirt he wore. "Don't see too many good-looking women coming in here to see this old memorial. Don't too many just plain folks come to see it either. Like everybody's forgot there ever was a Civil War."

Edna smiled. "I remember the Civil War from the history books, Mr. Eddings, but I didn't come out here to see this." She swung her arm up to take in the monument behind her. "I actually came to talk to you." She flashed her detective's badge. "I'd just like to ask you some questions about the cemetery and Ezra Rotheimer."

"What about that old goniff? Hell, he died before I was born."

"But you know something about him, don't you?" she asked, replacing her badge case in her purse and removing a ball-point pen and a small, wire-bound notebook. "From stories you've heard, things people have told you? We're investigating a series of strange events that happened over there."

"A lot of strange things have happened since Rotheimer took over that building on the lake and made it his museum," Eddings said smugly. "Like this little parcel of land you're standing on. It's not even part of Chicago. It's still Havenhurst Township. 'Course, nobody ever made an issue of it in the last thirty years or so."

She made a note of this.

"Now," he went on, "when they were excavating the land prior to the Columbian Exposition back in the eighteen-nineties, they found that a lot of the property Rotheimer owned over to the east was built on landfill. They packed it down, built some places up and supposedly put in some tunnels."

"Tunnels? Why?"

"Southside subway! Rotheimer was always looking for another way to make a buck. He figured to build a subway tunnel from over by the lake all the way to the Grand Crossing. Even started it. But he couldn't finish it."

"Why not?"

He stomped his foot on the ground. "Havenhurst! He'd have had to tunnel under the land here, and my granddaddy didn't want the peace of the dearly departed disturbed. There were some rumors that Rotheimer did go a ways underneath our land anyway. Of course, no southside-of-Chicago subway system ever became a reality."

"Then the tunnel was abandoned?"

"Yep. It's probably still there, though," Eddings said, squinting off in the distance as if concentration alone would allow him to see through the ground to the old tunnel's location. "It's probably the reason for the critters I find around here from time to time. Something unnatural about that landfill, if you ask me."

Eddings was beginning to remind Edna of her partner, Anderson, who liked to scare people with stories about the Museum. She decided to play along with the old man. "What kind of critters, Mr. Eddings?"

"C'mon. I'll show you." He walked off toward the road.

She started to offer him a ride, but instead told him, "Lead the way. I'll follow you in my car." She wasn't about to let anyone in her nice, clean police car who smelled as bad as he did.

She followed him about a quarter of a mile to a worn brick building, which looked to be as old as the Civil War monument they had just left. He disappeared through the front door before she could get out of the car. After a moment's hesitation, she followed.

The inside revealed that this structure served a number of purposes. It was a gardener's shed, tool room and storage area all rolled into one. It was also Luke Eddings' home, which was as disgustingly filthy as she figured it would be. But before she had the opportunity to be repelled by the sight and smell of her surroundings, he pointed to a skeleton assembled on the floor at the center of the main room.

Edna looked closely, but what she saw didn't make sense. She had never seen an actual skeleton of a horse, but she could have imagined that one would look something like this jumble of bones Eddings had assembled. At least half of a horse would.

"Well?" Eddings asked, nearly bursting with the excitement coursing through him. "What does it look like to you?"

She told him.

"You're almost right. But when I found it, the thing had only two legs, not four, and up here—" he pointed to an area in the vicinity of the rib cage "—was a couple of arms just like ours."

Edna eyed him skeptically. "And why didn't you attach the bones of those arms like you did the rest of the skeleton?"

"I did, but they decayed. Them things wasn't natural, lady. But then there's more unnatural stuff I've found out there over the years. Lots more."

What Eddings showed her were just jumbles of more bones, which the old man had apparently put together to resemble what he thought to be something unusual. She remembered a movie she'd seen on television years ago about an old man in the desert who put together what he thought was the skeleton of a flying demon, or a living gargoyle. Of course, in the movie, those things had been real.

"This here was a monkey with a human face," Eddings said, pointing to a pile of bones that looked like the leavings following a summer barbeque. "This was a cat with a set of wings growing out its back. This here was a snake with legs."

He went on and on, but nothing he described could be even remotely compared to what he was using as proof of its existence before the flesh had rotted off the corpse.

She finally stopped him. "Mr. Eddings, why don't you show me where you found these things?"

They were in walking distance of the edge of one of the freshwater ponds located in the cemetery. On top of a rise above this pond was a crypt as large as Eddings' brick shack. The name engraved over the crypt's mantle was "Rotheimer."

"Here they all lie, 'cept his missing kids, of course," Eddings prattled. "Nobody knows what happened to them, poor things. Maybe they're better off not being here."

Something made Edna tremble. She looked around. She felt as if they were being watched. There was no one in sight except Eddings.

At the top of the hill, however, there was brief movement at one of the filthy windows of the Rotheimer mausoleum. There, beneath decades of dust and decay, a startlingly blue eye stared down at Eddings and Detective Edna Gray.

22

OCTOBER 25, 1997
1:00 P.M.

Seymour Winbush had moved the executive offices of the DeWitt Corporation from the DeWitt Office Building on Lake Shore Drive over to DeWitt Plaza on North Michigan Avenue. The space occupied by the CEO, vice-presidents and executive staff of the multinational corporation took up the top three floors of the fifty-story building. This same space had once been the living quarters of Neil and Margo DeWitt, who had actually owned the giant corporation's far-flung empire. The DeWitts had been dead for sixteen months. Winbush blamed Larry Cole for the deaths of his former bosses.

E. G. Luckett went over all the information he possessed in his prodigious memory of the DeWitt Corporation as he was driven down Michigan Avenue by Cousin Gene Luckett. His hemorrhoids were making it difficult to sit comfortably. But his mind was still turning over the data on the Winbush/Cole situation.

But then, that was old news. Since September, when Cole had been hurt, Winbush had shown no more interest in the black cop. Maybe he was satisfied that Cole had suffered. After all, the cop had been demoted, his wife had left him, and he'd almost been killed out on that island behind the National Science and Space Museum. Perhaps this would atone for the deaths of the DeWitts. Two people who had rewritten the FBI profiles on serial killers, because they were a very rich, married couple.

No, E. G. thought, Winbush had called this meeting for another reason, which he would discover shortly as DeWitt Plaza came into view up ahead.

As Cousin Gene pulled the car to the curb, E. G. twisted his fleshy torso around in the front seat and opened the door. With some effort, he squeezed out onto the street. It took him a moment to straighten up. He was badly winded from this small amount of physical exertion. Gulping air, he turned to look back inside the Caddy.

"You know what time to pick me up?"

"Got it written down right in here," the younger man said, patting the notebook concealed in his inside coat pocket. Because Cousin Gene's memory was so poor when it was required to retain anything beyond female telephone numbers or measurements, Cousin Nadine had insisted that he write everything down. This led to E. G. recommending that Gene purchase a small notebook.

"I'm also going to pick up some more Preparation H for your hemorrhoids, E. G."

A couple of passerby picked up on that one. One of them, a young girl, snickered. The other, a neatly dressed gentleman of about sixty, gave E. G. a compassionate look.

With no other options available to him, E. G. Luckett slammed the car door and turned to cross the sidewalk to enter DeWitt Plaza. He couldn't help but vent the frustration caused through a combination of his anal pain and Cousin Gene's stupidity by hissing a very vicious "Imbecile!" under his breath.

He was forced to take two elevators to reach the penthouse. A smartly dressed young woman awaited him at the entrance to the forty-eighth floor, which was the first level of the three-story office complex.

"You must be Mr. Luckett," she said with a warm smile that E. G. knew was not for him personally, but was simply something the DeWitt Corporation paid her to put on display for their guests. "May I take your hat and coat, sir?"

She hung the coat and hat in a closet off an immense hall with a wooden floor that gleamed like glass. "Right this way."

Luckett waddled slowly behind her to a set of double doors halfway down the corridor. She knocked softly on the panel, waited a moment and then opened the doors. Before entering the room, E. G. glanced back over his shoulder at another set of double doors across the hall. That was the DeWitts' former library. It was there that Cole had begun building his case against the homicidal duo.

E. G. had never been invited up here and he was definitely impressed. The only way he could describe the room he was ushered into was "money." Marble, polished wood, crystal, indirect lighting and furnishings crafted for style and comfort graced the interior. At the center of all this extravagance sat Seymour Winbush.

Adopting his well-practiced mask of servility, E. G. walked toward the head of the DeWitt Corporation. Winbush, an aging, handsome, leonine-headed man, waited patiently for the elephantine Luckett to cross the office. He did not get up from behind his huge desk as Luckett struggled around it to shake his hand.

"It's good to see you again, Mr. Winbush, sir. You're looking very well. Keeping yourself in shape, I see. I could use a bit of that myself. Ha, ha." Luckett patted his own blimp-sized gut.

Winbush gave Luckett a look of barely concealed contempt. "Allow me to introduce you to the others I've invited to this meeting, E. G." Winbush motioned to the three men seated in the office, whom Luckett had pointedly ignored when he came in.

"George Doyle, Kyle Peters and Bill McElroy. This is E. G. Luckett, the city director of Public Safety."

As Luckett shook hands with each of the three men, he assessed them. Doyle looked like the administrative type, perhaps a lawyer, or an accountant. Peters came on like an artist. Maybe something just a little more disciplined, like an architect. Bill McElroy was also a big guy, but not like E. G. Instead, he was football-player big, like maybe a defensive tackle on the Bears. And he looked either pissed off or just plain mean.

E. G. slid into one of the softly upholstered, curved-seated easy chairs arranged around Winbush's desk. The chair was sturdy enough to take his weight, but the minute his rear end touched the cushioned seat, the pain of his inflammation caused him to wince.

"Something wrong, E. G.?" Winbush asked.

"No," Luckett responded with a pained expression. "Just a twinge. It'll pass." Not without something stronger than Preparation H, he thought.

"E. G.," Winbush began, "you're the only one who hasn't been brought up to speed on why I called this meeting. I'll let Mr. Doyle and Mr. Peters explain things. Then we'll get down to the reason I asked you in on this."

Doyle, the attorney, and Peters, the architect, formally in the employ of the late Harry McElroy of the McElroy Lakefront Development Company, laid out the same plan briefly for E. G. Luckett as they had for Eurydice Vaughn and Dr. Winston Fleisher at the National Science and Space Museum a few weeks earlier. They left out nothing; however, they didn't have the drawings, which Eurydice Vaughn had destroyed at the conclusion of that meeting.

"Tell him about my father," McElroy said in conclusion. "Isn't Luckett in charge of the cops? Maybe he can make them do something!"

Winbush gave the younger McElroy one of his bored expressions. "E. G. has already looked into your dad's death, Bill, and it was like everyone else has been telling you—it was nothing more than a heart attack."

"I don't buy that!" McElroy's face reddened. "What about these two? They were nearly unconscious, and that guy Fleisher was asleep. My father was slipped something by that woman."

Luckett cleared his throat. "I contacted the chief of detectives and had him look into your father's unfortunate passing. In fact, he assigned Commander Larry Cole, whom I'm quite sure Mr. Winbush will agree, is a very tenacious and thorough officer."

Winbush made no comment, nor would he look at Luckett.

"Commander Cole reported to me in my downtown office that your father died of a massive coronary, which was brought about by his life-style. As I understand it, your father was over sixty, smoked, drank and—"

"That bullshit doesn't mean anything, Luckett. My father was as healthy as I am!"

"William!" Winbush said in a voice that froze the flush-faced giant in place. "That'll be enough of that. We didn't come up here to berate E. G. or to argue about what happened to Harry.

"E. G., the reason we've asked you here is that the DeWitt Corporation is going to back Bill financially so that he can proceed with his father's plans for the development of the lakefront area around the National Science and Space Museum.

"Although Harry's death was an explainable tragedy," Winbush shot McElroy a hard look when the young man's head snapped up in protest, "we are concerned about other problems. We want to proceed a little more cautiously in our approach to the Museum. That's where you come in."

Although E. G. Luckett wasn't quite clear about what the CEO of the DeWitt Corporation was getting at, he gave no sign of this.

"In fact, my sources over at Eleventh and State report that Commander Cole has already done a great deal of the research for us."

When a few moments passed and Winbush didn't elaborate, Luckett asked, "And what kind of research is that?"

Again Winbush flashed one of his tolerant expressions in Luckett's direction. "Research about the Museum. Seems Cole and his old friends, Jamal Garth and Barbara Zorin, have been looking into some mysterious crimes that have occurred in or around the Museum over the years. All you've got to do is have Cole expand his research a bit."

"Expand it how, sir?" Luckett asked.

"To include the Museum's chairman of the board, Dr. Winston Fleisher, and its curator, a young woman named Eurydice Vaughn."

Luckett nodded his understanding. The only thing he had to figure out now was how he was going to get Cole to do this.

23

OCTOBER 30, 1997
DAWN

Eurydice Vaughn lived in a one-bedroom apartment in the twenty-story Lake Shore Drive condominium building just east of the Leamington Hotel, overlooking the National Science and Space Museum. She had occupied the apartment for five years and was considered a model tenant by management. She was clean, quiet, lived alone and had never been known to have a male caller. In fact, there were long stretches of time—days, sometimes even weeks—when she didn't set foot inside the apartment. The management believed Miss Vaughn's absences to be due to her duties over at the Museum. For their part, Dr. Fleisher and the rest of the Museum staff would not have been able to account for her whereabouts. However, she was at the Museum, but in a place where no one could find her.

The site of the current *Glassware from Around the World* Hall inside the National Science and Space Museum had originally been the site of Katherine Rotheimer and Jim Cross's workshop behind the Natural History Museum. Prior to construction of the brick workshop and the original structure that became the History Museum, Ezra Rotheimer had chosen that site as the point of origin for his lakefront subway system. A manmade cavern had been dug on the site and shored-up tunnels constructed from it in the direction of the Grand Railroad crossing, five miles away. As Luke Eddings explained to Detective Edna Gray, the walls of Havenhurst Cemetery finally stopped the nineteenth-century millionaire's scheme. So the excavated area was abandoned, but not forgotten. Now, in 1997, hundreds of feet beneath the surface, the cavern and adjoining tunnels were in use.

Electricity drained from the Museum powered the cavern's ceiling lighting system in the fifty-foot-high main chamber. It was this chamber that Rotheimer had originally planned as an underground version of Grand Central Station. Most of the station had been completed prior to abandonment of the project, and the place did resemble Grand Central, except that it was very dark, forbidding and empty.

Tunnels originally constructed to accommodate nineteenth-century trains ran off from four platforms around the station. Air shafts were sunk to provide ventilation to the surface. Most of these vents had been sealed off at ground level over the years; however, the largest one was still operational. It came out on Seagull Island.

A thorough, progressive-minded Rotheimer had even built executive and administrative offices into the upper level of the station. These offices now served a number of functions. Laboratories for chemical and biological experiments, operating rooms for humans and animals, a library, communications center, recreation center, and living rooms equipped with bedrooms, bathrooms and a kitchen— all these lined the upper level.

Dressed in the black Spandex body suit she wore on her nightly rounds through the Museum, Eurydice awoke in one of the bedrooms. The lights were off, leaving the twenty-foot-square area in total darkness. But she was aware that she was not alone. She could hear Homer's snore, which sounded like the rumbling growl of a grizzly. He was nearby.

Eurydice was lying on a bed that was actually more of a narrow cot, with a bare mattress thrown across the support springs. A coarse army blanket had covered her while she slept. She mused that Homer had probably covered her after she dozed off. She searched her brain to remember when. It had been after midnight. She had followed Larry again. She had even looked through one of the windows of his house. This was dangerous, but then she knew that she could move very fast if he caught a glimpse of her at the window and came to investigate. She was tiring, though, of these nocturnal games. She was also impatient.

Homer released a snore of such violence that the bricks in the walls seemed to vibrate. In the darkness, her face took on a mischievous expression of childlike cunning. Reaching down, she felt for his face in the dark. He slept on the floor. Whenever she stayed down here, which was often, he would end up right beneath her bed. That's where he'd always slept. She couldn't remember a time in her life, even when she was a little girl, when this hadn't been so.

She touched the deformed face. It was moist with perspiration. The same central-heating plant that serviced the Museum had been routed to pipe warm air in down here. Her room was directly under the vent. She could also smell the odor of Homer's morning breath. This touch, this smell and the heat of the darkness in the cell-like room were where she had come from. She had no memories of anything else until she'd gone to live above the surface as an adult. She, like Homer, was a creation of the Mistress. Only Eurydice had been a success.

Reaching down, she pinched his nose shut. He gasped and finally choked himself awake. She kept her hand around his nose. He let out a roar that shook the bricks, and reached for her.

Bouncing onto her feet, she bounded away from him. He pursued.

She darted down the balcony, passing the other rooms. He lumbered behind her, closing the gap with each stride.

The balcony came to an end at an ornate staircase leading down into the lower levels of the would-be station. Eurydice knew she could not outrun Homer on the stairs. Her only escape route was up.

A ledge ran around the top of the structure. It was seven feet above the floor of the balcony on which she was being pursued, but a leap onto the narrow iron railing would provide her with enough momentum to hurl herself across the space and try for a handhold on the edge. If she missed, the stone floor awaited fifty feet below. Without a second's hesitation, she leaped off the balcony railing and caught the ledge, her feet swinging beneath her. She was still laughing.

With another roar, Homer leaped from the balcony and landed beside her, but was able to support himself with only one hand. He wrapped his other arm around her waist and pulled her off the ledge. Laughing, they dangled by his lone grasp.

"What are you two doing?"

The amplified voice echoed through the underground cavern. Their laughter abruptly ceased. Homer swung back to the balcony and set Eurydice down on her feet.

"Stop that foolishness! What are you doing here, Eurydice?"

"I spent the night," she said as her head snapped up defiantly at the unseen interrogator.

Homer's head tilted toward the floor. One of his hands came up to touch her arm. She jerked away.

"You've already called enough attention to us when you saved that policeman. Your coming down here all the time will eventually cause someone to begin asking questions."

"No one's ever bothered us before."

A long minute of strained silence produced a tension that hung in the huge cavern like a shroud.

"I want to see you right now, Eurydice!"

"I've got to bathe Homer and fix breakfast. Then I'll come."

Homer tensed. Eurydice turned and rubbed his head. She noticed that his hair was starting to become a bit shaggy. After his shower, she would get the clippers. He was a wretched enough creature as it was. With the unkempt hair and the ragged beard he'd worn before she'd started trimming his hair, he didn't even look human.

Finally, the response came. *"As you wish."*

Eurydice smiled. She knew the Mistress could see her do this, but she was glad. She had won. It had taken her years, but she was beginning to assume an almost equal status with the Mistress. She also knew that no one lived forever. She altered the thought to, almost no one.

Homer howled with delight as Eurydice sprayed him with a garden hose. He did cartwheels in the stone-walled room with the large drain in the floor. There were eight shower heads arranged around the room. They were all turned on full-blast. He would dart under one or another of them from time to time and drink water straight from the faucet. She followed him, keeping the spray full-force on his body.

Finally, she shut off the hose, which was the signal for him to come over and sit on a stool in the center of the shower room. Obediently, he sat down.

They were both naked. Taking a bottle of liquid soap, Eurydice poured it liberally over a wet cloth, rubbed it to form a lather and then began to soap him from head to toe. She was aware that his body, no matter how misshapen, was a male's. He was unaware that she was a female of his species, as well as one possessing a stunning body.

Eurydice washed him with a cool outward detachment, but internally, she was in turmoil. The Mistress had imposed a number of strange rules on her existence. One of them was celibacy. However, this was another thing she was changing as she adapted to her half-life above. She'd realized long ago that she could never live up there permanently. In fact, she had no desire to do so.

But she possessed normal urges. Urges that caused her to begin looking at Homer in a different way when she reached the age of fourteen. By the age of fifteen, she had attempted an "experiment" with him. But it hadn't worked. He possessed no sex drive at all. His meager intelligence would not allow him to completely comprehend gender differences. When, with her awkward, adolescent blundering, she had attempted to interest him in her body, she succeeded in doing no more than terrifying him. After that, she couldn't even get him to wash her during their bathing periods together.

Eurydice had buried Homer under a mound of suds. Now she reached for the hose and rinsed him. When she finished, he emitted a spluttering sigh and waddled slowly from the shower area to get towels to dry himself with.

She watched him go. He had so few pleasures. It was a shame he would never experience the greatest physical pleasure of all. So far, despite the years she'd been up there, she had not engaged in sex. But she planned for that to change very soon.

Carrying her bottle of scented liquid soap, she stepped under the nearest shower head. She clamped her teeth as she turned the spray on cold. She stood under it for two full minutes, forcing her body to remain unflinchingly still. Then she adjusted the temperature to a more comfortable range and began to lather herself.

"Eurydice," Homer said from the other side of the shower room, where he had completely wrapped himself in towels, so that only his face showed.

"What is it, Homer?" Her eyes were closed against the soap covering her face.

"I saw you in the cemetery."

She rinsed off the soap and squinted at him through the spray cascading down her face. "You dreamed I was dead?"

"No. I saw you in the cemetery with Mr. Eddie."

She turned back to her shower. "Okay, I'll play. When did you see me in the cemetery with Mr. Eddie?" She knew that he meant Eddings instead of Eddie, but no matter how many times she'd tried to correct him, he still said it wrong. Of course Luke Eddings would never hear him say it anyway.

"But I wasn't in the cemetery last week," she said with her back to him.

"Yeah, you was."

"I wasn't."

"You was."

"I wasn't!"

It was time for Eurydice to go to work. She had fed Homer and been forced to listen to a few choice words from the Mistress about her behavior and the responsibilities of her position. Now she was dressed in a business suit and heels and her hair was combed. There was little resemblance between the wild, screaming amazon in black Spandex whom Homer had chased a few hours ago and the young professional now. But Eurydice realized that the wild thing was very close by.

She crossed the upper-level gallery of the subterranean cavern alone. As she walked past the Mistress's library, she stopped. The Mistress could be watching her now, but she didn't care. Eurydice stepped inside.

There were old books and new books, handwritten manuscripts, notebooks and drawings. A somewhat haphazard, dusty arrangement, though with some real gems hidden among the disorder. But she hadn't come in here to browse.

There were a number of photographs, as well as a couple of life-sized oil paintings. It was one of the paintings that she had come to view. It hung on the far wall beside the oil portrait of Ezra Rotheimer, which had originally been displayed in the Museum before "mysteriously" vanishing. She stopped and stared up at it.

The likeness in the portrait was not as accurate as photos of the period. The artist had been more flattering to the subject. In fact, the resemblance between the person this was intended to be and the rendering was vague at best. Eurydice had seen this portrait and the accompanying one of Rotheimer every day of her life. It was supposed to be Jim Cross. It came out looking like Larry Cole.

She studied it for another moment before turning to leave the library. She had fantasized about the man in this picture for years. Fantasies that at times had been erotic. That night on the island, she had seen the resemblance between the policeman and the Jim Cross likeness. This was when she'd decided to save Cole. Save him for herself.

As she headed for the passage to the surface that would deliver her to her office, she thought about the policeman. Eurydice Vaughn was a twenty-eight-year-old virgin. She intended for Larry Cole to be the man to change that condition for her. She intended for him to do this very soon.

24

OCTOBER 30, 1997
5:45 A.M.

Larry Cole's alarm clock went off. He had not been in a deep sleep, but merely dozing. It had been a long time since he had been able to sleep soundly for more than two hours at a stretch.

He swung his feet to the floor and sat on the edge of the bed for a moment. Lately he experienced a lingering depression that lasted through a substantial portion of the day. It was there with him now, like a weight chained to his back. The only way to deal with it was to ignore it, and the only way he could accomplish this would be to stay busy.

After a shower and shave, he went to the closet to remove his dress uniform. There was a lot of space in the closet. He and Lisa had shared it together. Now only his things were there.

He would be wearing the uniform today to attend the monthly command meeting, followed by a recruit graduation at the Police Academy. One of the few things the new superintendent had not changed since taking over the Chicago Police Department was the practice of having command officers, regardless of their assignments, attend such functions in uniform.

Before dressing, Cole checked the time. He was an hour and a half early. He could have breakfast at a restaurant near the Academy, but that wouldn't take long as he was seldom into more than tea and toast for his first meal of the day. That would still leave him too much time. Too much time to think.

He recalled that a couple of years ago, Dr. Drake had given a half-day seminar on stress reduction to command personnel. Cole had attended. The only thing he had come away from the seminar with was a self-hypnosis technique. He decided to try it now. As a precaution against dozing off while he was "under," he reset his alarm clock.

Clad in his bathrobe, he went downstairs to the den. Sitting down in his easy chair, he took a couple of deep breaths and willed himself to relax. He searched for an object to focus his attention on. He found an abnormality in the patterned edging at the top of a lamp shade across the room. He fought to clear his mind of all thought and external stimuli. The object of his concentration blurred, but he struggled to refocus his vision. It blurred again. At this point, as Drake had instructed, he began to count slowly; "one . . . two . . . three . . ." Cole closed his eyes and drifted into the first level.

He talked to Butch once a week on the telephone and had visited Detroit twice since Lisa had taken the boy there last December. At first their contacts had been painful, with Butch crying when they parted. But recently there'd been almost a formality to their farewells. It was as if the little boy was getting used to not having his father around. The idea of losing his son like this was the worst for Cole to bear.

On those trips and calls to Michigan, he saw and talked to Lisa. Like it was with Butch, the first couple of times had been rough. But then she too had become more relaxed. In fact, on his last visit, she had even kissed him good-bye. Nothing romantic, just a friendly peck on the cheek, but this provided him with hope. A false hope. Somewhere deep down inside himself, he knew she wasn't coming back to Chicago. He even considered the possibility that she wanted him to quit his job and come to live with them in Michigan. Then what would he do? No, he would be a Chicago cop until he either was forced to retire or died.

"Seven . . . eight . . . nine . . ."

He entered the third level, which was just before the last and deepest penetration into the subconscious. Dr. Drake had instructed his class to think of something pleasant at this stage. The image of Edna Gray flashed into his mind. His brows knit slightly before relaxing once more. The image of the young detective had not been conjured up by a conscious thought on his part. But, yes, her presence in his life was pleasant. Remote, but pleasant.

Cole was attracted to Edna, though she always seemed so tense around him. Whenever he attempted to have just a simple conversation with her, it was like pulling teeth. She would ask him to repeat things, as if she didn't understand what he meant, and at other times, it seemed that she went out of her way to avoid him. He was also afraid that his advances, if the point was stretched to its broadest possible extent, could be misconstrued as a form of sexual harassment of a subordinate by a command officer.

No, no one could ever prove anything like that, as nothing had actually passed between them. What had happened so far? Lunch together, a few words in the office, and once they left the building at the same time. He asked himself what he wanted from her. A lasting relationship? Marriage? That was ridiculous. He was already married. Then what did he want?

He possessed no answer for that question, but he had decided to adopt a different tactic with her. Basically, it entailed his doing no more than treating her just like another member of the Detective Division headquarters staff. For the past week, Manny or Judy had done all his driving, and he had managed to remain in the office until Edna was gone for the day. But he hadn't been able to gauge her reaction to this new approach, or rather lack of approach, because he'd been too busy.

"Ten."

Cole reached a state or plateau somewhere between consciousness and sleep. He was physically relaxed and his eyes were closed, but he was aware of everything going on around him. The National Science and Space Museum drifted through the relaxed blur of his twilight world. Then there was the figure in black rushing toward him out on the island, a flash of pain and after that . . . darkness.

He was in St. Anne's Hospital, lying on his back. Manny was nearby but sitting up in a chair, asleep. There was someone over in the corner of the room. It was the shadowy figure he'd seen out on the island. It moved closer. Came almost into the light and. . . . The image of Edna Gray popped back into his mind.

Slowly, Cole began extricating himself from the hypnotic state by reversing the procedure and sequence of numbers he had used to put himself under. When he reopened his eyes on the count of "one," he felt relaxed. Even the depression was gone. He was also wide awake. He checked the time. At first he thought his watch was wrong, but then he checked the desk clock. Thirty minutes had passed. But it didn't seem. . . . The buzzer on the alarm clock upstairs went off.

It had seemed as if he'd been under only a couple of minutes, but Dr. Drake had told them at the seminar that such time lapses were not unusual for someone under a great deal of stress. Well, he was always under more than the normal load of stress, whatever that could be, and if he didn't get in gear, he'd have the added problem of being late for the command meeting.

Although Cole and most of the other career cops found fault with the new superintendent, everyone had to admit he knew how to run a meeting. The superintendent himself called it promptly to order at 8:00 A.M. All participants were expected to be in their designated seats in the auditorium of the training academy and ready to get to work. Latecomers' names were taken and if an individual was late more than once, a record of this tardiness would be made and a superior officer dispatched to counsel that person. So far, in the ten months the superintendent had been in office, no one had been late more than once.

An agenda was passed out listing topics for discussion, with a designated time period for each subject to be discussed. If time ran out before the subject could be adequately covered, there was time allotted at the conclusion of the agenda for further discussion. If matters couldn't be resolved by then, it was either put off for review at a subsequent command meeting or, if urgent, sent to a designated panel of command officers for study and a prompt recommendation to the superintendent personally.

At the meeting's conclusion, Cole began collecting his things prior to heading for the graduation across the hall in the academy gymnasium when Govich came over to him.

"The superintendent wants to see you, me and Kennedy in the academy director's office before the graduation."

Cole checked his watch. The ceremony was due to begin in ten minutes. That meant they were wanted now.

The director's office was only a short walk from the auditorium.

First Deputy Superintendent Kennedy was waiting for them in the outer office.

"What's up, Terry?" Govich asked.

"Beat's me. The superintendent said he wanted to see the three of us. That's all I could get out of him."

"Is he angry?" Cole asked.

Kennedy smiled. "Corporate types like our new boss don't get angry, Larry. It doesn't fit their image." With that, he walked over to the closed door to the director's office and knocked. Then the three of them went inside.

25

B arbara Zorin didn't like the sound of it. "But, Larry, how did the superintendent find out about your investigation of the Museum and Seagull Island?"

"He didn't say," Cole said, lifting his third bourbon-and-water in the last hour and draining off a hefty portion of it. "And I don't really care. But I'll agree with him on one thing; if there's something going on over at that place, the chairman of the board and the curator have got to be either in on it or know something about it."

"That doesn't sound like the kind of thing the new top cop would say," Jamal Garth said skeptically. "After all, he makes a point of saying he's an administrator, not a cop, every time someone sticks a microphone in his face."

"I agree," Cole said. "Maybe a little bird whispered in his ear or somebody sent him an anonymous memo. Like I said, I don't care, but now we're completely legit. No more sneaking around and worrying about getting in trouble."

They were attending a meeting of the Brain Trust, which was a group formed during the DeWitt case. Then it had been composed only of mystery authors. Now Cole and his staff, to include newcomer Edna Gray, had joined the surviving members of the original group, Barbara Zorin and Jamal Garth. This Halloween Eve meeting was being held at Mama DeLeo's Pizzeria on West Taylor Street. They were in a partitioned-off dining room, where a large table was covered with a white cloth. Everyone was present.

"What does the superintendent figure the bottom line will be if we come up with anything, Boss?" Blackie asked.

Cole finished his drink and frowned. "I don't get it. Why is everybody looking for him to have an angle? There's a distinct possibility that over a hundred eighty capital offenses were committed at the Museum. Isn't that enough to get a police superintendent interested in doing some investigating?"

Blackie shrugged. "You got a point. I think I'd better go check on the pizzas. Since Ma DeLeo died, the kitchen help moves like they got glue stuck to the bottoms of their shoes. Might have to cart the food in ourselves. C'mon, Manny, you can give me a hand."

"Huh?" Manny was surprised at the request.

Blackie gave him a hard look. "You can help me get the pizzas."

"Oh, yeah." Manny struggled up from where he had been seated between a for-tonight vampish-looking Judy, who was made up like a 1920's flapper, and the usually quiet Edna.

"Blackie," Cole called after them, "while you're gone, see if you can get our waitress to bring us another round."

"Sure thing," Blackie said.

Out in the restaurant, Blackie led Manny toward the bar instead of turning in the direction of the kitchen. Manny thought they were heading that way in order to place the commander's drink order. When Blackie slid onto a bar stool, Manny remained standing until Blackie said, "Sit down, kid. We gotta talk."

Puzzled, Manny sat.

Blackie motioned for Jimmy DeLeo, owner by inheritance of the pizzeria but still tending bar, to bring them two glasses of draft beer. When DeLeo, a beefy man with hair worn in a slick-backed ducktail, set the beer down, Blackie instructed him to send another round to their party. Then he turned to Manny.

"Something stinks about this thing. I got the feeling we're being set up, and set up good."

"I don't get it."

"It's simple, kid," Blackie said, reaching for a cigar. "When Larry was doing this Museum investigation as a kind of hobby, it was okay. It was like therapy for him after all he'd been through. But I should have seen things going wrong when Edna showed up."

"What's wrong with Edna?" Manny asked with a frown. The sergeant had grown very fond of the pretty black detective in a completely platonic way.

"She's got a broken wing, Manny. She's been hurt bad in her life. I can see it in her face. Somebody's done her real wrong. I've seen that same look in the faces of abused children and battered wives. It's like every time somebody comes near them, they expect to be slapped or kicked."

Manny thought about this for a moment. He wasn't sure.

"Larry's finally coming out of the tailspin and all the bullshit he's been through this past year. Tonight he's letting his hair down. He'll be a completely new man tomorrow."

"By letting his hair down, you mean the way he's drinking?"

Blackie shot the sergeant a cross look. "I've known Larry Cole for more than twenty years and I've seen him ripped on booze maybe three, four times. The night Butch was born, after he was certain Lisa and the baby were okay, we left the hospital, went back to my place and polished off a whole fifth of Wild Turkey. Couple of other times after particularly heavy cases, we'd have a few, but when he's in the middle of a problem, Larry won't touch more than a beer or two. It's only after he thinks the problem is over that he unwinds a bit. I'd say that's what he's doing tonight."

"Oh," Manny said. Sometimes he really found it difficult following Blackie, but he usually discovered that the lieutenant was right in the long run.

"Do you think Edna's going to complicate things for him?" Manny asked.

Blackie sighed and shook his head. "I really don't know. Maybe she'll be good for him, but then what about her? Suppose Edna and the boss do get tight and Lisa decides to drop back into town. After all, she is still his wife. And she's got the ace."

Manny was ahead of the lieutenant this time. "Butch."

"Right."

Before they could resume the conversation, Jimmy DeLeo came down the bar. "Hey, Blackie, your pizzas are ready."

"Have them sent over to the table," he said, draining off the rest of his beer. "We're on the way."

Manny tried to duplicate Blackie's chugalug feat, but made it only halfway before a knot of gas formed beneath his breastbone. He managed to stifle a belch that felt powerful enough to pop his eyeballs out of his head as he followed Blackie from the bar.

Since Jimmy DeLeo had taken over the restaurant after his grandmother's death, he had changed a couple of things. One was the installation of a raised dance floor in the center of the main dining room. As this was a Tuesday night, the restaurant was not as crowded as it usually was on weekends, but DeLeo's always did a decent business. There were a few couples moving slowly on the dance floor to the tune of a romantic ballad being played over a quarter-per-record jukebox.

As Blackie and Manny headed back for the table, the sight of one of the couples stopped them. Larry and Edna were dancing. Their eyes were closed and they moved well together. Blackie turned to look at Manny. "Well, kid, here we go."

26

Larry Cole awoke slowly. His mouth was dry and he had that whoozy, shaky feeling that spelled "hangover." He looked around him. He was in a strange bedroom. Confused, he began trying to remember how he got there. As it came back to him, he felt a fingertip trace lightly across the scar on his left shoulder. He turned over. Lying next to him, Edna smiled and said, "Good morning."

"Good morning," he responded, reaching for her. With a smile, she came into his arms.

Later she snuggled up close to him and said, "I knew this was going to happen the first time I saw you."

"What did I do, give off psychic vibrations?"

"Yep. It was like I could read you."

"I didn't think I was that obvious."

She sat up and leaned down so that her face was inches from his. She looked deep into his eyes. "It wasn't obvious to anyone but me, Larry. I have a gift for reading people, or at least for feeling things about people. And you came across with the best vibes I've experienced in a long time."

"Thank you," he said, kissing her lightly on the lips.

"You're welcome. What would you like for breakfast?"

"I'm kind of a light early eater," he said, stretching, and realized that despite his hangover, he felt better than he had in a long time.

"Commander Cole," she said, getting out of the bed, "breakfast is the most important meal of the day."

He watched her walk nude to a corner closet.

She slipped on a robe and turned to him. "Everything you need to shower and shave is in the bathroom. Breakfast will be ready when you come out."

Twenty minutes later, he walked into the kitchen. A place was set for him with a glass of orange juice and a hot cup of coffee beside a gleaming plate. The *Times-Herald* was folded beside the plate. Edna carried a skillet from the stove. This was the first of three. When she was finished, she had piled the plate with five strips of bacon, what looked like a half-dozen scrambled eggs, grits swimming in butter and two huge biscuits.

"Do you really expect me to eat all of this?"

She was fixing a plate for herself over at the stove. "I want you to keep your strength up. I wouldn't want you getting rundown on me."

He ended up finishing most of the huge breakfast.

At eight-thirty, she walked him to the door. He had to go home and change clothes. His arm was around her waist.

"I don't mean to sound possessive, but when will I see you again?" she asked.

He stopped and turned to face her. "I'm free tonight. Why don't you come over to my place and I'll fix dinner for you?"

She looked down at the floor.

"You've heard about my cooking?" he joked.

She laughed. "No. It's not that. It's that I have heard about your wife leaving with your little boy and . . ."

"You wouldn't feel comfortable there, is that it?"

"Why don't we give that some time, Larry? You could fix dinner over here. I could even help."

"Okay, you're on. Steak à la Cole will sweep you off your feet."

"I've already been swept off my feet."

He changed at home and considered packing an overnight bag to take with him to her place tonight. "Stop it!" he said out loud. He realized he was moving way too fast for either of them. This was dangerous.

As he drove to the police gym for his own brand of rehab, he thought about the shaving cream, aftershave and deodorant. Each container had been unopened and waiting in her bathroom beside a brand-new razor. She had been expecting him. He wondered for how long. He felt a slight, tingling apprehension at the base of his skull. Maybe this had gone faster than he was aware of. That instead of being a part of the game, he was the game.

Parking his car in the lot at Thirty-sixth and Normal, he sat behind the wheel and thought for a moment. What was wrong with him? His wife had left him almost a year ago. He hadn't been out on a date, much less even looked at another woman, in all that time. So he was having . . . what was it they called it on the soap operas Blackie videotaped to watch every night? A fling? An affair? Why in hell not?

He got out of the car and walked into the gym. Despite the lingering vestiges from a bit too much booze and less than a full night's sleep, he had an excellent workout. Although it was a gloomy, overcast day with a hint of winter in the air, he found himself whistling as he walked into headquarters.

When he entered the outer office, Edna was at her desk, located between Judy's and Manny's. Judy was out and Manny was on the phone. He could see Blackie sitting in his cubicle, going over reports. Edna looked up at him and said a very normal, "Good morning, Commander."

He smiled and responded, "Good morning, Edna."

She returned to her computer.

He walked into his office. Hanging his coat on the rack, he found himself whistling again. He'd better get that under control too. Then he realized that he wasn't much for sneaking around. Never had been. But in this case . . .

There was a stack of messages on his desk. Nothing urgent. One from Dr. Drake, another from Barbara Zorin, one from a Loop attorney and the last from an "E. Vaughn." The name rang a bell.

Cole dialed the number on the message slip. After one ring, the phone was answered: *"National Science and Space Museum, Miss Vaughn's office."*

"This is Commander Cole of the Chicago Police Department, returning Miss Vaughn's call."

"Yes, Commander. Would you please hold?"

This was strange, Cole thought. He had been planning to get in touch with this Vaughn woman and Dr. Winston Fleisher later today anyway. He wondered why she had called him.

"Hello, Commander Cole. This is Eurydice Vaughn."

The voice sounded so familiar that Cole was certain he knew this woman. After a momentary hesitation, he said, "How do you do, Miss Vaughn?"

"I'm just fine, Commander. I know you're a busy man, so I'll get right to the point. Something turned up in our Lost and Found Department at the Museum that I'm sure you'll be interested in claiming."

"And what would that be?"

His intercom buzzed.

"I understand from the police-detail personnel assigned to the Museum that on the morning of September seventeenth, you lost a nine-millimeter Beretta automatic pistol out on Seagull Island. One was anonymously turned into our Lost and Found and I believe it's yours."

Cole's shock was muted by his intercom continuing to buzz. "Miss Vaughn, could you hold on a minute?"

"Of course."

Cole punched the intercom button. At least he thought he did.

"Commander?"

He looked down at the phone buttons. The intercom button was depressed. "Miss Vaughn, this must be—"

"This is Edna. Chief Govich wants to see you."

Suddenly, it hit Cole. Eurydice Vaughn and Edna Gray sounded identical on the telephone!

27

The Hughes Gulfstream helicopter flew over the southwest shore of Lake Michigan. The skyline of Chicago stretched for miles outside the starboard window of the aircraft. In the passenger seat beside the pilot sat Bill McElroy, heir to the McElroy Lakefront Development Company. He stared out unemotionally at the site below through a pair of dark aviator sunglasses.

"In about thirty seconds, we'll reach the Museum," the pilot said. McElroy merely nodded.

On cue, the Museum appeared on the ground, surrounded by parkland with autumn leaves turned to golden and red colors by the change of seasons.

"Isn't that beautiful?" the pilot murmured.

McElroy ignored him. "I want you to swing as low as possible over the Museum. Then circle back over the park. I want to take a look at that so-called Haunted Island out back."

The helicopter pilot complied. As they circled, the faces of people going into or leaving the Museum tilted up to look at them. A group of children exiting a school bus waved.

"Hey," the pilot said, noticing the children's costumes, "I forgot today's Halloween. I'd better get some candy on the way home tonight."

"Why? You got a sweet tooth?" McElroy's voice rumbled through the aircraft.

"No. For trick-or-treat. You know."

"Yeah. I know." McElroy turned to stare back out the window. "Bullshit like that is why you're still no more than a helicopter taxi driver. Now take me south like I told you."

The insulting crack angered the pilot, but he kept his cool. There were always a few strictly legit methods to get even with mouthy assholes like this McElroy. As the pilot banked sharply over the Museum and headed for Seagull Island, he hoped that his passenger hadn't eaten an early lunch.

Thirty minutes later, the helicopter landed on the roof of DeWitt Plaza. An ashen, gasping Bill McElroy struggled out of his seat and stepped onto the relative safety of the landing pad, fifty stories above the ground. The pilot smiled at his passenger's state and said a cheery, "I hope you enjoyed your flight, sir, and will fly Midwest Whirlybirds again real soon."

McElroy glared back at the pilot with as much fury as he could muster. "I'll get you for this, you sonofabitch! You did those loops and dives deliberately. You'll never get a cent out of me for your time!"

The pilot's grin widened. "I wouldn't sweat it, Billy-boy. We're on retainer for the DeWitt Corporation. Our contract has three years to run. The flight's already been paid for and we don't give refunds."

McElroy slammed the helicopter door shut and struggled over to the stairwell leading down into the building. By the time he got to the first level of the penthouse, his air-sickness had dissipated. He knocked at the entrance to the study before entering. Seymour Winbush was at his usual post behind his desk.

"How did it look?"

"Like a fucking museum in the middle of a fucking park!" McElroy said angrily, snatching off his parka and tossing it on one of the chairs in front of Winbush's desk. "If it was up to me, I'd bulldoze the whole goddamned thing and start from scratch. On top of that, the fly jockey you gave me's a real smartass. The next time I see him, he's gonna lose a few teeth!"

Two spots of color appeared high up on Winbush's cheeks. "You know, you can really be insufferable at times, William. If it hadn't been for your father, you'd have ended up on the unemployment line."

McElroy's face creased into lines of anger, but he held his tongue. As the CEO of the DeWitt Corporation's face reverted to its usual pallor, Winbush said, "And I abhor profanity, so leave your gutter language outside."

"Yes, sir. I'm sorry, sir, but I was upset," McElroy said contritely.

Winbush cleared his throat. "Now I'll start at the beginning once more. How did it look to you?"

"To start off, we're going to have to level everything around the Museum," McElroy said with some degree of authority. He possessed an engineering degree from Harvard, where his father and Seymour Winbush had been classmates in the forties. "Some blasting will probably be necessary to get the old tree roots out of the ground. This could cause some structural damage to the Museum. We've also got to worry about flooding, with the lake being so close."

"We can repair any damage done by blasting or flooding later," Winbush said.

"So when can I start?"

The CEO leaned back in his chair and adopted a reflective pose. "We're going to have to grease some palms and pull in some favors, not only at the local level, but also in Washington. We can figure on some stiff opposition from environmentalists, school groups, church organizations and the like, which will make most of the politicians run for cover."

"So what's the use? Why waste our time?"

Winbush turned his washed-out gray eyes on McElroy. "Because your father wanted it, William! That's enough for me and it should be enough for you."

"I understand that, sir," McElroy managed as politely as he could. "But we're going to need all the help we can get. There'll be right-of-way problems, zoning restrictions, permits to excavate, permits to blast and permits to build. I mean, if the skids on this thing aren't greased slick, it'll be like—" he swallowed the expletive "—pouring money down a rat hole."

"I anticipate getting all the help we'll require for this project," Winbush said, once more dropping into his reflective state. "If the Museum is discredited or somehow seen to be dangerous, public opinion will be on our side. Then the politicians will fall in line and everything we need will be ours for the asking."

"It was dangerous enough for my father," McElroy said. "And I know who was responsible for his death."

Winbush didn't reply. He also didn't see the need to say what was on his mind. The CEO of the DeWitt Corporation still hated Larry Cole, but he also respected him. So, he figured that if there was something going on over at the Museum, the policeman would find it. In fact, Winbush was counting on this.

28

OCTOBER 31, 1997
1:10 P.M.

Cole, Manny and Edna walked through the main entrance of the
National Science and Space Museum. They proceeded to the
information desk in the main rotunda. After identifying themselves,
they were turned over to a uniformed security guard, whose job it
was to escort them to the curator's office.

As they walked along, Cole and Manny marveled at the exhibits
that had been added since the last time they were there. Edna felt a
certain pride at their reaction, as this place was almost like her own
personal possession after all the time she had spent working in it. In
fact, if it hadn't been for the Museum, she wouldn't have met Larry.
She corrected her thoughts to call him Commander Cole.

The Museum was crowded for a midday afternoon. Most of the
visitors were children dressed in Halloween costumes. Free candy
and Halloween favors were being given out at various locations by
Museum staff employees, who were dressed as spacemen, cowboys,
court jesters and Civil War soldiers.

"This is something they do every year," Edna explained. "Ezra
Rotheimer himself started the practice back in nineteen-seven. Any
child without a costume is provided with one free of charge. The
children are also given bags for the fruit and candy being passed out.
Free movies and cartoons are shown all day in the Theater of the
Future."

A group of children, dressed in a myriad of costumes and with
plastic masks over their faces, ran past. They dragged multicolored
shopping bags filled with candy behind them.

Manny watched them wistfully. "Wouldn't it be just great to put on a costume and go trick-or-treating like we used to when we were kids?"

"Rotheimer thought of that too," Edna explained. "At six o'clock tonight, there will be a costume party for adults. They'll be giving out candy and fruit like now, but also small bottles of liquor and other adult goodies."

"Is this party for the general public?" Cole asked as they boarded an elevator at the rear of the Museum.

"I'm afraid not, Commander," she replied. "It's invitation only, and the Museum Funder's Club expects healthy donations from those attending."

"Have you ever attended?" Cole asked.

"No, sir. I haven't been in the Museum before eleven P.M. or after seven-thirty A.M. in all the time I've been on the detail. I just heard about the masked ball."

The silence of the empty, carpeted corridor on which the elevator doors opened was far different from the noise downstairs. As the guard escorted them past a miniature-car display, Cole and Manny slowed to study the painstakingly accurate replicas.

"This is my car, Manny!" Cole said. "A nineteen fifty-nine Thunderbird convertible. I think this is the most beautiful automobile ever made for the American road."

Edna stopped with Cole. The guard proceeded a few feet beyond them and stopped as well. He was used to escorted guests dallying at a display. Manny merely glanced at the classic Thunderbird before being drawn to a miniature Rolls Royce Silver Cloud opposite the T-Bird.

"You a rag-top man, Commander?" Edna asked.

Cole nodded. "I owned a couple of Mustang convertibles over the years, but lately I've been strictly into hard tops. Someday maybe I'll own one of these."

They rejoined the guard.

At a set of double doors three-quarters of the way down the corridor, the guard stopped and knocked before entering. Raised brass letters on the door announced the occupant: EURYDICE VAUGHN, CURATOR.

A secretary got up from her desk when they walked into the large, carpeted outer office. "Thank you, Officer," she said, dismissing the guard. Then she turned to them. "I'm Janice Cotton, Miss Vaughn's secretary. Commander Cole?"

"I'm Cole," he said, extending his hand. "This is Sergeant Sherlock, and Detective Gray."

The secretary nodded, but a frown of confusion faded her smile. "Won't you have a seat?" She motioned to a reception area over by the windows looking out on the exterior of the Museum. "I'll tell the curator that you are here."

The three cops exchanged questioning glances. When they were alone, Manny asked, "Hey, Edna, you ever get the feeling your presence wasn't required?"

"Or wanted either, Sarge," she added.

"Miss Cotton did give the impression that she thought I was coming alone," Cole agreed.

"We couldn't let you do that, Boss," Manny said. "These museums can be dangerous places."

He had spoken in jest, but Edna said a very serious, "This Museum *is* a dangerous place."

The secretary came back into the outer office. "The curator will see you now."

With Cole in the lead, they crossed the office to the door.

Eurydice Vaughn stood up when they entered. She extended her hand to Cole. "How do you do, Commander?"

"Very good, Miss Vaughn. This is Sergeant Sherlock."

The curator did not extend her hand to him, but merely nodded.

Cole turned to Edna, but she had already stepped forward and offered her hand to the curator. Eurydice Vaughn stared at the detective, but did not take the offered hand. There was a noticeably remote hostility in her gaze. Edna's look also contained hostility. The women projected a mirror image of emotion. A mirror image that Cole and Manny noticed also extended beyond emotion. With a startling impact, they both saw the remarkable resemblance between the curator and the detective.

Eurydice Vaughn produced a varnished wooden box, which she handed to Cole. Opening it, he found the gun he had lost out on the island. He checked the load. It contained the same number of rounds as he remembered. It had also been recently cleaned.

"Was this the way it was turned in to your Lost and Found?" he asked the curator.

"Yes, box and all."

"I'd like to talk to the employee who accepted it."

"Why?"

"I'd like to know who found it. Questioning him might give me some clue as to what happened out there that night."

"I don't think that will help you," the curator said. "You see, no one in Lost and Found actually saw who turned it in. It seems that the box and its contents simply appeared on the counter during one of our busier periods of the day."

"Maybe a ghost put it there," Edna said.

The curator turned to stare at the detective. "I don't understand what you mean."

"I was advancing a theory, Ms. Vaughn. By the way, you're not a Mrs., are you?"

"That wouldn't change the Ms. if I were."

"Of course not. I forgot the section of the feminist rules-and-regulations manual covering that precept," Edna said. "Like I said about the ghost, I was advancing a theory."

"Talking about ghosts sounds more like fantasy than theory."

"Not necessarily," Edna countered. "Sherlock Holmes once said that after all possibilities have been exhausted, then whatever remains, no matter how fantastic, must be the solution."

There was a cameo brooch pinned above the left breast of the curator's white-silk blouse. She reached up to finger it as she said, "I didn't know Conan Doyle was required reading at the Police Academy."

"You'd be surprised what is required at the academy."

Cole and Manny felt a lethargy drop over them as if they had become ensnared in a heavy net. They were aware of most of what was happening in the office. They could hear and see, but suddenly there was an unreality about everything. Eurydice Vaughn and Edna Gray seemed totally unaffected.

"But ghosts or mysterious happenings are part of the Museum's legacy," Edna was saying.

"Do you know a great deal about the Museum, detective . . . ?"

"Gray. Edna Gray."

Eurydice's hand came away from the brooch so abruptly that she banged her fingers on the edge of the desk.

"That must have hurt."

"It's nothing. I have a high pain threshold. What were you saying?"

"You were asking me if I knew a lot about the Museum. As a matter of fact, I do. I was on the police detail here for almost three years."

Now the curator stared intensely at Edna. "I thought I knew most of the detail people."

"I worked straight midnights. We saw very few staff people that late at night."

"Oh."

"So I do know that some of the things that have happened around here can't be explained easily. Such as the disappearances both inside and out on the island. If it's not ghosts, then maybe there's someone hiding in the walls, like a Museum version of the Phantom of the Opera."

"What did you say?" The curator sat forward on the edge of her chair.

For Cole, it was like dozing off and forcing himself awake. He blinked his eyes and shook his head a couple of times. He looked over at Manny. The sergeant was sitting up rigidly in his seat, staring blankly off into space. Cole checked the curator and Edna. He became instantly aware of the tension surrounding them.

"I think I need to get some air," he said, getting shakily to his feet.

"Larry, are you okay?" Edna asked with alarm. She jumped up and rushed over to him.

"I'm all right. See about Manny."

As Edna turned to the sergeant, Cole looked at Eurydice Vaughn. The curator had stood when Edna did. But she was not looking at Cole. Instead, her total attention was on the detective who was helping the groggy Manny Sherlock to his feet. And the gaze on the curator's face was of such intense fury that Cole felt as if it possessed a physical presence of its own.

Edna helped Manny to the front door of the Museum. Cole managed to make it alone. Eurydice Vaughn followed them, asking repeatedly if she could get personnel from the Museum dispensary to help. Cole declined the offer.

Gulping fresh air seemed to revive Manny, whose face was pale.

"I'm going to take him down to the car, Commander," Edna said.

"I think I can walk now," Manny told them, managing to stand on his own.

Edna spun on Eurydice. "What happened to them up there, or is that another little mystery of your Museum?"

Eurydice flared back, "I haven't the slightest idea what you're talking about! It was probably something they had for lunch."

"Like the man who died in your staff dining room a couple of weeks ago?"

Eurydice actually took a menacing step toward Edna.

Cole intervened by stepping between them. "I think the allegations have gone far enough. Would you wait for me in the car, Edna?"

The detective's eyes were locked with the curator's, and for a moment it didn't look like she was going to obey. Then she slowly turned and followed Manny.

A few minutes later, Cole joined them at the police car.

"I think I'd better drive, Commander," Edna said. "You still don't seem like your normal self."

He nodded and slid into the front passenger seat. Manny was already in the backseat, his head resting on the cushions. As she put the car in gear, he asked, "Wow, what happened?"

"She did something to you," Edna said.

Cole asked, "If Miss Vaughn did do something to us, why didn't it affect you?"

"I don't know, Commander!"

"Take it easy, Edna," Cole said. "You're going to bust a blood vessel in a minute."

As they pulled onto Lake Shore Drive, she checked the rearview mirror. Manny appeared to be asleep. She checked Larry. He seemed to have made a full recovery. As she watched out of the corner of her eye, he pulled a white, square envelope from his coat pocket and opened it.

"Would I be prying if I asked what that is?" she asked.

He was still reading. "Miss Vaughn gave it to me. It's an invitation to tonight's Halloween party at the Museum."

"You're not going, are you?"

"Yes, I am."

29

L arry Cole sat at his desk and stared at a message slip. On it was the name and number of Attorney Ronald Cohen, whose office was on West Madison Street in the Loop. When they got back from the Museum, Cole had returned the lawyer's earlier call.

Cohen got right to the point, *"Commander, I will be representing your wife, who is seeking a legal separation from you and custody of Larry Cole, Jr."*

Cole felt as if the bottom had just dropped out of his life.

Cohen continued. *"I'd like to arrange a meeting with you in my office at your earliest convenience."*

"Will Lisa be there?"

"In a way. We'll be discussing this via conference call. Mrs. Cole will be in one of my colleagues' offices in Detroit. Of course, you can bring legal representation."

Cole's anger flared. "You can count on it!"

They settled on a date for the following week. When Cole hung up, he felt as if he'd been kicked in the head. He couldn't understand how the woman he had fallen in love with, courted, married and had a child with, could do this to him.

Tomorrow he would find himself a good divorce lawyer. He wanted the best because he didn't plan to give up his son. At least not without one hell of a fight. Then he would—

His intercom buzzed. Cole snatched up the receiver. "Yes?"

There was a momentary silence. Then Edna said, *"Commander, I was just about to lock up the office. I wondered if you needed anything."*

He'd forgotten all about her in the confusion at the Museum and then this call from . . . it took him a moment to phrase the words, "his wife's attorney," in his mind. "Could you come in here for a minute, Edna?"

"Yes, sir."

There was a knock on his office door, followed by her opening it and stepping inside.

He stood up and walked around his desk to face her. He stopped a foot away. She looked up at him.

"I'm sorry I was abrupt on the phone just now," he said, "but I just had something of a problem call."

"Anything I can help you with, sir?"

He reached out and gently grasped her shoulders. "We're alone now. You can drop the 'sir' and the 'Commander.' "

"Is there anything I can do to help, Larry?"

He smiled, leaned down and gently kissed her forehead. "No. I'll work it out. I'm sorry it made me edgy with you. That's not the real me."

Her face finally cracked in a smile. "You've got a right to be edgy. You go through a lot."

He released her and returned to his chair behind the desk. "We still on for steak à la Cole?"

"Definitely. Then you're not going to the Museum tonight?"

"I'm going over there for only an hour or so, Edna. Then I'm coming straight to your place for a late supper."

"You wouldn't be going back to see the curator again, would you?"

"Do you think that's why I'm going?"

"I can't say, Commander."

Cole took a deep breath. "I am working on a case, Edna."

"You shouldn't be going alone! Eurydice Vaughn did something to you and Manny today. Maybe to me, too, but I just haven't reacted to it yet. If she gets you inside that place alone tonight, you might become the next 'Missing: Presumed Dead' case!"

"Like I told you before, I'll be at the Museum for only an hour or so. There will be plenty of people around, if the understanding I got from you earlier is correct, so I'll be perfectly safe. After all, I am a cop."

With a shrug of resignation, she said, "I understand."

He stared at her. Her eyes were focused at a location somewhere over his right shoulder. "Will I still be able to see you later?" he asked.

"Okay," she said before letting herself out the door.

"You're doing real well today, Cole," he said to himself. "Real well."

Edna was still at her desk when he came out of his office a few minutes later.

"I thought you were leaving," he told her.

She looked up at him and smiled. "I have a couple of things to finish. I'll be at the apartment when you get there."

He perked up a bit. "I promise. Before eight."

As he walked to the double doors at the entrance, she called after him, "Larry?"

He stopped and turned around.

"Be careful." She blew him a kiss.

He winked back. He was whistling when he walked out.

Edna's face became deadly serious as soon as Cole was gone. Her mind worked ferociously for a moment, weighing proposals and counter-proposals. Finally, throwing caution to the wind, she snatched up the phone.

It rang twice before it was answered, *"Hello?"*

"Judy, it's Edna. Are you still going to help me?"

"Help you? I'm going with you! This is definitely a job for the Mistress of Disguise/High Priestess of Mayhem."

"Judy!"

"And company, of course. How soon can you get here?"

"I'm on the way.

30

Eurydice Vaughn was dressing for the Halloween party. Homer shuffled around in the subterranean room behind her. He was excited, as this was the one day of the year when he could mingle with normal people. But he, like everyone else at the party, would be in costume.

She was combing her hair to hang to her shoulders. She wore a simple, low-cut cotton blouse with balloon sleeves, a flaring black skirt and flat shoes with no stockings. Other than a wide black belt and a black mask, this would be her entire costume.

She stared at her reflection in the mirror. Her mind kept returning to the encounter with the female detective in the office that afternoon. There was something odd about her. Something odd and terribly familiar. Even the name, Edna Gray, was like one she knew. But her conscious mind, possessing an awesome, nearly eidetic memory, could recall no such person in her life.

Eurydice studied her face. Wearing her hair like it was now combed, and with a bit more flesh on the cheeks and sadness in the eyes . . .

"Eurydice, when are we going to the party?" Homer wailed.

She snapped out of her reverie. "In a moment, Homer. I'm almost ready."

"You take too long. I want to go!"

She applied a light coating of lipstick and reached for a pin. The one tonight would be a simple oval of solid gold. A Virgin pin. Very apt. The trigger on the back side would release an aromatic, which affected anyone within twenty feet of her. The Mistress had perfected the aromatics. Different scents, and a few odorless ones, did various things. Some could block oxygen intake to the bloodstream, which could be fatal to hypertensive, heavy smokers like Harry McElroy. Others placed an inhaler in a pliable, hypnotic state and could result in memory loss. Some possessed an aphrodisiac effect.

The one she held now contained the last scent. It would be directed at only one person when they were alone.

She undid the clasp and was about to pin the brooch over her left breast when she stuck herself. She studied the drop of blood expanding from the tiny hole in her finger. She was immune to the aromatics. She wondered if the Mistress had planned this or whether her biological makeup made it so. Another odd thought struck her. Edna Gray had also been unaffected by the aromatic. It should have placed her into the same stupor as Sherlock and Cole. Eurydice had planned something for the commander. Just a simple physical examination while he and his companions dozed. But the female detective had shown no reaction.

Snatching a tissue from the box on her dressing table, Eurydice stood up and said, "C'mon, Homer, we're late."

"Not my fault," he grumbled.

As they headed for the passageway to the surface, she asked, "Homer, do you remember when I . . ."

His head swung in her direction. He waited.

She struggled to find the right word. She didn't want to say "created."

She decided on, "Do you remember when I came here?"

His head bobbed up and down. They were approaching the foot of the staircase that led up into the darkness under the Museum. She stopped.

"Tell me about it."

His massive shoulders hunched into a shrug as he spluttered, "You cried a lot. I want to go to the party." With that, he vanished up the stairs.

After a moment, she followed.

From an unseen vantage point, they had been observed. The ancient voice of the Mistress purred, "Getting curious, daughter? Now, we really can't have that, can we?"

31

"This will need only one more stitch," Judy said as she cinched Edna into the sequined evening gown.

Standing in front of the full-length mirror, Edna studied her reflection. "You didn't have to go to all this trouble, Judy. I've got gowns like this at home."

"Are they silver-sequined?"

"No. But what's the difference?"

Judy stood up. "My dear, dear Detective Gray, this is not merely a dress, it's part of a costume. Now for the tiara."

From the dresser beside the mirror, Judy picked up a simple tiara consisting of a couple of metal bands and a white stone in the center. She affixed the tiara's clips in Edna's hair.

"The cape." Judy removed a short cape from the same garment bag the sequined gown had come in and helped Edna fasten it around her neck. "And finally, the pièce de résistance."

From the dresser jewelry box, Judy removed a silver necklace with a medallion containing a white stone that matched the one in the tiara. The necklace was large enough to go over Edna's head. The medallion hung between the cleft of her breasts.

"Now what?" Edna asked, somewhat dismayed by what stared back at her from the mirror. The only way she could properly classify it was to term the sight "tacky."

"This is what makes it all work." Judy handed her a tube-like device with straps for attaching it to her forearm.

"What's this?" Edna asked as Judy began strapping it on for her.

"A Vanisher."

"A what?"

"A Vanisher," Judy explained patiently. "It works on a gravity principle, but you've got to be careful to make sure the pellets roll clear of the hem of the gown. They have a small charge that shouldn't be hot enough to ignite—"

"Judy, this is an explosive!"

"Trust me. You wanted a dynamite costume and you've got one. No pun intended. Now I'll show you how it works."

Judy stepped up beside Edna. Both women were visible in the bedroom mirror. "With your right hand, you grasp the sapphire, using your thumb and index finger like this."

Edna mimicked the Mistress of Disguise/High Priestess of Mayhem.

"Then imperiously raise your left arm thusly."

Again Edna followed Judy's directions. She felt something shift in the device on her arm. An object was expelled from the bottom of the tube. Edna watched it bounce on Judy's varnished-wood floor. It appeared to be no more than a small ball of multicolored paper. Then it exploded.

Edna screamed as a cloud of dense white smoke enveloped her.

"Relax," Judy said. "That's the effect. Every time you raise your left arm, you'll release a pellet. When the smoke comes up, you're supposed to vanish."

"But I'm still here, thank God."

"You should stand in a doorway or in front of something you can duck behind before you use it. That way, it'll seem like you vanished. Get it? That's why it's called a Vanisher."

Edna managed to nod. "How many pellets do I have left?" She kept her left arm rigidly down at her side.

"Ten," Judy said before correcting, "You can make that nine now. I'd better get into my own costume."

Edna looked back at the mirror. "By the way, who am I supposed to be?"

Judy was in the closet across the room. She stuck her head around the edge of the door. There was surprise on her face. "You're Azura, Queen of Magic. The nemesis of Flash Gordon in the nineteen thirty-eight serial *Flash Gordon's Trip to Mars*, starring Buster Crabbe."

"So who are you going as?" Edna raised her arm a bit but quickly dropped it when she felt the pellets shift.

Judy's head popped around the edge of the door again. Her hair was completely covered with a flesh-colored skullcap. "Why, your partner in crime, Ming the Merciless, of course."

Edna looked back at Queen Azura staring at her in the mirror. The things she did for love.

32

OCTOBER 31, 1997
6:00 P.M.

Larry Cole trotted up the steps to the main entrance of the Museum. Two guards, dressed in 1890s' Chicago police uniforms, with long coats and helmets, were checking guests in at the door.

Cole presented his invitation.

"You'll have to put on a costume, sir," one of the guards said.

"And where would I go to get one?"

Eurydice Vaughn's secretary stepped forward from the side of the entrance. "The curator has seen to this guest's costume requirements," she said. "Would you come with me, Commander?"

She escorted Cole back through the main rotunda in the direction of the elevator they had used to get to Eurydice Vaughn's office earlier. As they walked along, the secretary was silent.

"Where is the party held, Miss Cotton?" he asked, making small talk.

"In the West Hall. There will be someone available to escort you after you change."

They exited the elevator.

"And what kind of costume has Miss Vaughn arranged for me?"

She stopped at a door on the opposite end of the corridor from the curator's office, then stepped forward and turned the knob, revealing a small office with a private bathroom. "Your costume is hanging inside," she said before turning and walking away.

Cole watched her go. "Friendly type," he murmured under his breath.

At the door to the curator's outer office, Janice Cotton hesitated. She could do this, she told herself. She'd done it before. It was simply in and out. Then she'd go home and get very drunk like she did every

Halloween. By tomorrow, she'd be hung over and what she was about to see would be forgotten. She opened the door.

"Hiya, Janice," a male voice called from the waiting area.

She nearly screamed before realizing that it was only Jonathan Gobey, who was on the Museum staff. He was seated in one of the leather armchairs. There were two men with him whom Janice recognized as maintenance workers. They were dressed in Three Musketeers costumes. Together, they stood up.

"All for one and one for all!" Gobey said lamely. "I'm Athos." He turned to the worker on his right.

"I'm Porthos!" the second man said in a deceptively deep voice for someone who weighed no more than a hundred and sixty pounds.

"I'm Artemus," the third and heaviest of the trio said.

"It's Aramus, not Artemus," Gobey scolded.

Janice Cotton didn't have time for this nonsense. She still had an emotional hurdle to overcome. Ignoring them, she walked to the door of the curator's office and knocked. She waited until she heard Miss Vaughn call, "Enter," before venturing inside.

When the secretary had closed the door behind her, she refused to look in the direction of the simple blue-cloth couch against the far wall. She instead focused all her attention on Eurydice Vaughn. The curator was seated behind her desk, reading through a file. She didn't look up when her secretary came in. Janice crossed the room to stand before her.

"Well?" the curator asked.

"The commander is in the changing room. He should be ready in a few minutes."

"Excellent! On your way out, send in the Three Musketeers. They're going to help me play a little practical joke."

"Yes, ma'am."

The secretary turned to leave. She still had not looked in the direction of the couch. She was just starting to think that she would make it this year when the curator's voice stopped her.

"Janice."

She halted. Caught off guard, her eyes flicked involuntarily in the direction she'd been avoiding. Her blood ran cold at what she saw.

The curator was talking. "You did a nice job. Thanks. That will be all for tonight."

Janice Cotton ran out of the office.

Eurydice glanced up from the file and looked over at the sight that had scared her secretary not only on this Halloween, but also on the past two Halloweens. That thing had been Death. The Grim Reaper himself. All seven feet of him. Only Eurydice knew that it was Homer beneath the black costume with the skeleton mask. Actually, Eurydice mused, Janice had been lucky. Had she caught a glimpse of Homer without the costume, she would probably have been taken straight to an insane asylum.

"I don't think my secretary likes your outfit, Homer."

A grunt came from beneath the full-length costume.

When the Three Musketeers, led by Jonathan Gobey, came through the office door, Eurydice was again reading the file. As the three men gave the menacingly silent figure of Death questioning glances, she read the passage in one of the attachments to her Commander Cole file.

"The student is an excellent athlete, which his full football scholarship will attest to. However, he is also a gifted fencer, who will be an asset to next year's University of Iowa fencing team."

The comment was more than twenty-five years old, but Eurydice had found it interesting. She wondered how much of this sword-fighting prowess Cole had retained since his freshman year of college.

She looked up at the Three Musketeers. "Now listen to me very carefully. I don't want any mistakes."

Each man gave her his undivided attention as Death looked on silently from across the room.

33

L arry Cole placed the black hat with the silver band on his head and stepped back from the mirror. The costume fit perfectly, right down to the boots, pants and shirt. Donning the cummerbund, black mask and cape succeeded in totally altering his appearance. He found it difficult to recognize himself behind the disguise of El Zorro, reflected back at him.

A smile split his face under the mask. This had always been one of his fantasies. So, it was like Manny said earlier, the same as being a child again and going out for trick-or-treat.

The only thing he had yet to put on was the sword. It was on the dressing table by the sink. Cole picked it up. He had expected a fencing foil, but this was a real, tempered-steel sword. He unsheathed the blade. The gleaming, razor-sharp metal sparkled in the light. Despite the weight, he found it fairly simple to handle. He made a couple of quick thrusts. He fingered the sword's edge. It was sharp, and the point could easily puncture flesh.

This was not the type of prop for a Halloween party. He would have left it, but the costume would be incomplete without it. He slipped the sheathed sword into the cummerbund and anchored the Beretta on the opposite side before checking his appearance once more.

"El Zorro, you are one bad-looking dude!"

Cape flaring behind him, Cole headed for the door.

He was crossing the office when he heard the scream. It came from right outside the room. He snatched open the corridor door and stepped out.

A masked woman with long, dark hair raced past him as if the Devil himself was chasing her.

"Miss, wait!" Cole called, but she kept going. The sound of running footsteps carried to him from an adjacent corridor. Cole turned in time to see three masked, costumed men round the corner and head in his direction. They pulled up some fifty feet away and stopped.

The tall, lean one in the middle stepped forward. "What have we here, Musketeers? A masked bandit standing between us and our pleasure with the tavern wench?"

Cole smiled. "Look, guys. I was on my way to a party and—"

"Silence, fool!" the one on the left shouted.

"Athos," the one on the right said, "perhaps we should teach this masked moron a lesson."

"Yes, Porthos, I think you're right."

"Please, sir," came a tearful voice from behind Cole. He turned. The girl who was being chased cringed over by the pedestal on which rested the replica of the Thunderbird he had admired earlier. "Help me. They're drunk and want to hurt me."

"Okay," Cole said. "This must be some kind of game you people play on Halloween and that's okay by me, but I'm not here to play games."

"A coward!" Athos crowed.

"A fool and a coward!" Porthos echoed.

The last one remained mute, but drew his sword from a sheath beneath his tunic. The two others followed suit.

For just an instant, Cole considered pulling the Beretta and putting an end to this foolishness. But then he noticed that the Three Musketeers carried normal fencing foils, with guards over the tips. No one could be hurt by those things.

"Please help me," the woman cried softly behind him.

The grin spread slowly under the mask of Zorro. "I guess you boys aren't from around here or you'd know who I am."

"We'll put that on your tombstone, chump!" said the one whom a process of elimination told him would be Aramus.

"I see you talk my language," Cole replied. Then he yanked the sword from its sheath, wrapped the tail of his cape around his left arm and dropped into his fencing stance. He hadn't done this in a long time, but it came back to him quickly. He rocked back and forth, making sure his weight was evenly distributed.

The handle of the blade fit well in his fist and it felt good. In fact, he was looking forward to this little fencing match. Of course he'd have to be careful with the razor-sharp blade. Maybe slice through one or two of the mouthy Musketeers' foils for effect. This was going to be fun.

"Which one of us goes first?" Athos asked his companions.

"Why quibble?" Zorro said in a voice than stunned the Musketeers. It sounded as if a different man had addressed them. "I'll take all of you at once. After all, it took the three of you to chase after one defenseless girl." The tempered steel whistled through the air.

For a moment, the Musketeers hesitated. Then Porthos bellowed, "An insult!"

"The honor of the King's Musketeers must be avenged!" Athos howled.

"Let's get this punk!" Aramus shouted.

They rushed down the hall toward the caped figure in black.

34

OCTOBER 31, 1997
6:21 P.M.

Police Officer Andrew Anderson had decided to modify his police career after his partner, Edna Gray, had accepted the temporary assignment to Detective Division headquarters. However, his change had not been as decisive as Acting Detective Gray's. He had simply moved from the midnight shift to the afternoon watch. So he was on duty when there was a knock at the door of the private police command-post entrance at the far southeast side of the Museum.

His partner, a young officer named Alex Reed, who was studying English literature at the University of Chicago, looked across at Anderson. "You expecting anyone?"

"Could be the sector sergeant," Anderson said, turning back to his paperback book. "You'd better check it out."

Reed got up and crossed the command post to the steel-reinforced door. He opened it.

Anderson felt cool air rush into the room. It wasn't cold yet, but then it wasn't the type of weather you go around leaving doors open in either. After a moment, he bellowed, "Reed, would you close the damned door?"

There was no response. Finally, Anderson was sufficiently annoyed to spin his chair around and glare at the open door. What he saw froze him into total immobility.

They had slipped up to his desk silently. Reed was still over by the door with his hand clamped over his mouth to stifle his laughter. When he saw the look on Anderson's face, he could no longer contain himself. He staggered outside and was convulsed with hysterics.

"Edna, is that you?" Anderson managed to say.

"I'm undercover tonight, Anderson," she replied. "If you must speak to me, you will address me as Azura, Queen of Magic."

"And Empress of all the Martians," the cadaverous figure with the shaven head, penetrating eyes, Fu Manchu mustache and beard rasped.

"We're going to the Halloween party as backup for Commander Cole," Azura explained.

"It's supposed to be invitation only."

"So, we're part of security for the affair. I know the curator personally. She'll be glad for the extra help," Azura said. "Just keep it under your hat, and if we come up with a good pinch, we'll put you on the paper. That goes for laughing boy out there too."

The other policeman could still be heard howling through the open door.

"C'mon, Ming," Azura said. "We've got work to do."

As they walked to the connecting door leading into the Museum, Ming the Merciless whispered something to Azura. At first the Queen of Magic shook her head, but in the long run, she agreed.

Opening the inside door, the two costumed figures proceeded through it. Then Azura stopped and turned to face the still-staring Anderson.

Her right hand came up to touch the white sapphire hanging around her neck. "Remember that Azura, Queen of Magic, sees all, so do not disobey me."

The now teary-eyed Reed staggered in from outside and witnessed, along with Anderson, what happened next.

She raised her left arm above her head. There was a soft pop, followed by the silver-sequined figure becoming immersed in white smoke. The smoke evaporated rapidly, but when it was gone, the woman whom they knew as Officer Edna Gray had vanished. The door leading into the Museum was also closed.

Reed went back to his textbook. Anderson picked up his adventure-novel paperback. A few minutes of silence passed. Finally, Reed looked across at his partner.

"Andy?"

"I don't know how she did it, Reed, so don't ask me!"

Reed looked back at the closed door once more and then buried his head in his book.

35

The battle in the corridor outside the curator's office was not going well for the Three Musketeers. Despite their superior numbers, the black-masked figure had parried them, pummeled them and even cut the pants off of Aramus. For their part, they had been unable to lay a foil on their adversary. And throughout the battle, Zorro added insult to injury by continuously laughing at them.

But all had not gone completely well during this impromptu fencing match. The four men had knocked over six of the pedestals on which the miniature cars were displayed. Two of the replicas, the Rolls Royce Silver Cloud that Manny had admired, and a 1950 Jaguar roadster, were completely destroyed during the melee.

Now Zorro had Athos backed against the wall. Porthos and Aramus had been respectively disarmed and forced to withdraw from combat for modesty's sake. Athos had at least made a fight of it, however ill-prepared he might have been. The Musketeer raised his flimsy foil to ward off the advancing masked man. Zorro's heavier, sharper sword came up and snapped the foil in two.

Snatching off his hat and mask, the Musketeer dropped the remaining stub of metal and raised his hands in surrender. Zorro continued to advance.

"Please, sir," he pleaded. "It was only meant as a joke. We wouldn't have hurt you."

"Hurt me!" Zorro laughed. "How absurd! You and that pair of buffoons couldn't hurt me. Now you know who I am!"

"Yes, sir."

The sharp sword point was only millimeters away from the fake Musketeer's midsection. He was painfully aware of its proximity.

"Thank you for rescuing me, kind sir." It was the woman they had chased. As the battle concluded, she advanced down the corridor. Now she stood only a few feet away.

"I am the friend of all poor and downtrodden people," Zorro said, keeping his sword at the Musketeer's stomach. "But this rascal must be punished for what he tried to do."

"Please," the Musketeer pleaded, looking frantically at the woman.

"Spare him," she said, "and I will give myself to you freely."

The man in black shook his head. "I require no reward for my services. Although your offer is tempting." The sword point was extended to make contact with the Musketeer's body. It would take but little pressure to puncture cloth and then flesh. "As for you, my lecherous Musketeer, I'm going to leave you with a little souvenir of this meeting."

The sword point moved with blinding speed. The Musketeer screamed, but then there was no pain. Looking down, he saw that the letter "Z" had been carved on his tunic.

"Now take the rest of your ruffian band and get out of my sight."

The Musketeer jumped to obey. His frightened companions, with Aramus being forced to hold up his pants, followed him down the corridor. They were soon gone.

The man in black turned to face the woman he had rescued.

"My hero," she said with undeniable passion in her voice.

He smiled at her. "I'll say one thing for you people, you do know how to throw a party!" The voice was Larry Cole's, not El Zorro's.

36

Edna, as Azura, Queen of Magic, and Judy, as Ming the Merciless, made their way through empty, dark Museum corridors toward the West Hall, where the costume ball was being held. As they approached, they could hear a band playing.

"Sounds like they've got a whole orchestra in there," Judy said.

"I've heard they always do. Some thirty-odd pieces. I understand they do a lot of ballroom dancing, like the fox trot, the rumba, waltzes and that kind of thing."

"Not my cup of tea."

"You don't dance, Judy?" Edna asked.

"Yeah, but I'm strictly a 'let's-get-down-and-party' girl." To emphasize her statement, Judy snapped her fingers and swung her hips provocatively beneath Ming's robes.

Edna laughed, then quickly said, "Damn!"

"What's wrong?"

"We don't have masks. They won't let us in the party without them."

"Not to worry," Judy said, reaching into a pocket beneath her robes. "I brought these along. I was just looking for the right moment for us to put them on."

She handed Edna a silver mask that matched her outfit perfectly. Judy's mask was a deep burgundy, which went well with Ming's robes.

Edna was just slipping the mask over her head when they turned the corner across from the entrance to the hall where the ball was being held. To keep from activating the Vanisher, she used only her right hand. The doors of the hall were open and a large group of people was visible, either dancing or mingling around inside. A security guard, dressed in one of the antique police uniforms, saw Edna just as she struggled to pull the mask down over her face. He called to her, "Miss Vaughn!"

Her mask in place, Edna stopped. Judy proceeded a step or two past her and halted also. The Mistress of Disguise/High Priestess of Mayhem turned around to see what had happened to her companion. The security guard left his post and crossed the wide exterior corridor toward them.

"What's wrong?!" Judy stage-whispered.

"He thinks I'm the curator!" Edna said, barely moving her lips.

"So?"

"I'm not the curator, Judy!"

The guard came within earshot. "Miss Vaughn, Dr. Fleisher's been looking all over for you. He wants to see you right away."

"The curator will be right there," Judy said.

The guard looked at the Ming the Merciless costume. For a moment he was about to question who this masked figure was, but then, that was none of his business. He'd delivered his message. He turned and walked back to his post.

"You can do this, Edna," Judy urged.

"Do what? Impersonate Eurydice Vaughn? You gotta be crazy!"

"You said you wanted to help the commander, right?"

"But how can I do that, pretending I'm somebody else?"

"Intelligence-gathering, girl! They'll say things to Eurydice Vaughn they'd never say to a cop. Plus, Manny said you and this curator could be twins."

"Manny's either blind, crazy or both."

Though the security guard had returned to his post, he was staring curiously back at them.

Judy noticed his scrutiny. "In a minute, you're going to blow this thing for both of us."

Edna's eyes, beneath the mask, swung from Judy to the entrance of the ballroom and back again. After a second's longer hesitation, she said, "What the hell? I always wanted to be a stuck-up bitch."

With that, she headed for the ballroom entrance. A smiling Judy followed. "You're getting to be more and more like me every minute."

37

D r. Winston Fleisher, decked out in a black coat, ruffled shirt and fake Van Dyke beard, had drunk two glasses of champagne and was flying.

"Who am I?" he gushed as he stepped in front of one unsuspecting guest or another and struck a scholarly pose.

He'd gotten a number of different opinions.

"John Wilkes Booth."

"No."

"Simon Legree."

"No!"

"Freddie Kruger."

"Who's Freddie Kruger?" Fleisher asked with dismay.

No one had come up with Edgar Allan Poe. That was because he hadn't taken Eurydice's advice and attached the stuffed raven to his shoulder.

He was looking for a place to sit down and wait for his head to stop spinning, when the mayor arrived. As Eurydice had yet to put in an appearance, the chairman straightened his spine and crossed to the ballroom entrance.

"Good evening, Your Honor." Fleisher's speech was a bit slurred.

"Winston, good to see you again." The mayor, who was dressed as Hack Wilson in a vintage Chicago Cubs baseball uniform, pumped the chairman's hand.

The two men flanking the mayor were dressed the same as all the security guards, in turn-of-the-century police uniforms.

There were numerous other guests to greet, most of whom were masked; however, a coterie of escorts was assigned to accompany certain VIPs from the entrance to the Museum to the West Hall. A card with the VIP's name and title on it was provided for Fleisher's information. Usually, Eurydice shared this task with him. Again he looked around for her.

There were all types of costumes in evidence tonight, from four-legged creatures—dinosaurs had been popular the last few years—which took two bodies to operate the fore and hind legs, to some guests wearing 1920s' clothing as costumes. The only thing about these half-century-old costumes was that those wearing them looked old enough to have been around when the clothing was new. There were a fair share of professionally costumed action heroes and a John Wayne cowboy lookalike, who strode by the inebriated Fleisher with a saunter so authentic it was eerie. There were tramps and kings, empresses and harlots. The National Science and Space Museum's Halloween Ball. The social event of the season!

Suddenly, Fleisher realized he wouldn't be able to recognize Eurydice even if she was standing right beside him. As he looked out across the hall, which was filling to capacity rapidly, he noticed any number of shapely females. Last year, Eurydice had come dressed as Cleopatra in an outfit that would have rivaled Liz Taylor's film costume. But the year before, she had come dressed as Charlie Chaplin's Little Tramp. So she could be anybody and there were a lot of bodies in the room. One of the security guards approached him.

"Miss Vaughn asked me to help her find you, Dr. Fleisher," the guard said.

The chairman stared past him at a figure, who gave the chairman a very solemn, evil-tinged bow.

"Ming the Merciless?" Fleisher exclaimed. "Eurydice, that is brilliant!"

The guard nervously cleared his throat. "I think that this is Miss Vaughn, Doctor."

Somewhat bleary-eyed, Fleisher turned to look at the woman in the sequined dress. She stared back at him from beneath her silver mask.

"She's Azura, Queen of Magic, Empress of all the Martians," Ming said.

"The old Flash Gordon serial! Really very top-drawer costumes."
The chairman struck a pose. "And who am I?"

Azura started to say Simon Legree, but Ming was too quick for
her. "Edgar Allan Poe."

Fleisher was stunned. Then he leaped forward and planted a kiss
right on Ming the Merciless's bald head.

"You've made my entire night!" he said just as an escort in a
court jester's costume led three people over to him.

Fleisher had left his glasses back in his office and couldn't make
out the print. He handed the card to Eurydice.

The woman in the silver mask took it. She flashed a warm smile
at the new arrivals.

"Dr. Fleisher, allow me to introduce Mr. Edward Graham Luckett,
Director of Public Safety; his nephew, Mr. Eugene Luckett, and Miss
Pamela Harper."

Luckett was dressed as Abraham Lincoln; however, he looked
more like a Quaker due to his obesity. Cousin Gene wore a Rambo
costume, replete with wig, the required mask, bandolier, plastic M-
16, and a real twelve-inch hunting knife in a leather sheaf strapped
to his waist. The younger Luckett was also a body-building fanatic,
possessing pectoral muscles now exposed beneath a skimpy vest he
wore only at his uncle's insistence. Whenever he caught someone
looking, Cousin Gene would flex his chest muscles for effect. Pam
Harper, one of Gene's on-again, off-again girl friends, was a shapely
young lady who was also into exposing as much of herself as the law
would allow her to. As such, she wore a "genie" costume, which,
she'd explained to Gene's stuffy uncle when she got in the car, was
from ". . . like in *I Dream of Jeannie* . . . you know, the television
series."

After the introductions, Dr. Fleisher cried "Wonderful!" as he
shook hands with the new arrivals and wondered if he could chance
another glass of that excellent domestic champagne. "This party is
going to be a tremendous success."

Dr. Fleisher was about to ask the curator what was wrong with
her voice when Eugene Luckett stepped forward. "Miss Vaughn, I've
heard so much about you that perhaps I could have this dance?"

The band had just begun playing a waltz.

"Of course," she said with a smile.

That's his Eurydice, the chairman thought as he turned to the director of Public Safety and the young woman with him. But they were already heading for the bar. He looked around for Ming the Merciless, only to find that the mysterious figure had vanished.

38

The Zorro-costumed Larry Cole walked through the dark Museum corridors with the woman he had rescued from the bungling Musketeers. She had not removed her mask. After they'd left the disaster area outside the curator's office, she had taken his arm. As they walked along, he was conscious of one of her breasts rubbing against him.

"Won't someone be angry about the mess back there?" Cole asked.

"Don't worry about it. I'm sure those items can be replaced."

Cole noticed that she spoke with an accent. It was possibly Spanish and it was faked. Tonight was for make-believe anyway.

"What's your name?" he asked.

She stopped and looked at him. Although she was wearing flat-heeled shoes, her forehead was at the level of his eyes. "Must we use names?"

The invitation was obvious. He leaned forward a bit. She met him halfway. The kiss began tentatively, but increased in passion rapidly. He crushed her to him and felt her arms go around his neck. He felt her press her body against his as a groan escaped from deep within her.

Suddenly, he broke the embrace and stepped away from her. He was looking off down the deserted gallery in the direction they had come from.

"What's wrong?" she asked in a husky voice as she straightened her mask.

"I heard something," he said, his hand going to the hilt of his sword, although he thought first about pulling his gun.

She stepped toward him. "This is an old place. It makes a lot of strange sounds."

"No," he said. "That was a footfall. There's somebody out there."

She attempted to take his arm again, but he gently pulled away.

"Wait here. It could be our Musketeers coming back for another beating."

He trotted back down the gallery. Quickly, she followed, keeping up with little effort.

The gallery was a huge trophy room. Awards were on display from the victory batons of Roman generals to replicas of Super Bowl trophies. Dim night-lights backlit the trophy cases, but for the most part, the immense room was in darkness.

Cole stopped at the end of the gallery and drew the sword. He was certain he'd heard something, and whatever it had been came from right around the area where he now stood.

The woman came up behind him but stopped some twenty feet back. He turned to find her staring at one of the cases. As he watched, she appeared to motion with her hand. He thought that out of the corner of his eye, he caught a brief movement that came from the case she was looking at. But when he turned to look at it, there was nothing there.

Cole walked over to the case. There were a number of trophies displayed inside it. Football, basketball, baseball and tennis. Nothing struck him as being of much consequence. At least not to him. But he wasn't interested in the contents of the case anyway.

He stared at her. In the poor light of the dimly lit Museum, he could barely see her masked face. "Who are you?" It was a demand.

"I thought we weren't going to worry about names tonight."

"Change in the rules. Now, who are you?"

"I'll tell you only . . . if you can catch me!" With that, she darted off down the gallery.

Cole sheathed the sword and pursued. She was fast, but he figured he would catch her eventually. He was wrong.

As they ran off, the trophy case moved with an ease that would have amazed Cole. From behind it stepped the figure of Death. As the case slid noiselessly back into place, the skeleton mask turned in the direction of the running pair. Then the giant Grim Reaper took up pursuit. But he was not chasing them both, only the caped figure of Larry Cole.

39

Gene Luckett was an excellent dancer. He led Edna around the floor with an impressive deftness. Light on his feet, he never missed a step.

Edna was glad he believed she was Eurydice Vaughn. She also got the impression that her partner had other things on his mind than just a simple dance; if he went much further, the director of Public Safety's nephew was going to end up with a hard knee to the groin.

"I understand a number of people are interested in your Museum, Miss Vaughn," Gene said. He was squeezing her shoulder as if testing the ripeness of a melon in a supermarket.

"We set a record attendance figure last year."

"I don't mean Museum visitors. I'm talking about people my uncle tells me are interested in developing the lakefront and the land around the Museum."

"Oh, I wasn't aware of that," she said.

The music stopped and the dance ended. They were on the opposite side of the hall from the spot where they had left Dr. Fleisher, Luckett and Pam Harper. He didn't seem to care.

"I thought Harry McElroy made his pitch for developing the lakefront to you and Dr. Fleisher personally." He sounded skeptical.

Edna remembered the name Harry McElroy from the Twenty-four Hour Incident Report. He had succumbed to a heart attack after eating lunch in the Museum's executive dining room.

"Your name's Gene, right?"

"That's right."

"Well, why don't you call me Eurydice? Take me over to the bar and buy me a drink?"

"An excellent idea, Eurydice."

Edna noticed Dr. Fleisher near the entrance, talking animatedly to a couple whose costumes were strictly out of American Gothic. A masked woman in a white blouse walked rapidly past them and actually ran across to the opposite side of the hall.

"Anything wrong?" Gene asked.

"Just checking on Dr. Fleisher," Edna said, looking around once more. "Why don't you tell me more about this lakefront development project?"

"The DeWitt Corporation is interested in carrying on Harry McElroy's work."

They reached the bar. Gene ordered drinks from a female bartender wearing a red vest and a fake handlebar mustache.

Edna went back to her surveillance of the room. She saw Ming the Merciless on the other side of the dance floor. A man in a black costume appeared at the entrance to the hall.

Zorro, Edna thought, and that was one fantastic costume. Then she noticed the way he walked and carried his shoulders. It was Larry Cole.

Gene walked over with their drinks. "Shall we find a remote corner and talk?"

"This is probably as quiet a place as we'll find tonight, Gene."

"I would think there would be someplace more private in the National Science and Space Museum."

"Not tonight."

She looked over Gene's shoulder and saw Larry moving slowly around the room. He appeared to be looking for someone.

"Bravo! Bravo, sir!" Dr. Fleisher shouted on the other side of the room.

All eyes turned in his direction. The chairman was applauding the entrance of a giant figure in black robes carrying a scythe. His mask was a skeleton's face.

"Death, as always," Fleisher bellowed drunkenly, "pays our annual masked ball a visit!"

"How gruesome," Gene sneered. "You'd think people could use their imaginations and come up with more cheerful costumes."

Edna started to say, "Like Rambo," but she noticed that Death moved with a single-minded purpose. A single-minded purpose in the direction of the costumed Zorro.

"Excuse me," she said, handing Gene her glass.

"Hurry back," he called.

The band was playing a slow melody suitable for a two-step. Dodging around a few couples, she reached Zorro.

"Commander Cole, how are you this evening?"

She watched his lips tighten in a grimace.

"Don't you remember me?"

"I'm not as good as you are at recognizing people wearing masks."

"You were in my office only a few hours ago and you're my guest tonight," she said. "Still don't recognize me?"

"Oh, Miss Vaughn. I'm sorry. Nice costume. Azura, Queen of Magic and Empress of all the Martians, right? I've got a friend who has one just like it." He reached down and lifted the hem of her cape. "Right down to the Vanisher."

Edna felt as if she was skating across very thin ice. "Why don't we dance?"

He was looking around the room again.

"Commander?"

As he turned back to her, the enormous figure of Death loomed behind him. Edna almost screamed as it leaned down toward them. It hesitated for a moment, seeming to study them before straightening up and walking away. Cole had been unaware of its presence. Edna's heart was in her throat.

"Okay, one dance," he said. "But then I've got to go."

As she stepped into his arms, she asked, "Hot date?"

He smiled. "You could say that. I'm doing the cooking."

She could have kissed him.

40

The imposing figure of Death moved easily through the crowd attending the Halloween ball. It startled many and frightened even more, but then, this was a costume party and, in the spirit of the New Orleans' Mardi Gras, people were more willing to tolerate, even to laugh, at bizarre sights.

The guard at the entrance to the hall watched Death pass. A short distance down the corridor, Death stopped.

"Why didn't you take him, Homer?" a voice demanded.

The voice was Eurydice's and came from behind him on the left.

"He made it to the party before I could catch him. Why did you change your costume, Eurydice?"

"What are you talking about now?"

"Why did you dance with him?"

"I haven't got time for this. Follow him when he starts back upstairs. Just do what I told you!"

Homer shrugged and ambled off. The corridor went silent once more.

41

Cole couldn't figure out what was happening to him. He had spent ten years being faithful to one woman. He had spent last night in another woman's apartment, been passionately kissed by a total stranger in a dark museum gallery, and now the Museum curator had her head on his shoulder and her arms wrapped tightly around him as they danced. He wondered if it was something in the air.

The dance ended. His partner stepped away from him. "We must do that again soon."

Rambo walked over, carrying two glasses. "You forgot this." He handed one of the glasses to Azura. E. G. Luckett and Pam Harper joined them. Luckett turned to look at Cole. "Nice costume."

"So's yours."

"But yours has such flair. A man of action and adventure. The mask is part of what you are."

"Excuse me a moment," Azura said. "I have to escort my guest to the door. He has to leave."

"Of course," Rambo said with a bow. "Oh, by the way," he called to Zorro. "I don't think I caught your name."

The man in black turned and smiled. "I am known by many names, but you can call me Zorro, the Fox."

With that, he turned, took Azura's arm and walked away.

"Now I'd call that taking a costume much too seriously," Luckett said.

"Looks like a fag to me," Rambo sneered.

"I think he's cute," Pam added.

In response, remaining in character as Rambo, Cousin Gene grunted.

Judy Daniels had kept Edna under a very close surveillance since she'd been asked to dance by Gene Luckett. And the Mistress of Disguise/High Priestess of Mayhem was forced to admit that the fledgling undercover police officer, disguised as Queen Azura, was good. She'd faced the unexpected with a slow, deliberate cool. She'd even carried off her impersonation in front of the director of Public Safety.

Edna walked Commander Cole into the corridor outside the ballroom. They exchanged a few words before the gallant Zorro kissed her hand and walked off into the shadows of the darkened Museum. Judy slipped up behind Edna.

"Where's he going?"

"To an office on the administrative level to take off his costume."

As they watched, he turned a corner at the far end of the gallery and disappeared from view. A moment later, he was followed by the mammoth figure of Death.

"Where did he come from?" Judy gasped.

"It's where he's going that worries me. C'mon."

They ran down the corridor toward the front of the Museum.

42

Jonathan Gobey and his two inept Musketeers retreated to the stone bench in the *Glassware from Around the World* Hall. They opened a full bottle of Remy Martin cognac and passed it around. The booze had been part of their reward from the curator.

"That guy was a professional," Gobey said.

"He toyed with us," Mays added.

"Let's just go find this guy and kick his ass!" Drew said.

They staggered from the hall and went in search of Zorro.

43

Homer was confused. Eurydice was doing some crazy things. One minute she was in one costume, the next in something else. She'd told him to get the man in black, then she had danced with him. He'd planned to get the man for Eurydice and go back to the party, but had lost sight of him. Still, he knew where he was going, so there was no need to rush.

Homer turned into a corridor that ran perpendicular to the curator's office; he came to a dead stop. There, standing some thirty feet away from him, was Eurydice. She was wearing the silver thing.

"You are to turn away from this place, Death, and trouble us no more," she intoned, pointing her right index finger at him. "I, Azura, Queen of Magic, command it!"

"Huh?" Homer gasped. "Eurydice, I . . ."

As he stared at her with confusion raging inside him, she touched her right hand to the stone hanging from her neck and raised her left arm above her head.

The puff of smoke frightened Homer and he nearly ran back the way he had come. But even his infantile mind rationalized that Eurydice, or at least the woman he thought was Eurydice, would never hurt him.

He looked back at where the woman had stood. She was gone.

A grunt escaped from Homer. Only two people on Earth were capable of interpreting the sound he made. They—the Mistress and Eurydice—would have labeled it as one of surprise. It was followed by another. This was a sound of glee. He hopped into the air. It was a game! Eurydice, wearing the silver thing, wanted to play a game with him! And this was a good night for it too. Would get him in a good mood for the party. Roaring, he raced toward the last spot he had seen the woman in the silver thing. The chase was on.

The roar echoed through the empty halls of the Museum. The guard at the entrance to the ballroom heard it, some of the party-goers, including Luckett and Cousin Gene, heard it, and Larry Cole heard it.

Inside the office, where his suit was hanging, Cole snatched off the black hat and mask. He was about to leave when he heard a noise. He froze and listened. Then the doorknob started to turn.

44

OCTOBER 31, 1997
7:40 P.M.

Judy Daniels heard the roar. She pulled a .38 Colt Detective Special from an ankle holster, stared up into the darkness at the top of the steep staircase and felt her legs start to tremble.

"C'mon, Edna," Judy said to herself through clenched teeth. "Move it, girl, so we can get out of here."

The sound of high heels clicking rapidly across the stone floor upstairs carried to Judy. A second later, Edna appeared at the top of the stairs. She stopped and slipped out of her heels; however, the gown was tight around her knees, obstructing running. Reaching down, she yanked at the seam, ripping it up the side. Then she dashed down the stairs. Near the bottom, she nearly fell but Judy caught her.

Edna was breathing hard from a combination of exertion and fear. Snatching off the silver mask revealed a terror on her face that reinforced Judy's.

"What was that noise?" Judy asked.

"Death! And he's after me!"

They could hear the rapid footfalls at the top of the steps.

"Wait!" Judy shouted.

Reaching beneath Edna's cape, she deftly unstrapped the Vanisher. As soon as it came off, the figure of Death appeared at the top of the staircase. The two women fled into the dark as he leaped down toward them.

Jonathan Gobey led Mays and Drew into the office. The Zorro costume hung in the bathroom. They walked toward it.

Drew picked up the sword. "This is a steel saber. No wonder he was able to outfight us!"

"Let me see that," Gobey said. "It's from the new collection. Do you know how much this is worth?"

There was a noise outside in the office.

"What was that?" Drew asked in a trembling voice.

"Sounded like a door closing," Gobey said.

"We'd better check it out," Mays whispered.

Cautiously, they returned to the outer office. It was empty. The corridor door was closed.

"It didn't close on its own," Drew said.

"Probably just the wind," Gobey added, returning to the bathroom.

"There's no wind in here," Mays said. "But what are we gonna do now? The guy's not wearing the costume. How will we recognize him?"

"To hell with him," Gobey said from the bathroom door. "What about me?"

45

Judy and Edna sprinted toward the command-post office. Their pursuer was getting closer.

Up ahead Judy saw a haphazardly arranged metal sculpture. One of its pointed appendages extended out six feet above the floor.

As they approached the sculpture, Judy leaped and hooked one of the Vanisher's straps over it. The device was suspended upside down. Instantly it dislodged a pellet, which struck the floor and erupted to emit a cloud of smoke.

On the other side of the smoke, Judy spun around and raised her gun. She aimed it back down the corridor. She knew their pursuer was big, and obviously fast. Now the Mistress of Disguise/High Priestess of Mayhem would find out if it was bulletproof.

Edna saw what Judy was doing and reached for her own gun, a .25-caliber Beretta automatic that had been anchored at the small of her back. She swung her gun up and pointed it in the same direction Judy aimed. As the Vanisher dislodged pellet after pellet, exploding to form smoke clouds, the two women continued backing down the corridor.

Homer was cunning. He realized that something about Eurydice was wrong. He could tell the two were heading in the direction of the guard place. The Mistress had ordered him to avoid this area; that is, at ground level. Homer scrambled atop a display case, and using guide wires supporting exhibits hanging from the ceiling, climbed high above the two women now racing down the corridor.

By the time Judy activated the Vanisher, he was directly over their heads. Beneath his Death mask, he frowned. He stared down at the unmasked woman in silver. Then he silently crept away.

46

L arry Cole walked out the front door of the Museum. The guard on duty said a cheerful, "Calling it an early night, sir?"

Cole smiled back. "They party just a little bit too heavy for me. Good night."

"Good night," the guard said as he watched Cole trot down the steps to his car.

47

The cognac bottle was empty. Gobey, Mays and Drew staggered toward the ballroom, where the Halloween party was now in full swing.

"I mean," Drew slurred, "who the hell does she know anyway? We never had a curator younger than fifty in all the years I been here."

"How long you been here, Drew?" Mays, who was equally drunk, asked.

"Seven years."

"How many curators have they had in that time?"

"Two. Fleisher and Vaughn."

They exploded with uncontrollable laughter.

"Wait a goddamned minute!" Mays said. "Let's ask somebody who'll know what he's talking about. What do you say, Jonathan? Hey, where'd he go?"

Drew also looked around. "He was here a minute ago. Jonathan?"

"Jonathan?"

Two galleries away, the giant figure of Death moved toward a case in the *Glassware from Around the World* Hall. Over his shoulder he carried the unconscious body of a man dressed as Zorro.

There are more bizarre stories in reality
than any of us could imagine.

—J. Garth.

48

Umberto Giampi was an Italian immigrant who had been living in the United States for two years. As he was determined to make his fortune before he qualified to become a naturalized citizen, he worked three jobs. To save money, he slept on a cot in a spare room of his sister's house and spent money only for rent, food and a new Chevrolet compact, which was his sole concession to life in his new homeland. He had saved fifty-two thousand dollars and was planning to open a hot-dog stand on South Commercial Avenue when he reached the hundred-thousand-dollar mark. Then Umberto felt he would become a real American capitalist, like John D. Rockefeller, Conrad Hilton or Ezra Rotheimer, whom he had read about back in Italy.

Now, as the sky brightened over the lake, Umberto drove south on Lake Shore Drive, approaching the National Science and Space Museum, returning from the office-cleaning job he held three nights a week. If he made it to his sister's house by six, he could manage two hours' sleep before he went to work in his brother's dry-cleaning plant. His hands gripped the steering wheel tightly as he squinted at the road ahead. For the third time since he entered Lake Shore Drive at Randolph, his eyes shut. He dozed for perhaps a second or two before snapping himself awake to see a man standing in the road before him!

Umberto Giampi yanked the wheel, causing the compact to skid on the pavement, which was slick with morning dew. He lost control and the car went into a spin. Finally, it came to a halt facing north in the southbound lanes. Then Umberto saw the body.

His heart raced as he opened the car door and got out. A couple of cars went by in the northbound lanes, but slowed only momentarily before racing off toward the Loop. Slowly, he approached the prone figure. It was wrapped in some kind of black coat or cloak and he couldn't tell if it was a man or a woman. It didn't move. He bent down and touched the shoulder. There was no response, but he could tell that there was warm flesh beneath the black cloth. He reached out a trembling hand and turned the body over. What he saw made him gasp in horror. The face was masked!

Umberto stumbled backward, scrambled onto his hands and knees and began crawling away as fast as he could. Then he heard the siren.

It came from the direction of the Museum. Through the ever-brightening early morning light he could see twirling blue Mars lightbeams approaching. He briefly considered flight, but then realized he could never escape. Suddenly he had an idea. The masked man he hit was probably a robber. Umberto Giampi's mind worked rapidly. The robber had been standing in the road in an attempt to stop him! The masked bandit was probably armed! As the police car skidded to a stop, the immigrant worker began fashioning a lie.

49

L arry Cole awoke early. Dinner the night before had been quiet, but he did notice that Edna seemed excited. Well, he felt a bit excited himself.

After dinner they made love before falling into an exhausted sleep. He had slept six hours, which was something of a record for him of late. At about 5:00 A.M., he awakened.

Carefully, he slipped out of bed without disturbing Edna and put on his shorts. He walked through the darkened apartment to the kitchen and drank a glass of water. In the living room was a bookcase that contained the latest books by Barbara Zorin and Jamal Garth. He was about to pull one out when he noticed the framed photos on top of the bookcase. He studied them.

There were four pictures in all. One was of a handsome, medium-brown-complexioned black man. His bushy Afro hairdo dated the photo to the late sixties or early seventies.

The woman in the second photo bore a striking resemblance to Edna. The hairdo was again circa early seventies. Cole speculated that she must be Edna's mother. The next photo was of two laughing little girls with a remarkable resemblance to each other.

He merely glanced at the last photo of the woman and the oldest girl. It made Cole uneasy. There was something wrong with this picture, a coldness and absence of life. It reminded him of Edna. Not Edna all the time, but once in a while when she became remote, like in his office last night before he went to the Museum. Cole looked back at the happy children.

"That's me and my sister, Josie. The others are of my mother and father."

Cole turned around. Edna, clad in her nightgown, was standing at the entrance to the bedroom. She came over and he wrapped his arms around her as she cuddled against his bare chest.

"You and your sister looked amazingly alike as children," he said. "Do you still favor her as much?"

He felt her shiver violently.

"Hey," he said with concern. "You're freezing. I'd better get you back to bed."

Under the covers again, she was still trembling.

"Are you okay?" He placed the back of his hand against her forehead. It was cool.

"Just caught a chill." Her teeth chattered. "I'll be okay in a minute."

He pulled her close to him and they lay like that for a full five minutes before the heat of his body warmed her.

"I think you're coming down with something, Edna. Maybe you should stay home today."

She pulled his arms tighter around her. "Would you stay with me?"

He thought for a moment before answering. "That's an idea. I haven't had a day off in a while. I don't think Govich would mind. You know there will be talk."

"Would that bother you?"

"It's not me I'm concerned about."

She laughed. "So two people, who happen to work in the same office with about fifty others, decide to take off on the same day. Who could make anything out of that?"

"You've got a point."

They became quiet and still again. After a few moments, he said, "You didn't tell me if you and your sister still favor each other."

She didn't respond immediately. When she did, her voice was very subdued. "Josie was one of the Museum's 'Missing: Presumed Dead' cases. She disappeared in the *Glassware from Around the World* Hall on the afternoon of August seventh, nineteen seventy-two. No one ever saw or heard of her again."

"Did they search the Museum?"

"They searched it and the park around it. A Detective Mulcahy from the Missing Persons Section was assigned to the case. He was a freckle-faced old Irishman who always reminded me of Santa Claus. He never stopped looking for Josie. Even after my mother died. He retired when I was still in the Police Academy. I went to his retirement party and he made me promise that I'd keep looking for her."

"Have you?" Cole asked.

"I guess so, but after all this time, what's the use? She's like all the rest. Something happens to them in there and they're never seen or heard from again. Perhaps there is something supernatural about the place."

"I don't believe that. Maybe I can't explain exactly what happened to me out on that island, but what I saw was no ghost and my injury was caused by something that exists in this world."

"Larry," she said softly, "I've got a confession to make."

"Not now," he said, blowing gently on the back of her neck.

"But I've got to tell you about last night."

"I said not now." He began nibbling gently at the flesh of her shoulder. "That's an order."

"You're not going to pull rank on me in bed, are you?"

"Definitely." He turned her over and covered her mouth with his.

50

Homer stumbled down the winding stone steps beneath the *Glassware from Around the World* Hall. He was very drunk. This had been the best party he had ever attended. A brunette in what he heard some people call a "Harem" costume had danced with him a lot. People had bought him drinks he had sipped through a straw that fit into a hole in his mask.

When the sky began brightening outside, Homer headed for the ballroom exit. A man dressed in a "Rambo" costume, who was as drunk as Homer, stepped in front of him.

"Yo, Death," the man said, swaying from side to side as he waved a large knife through the air. "I wanna see what you really look like. Take off the mask."

Through the robe, Homer reached out and grabbed the wrist of the knife hand. The man struggled, but it didn't do any good. Homer forced him to the floor before taking the knife away. He then stepped on the blade while pulling the handle upward and snapping the knife in two.

With another grunt, Homer walked away as people rushed over to attend the injured Rambo. The giant in the Death costume had broken Rambo's wrist in three places.

But now Homer didn't feel so good. He was having trouble negotiating the staircase and he kept blundering into the walls. He had never been allowed to stay at a party so long. Usually, no later than 1:00 A.M., Eurydice would come and get him. But he hadn't seen or heard from Eurydice since about 8:00 P.M.

At the bottom of the staircase he stepped into the huge subterranean cavern that had been originally constructed as a railroad station.

Snatching off the mask and robe, he dropped them, along with the scythe he had carried all night, on the floor.

He staggered a couple of steps along the gallery and slumped to the floor, his back to the railing. Instantly, he was asleep and snoring.

A rumbling noise began on the opposite end of the gallery, making the floor vibrate. Oblivious to it, Homer slept on.

The origin of the sound rounded a corner and came within sight of the sleeping, shirtless giant. The rumbling stopped briefly. Then one of Homer's roarlike snores carried the length of the gallery. The rumbling started up again, coming toward Homer.

He was awakened by a searing pain across his chest. He screamed and leaped to his feet, but the twelve-foot rawhide bullwhip snaked out and wrapped around his ankles. He fell heavily to the floor. He would have been strong enough to fight off his attacker, but then a metal rod made contact with his side and he spasmed rigid as ten thousand volts of electricity coursed through him. He screamed in pain and terror. Then his tormenter raised the bullwhip again.

Eurydice was on the stairs leading down from the Museum when she heard Homer's screams. She raced to the bottom of the steps and out onto the gallery, less than twenty feet away from him.

The scene before her she had seen repeated many times. Homer was being beaten by the Mistress; but this was the first time since Eurydice had gone to work above the surface.

"Stop!" Eurydice cried.

The Mistress spun toward her.

Old age had done everything to the Mistress but kill her. Her flesh had withered into near mummification. Only a few white wisps clung to the liver-spotted skull. Her weakened limbs permitted only a crawl. But after over a century of life, the Mistress's brain, eyesight and hearing were nearly as keen as Eurydice's.

The Mistress was seated on an electronically powered cart with wheels of sectioned metal that could be mechanically altered to change their shape. This enabled her to climb or descend stairs in the subterranean chamber and had she desired, to climb to the Museum above.

The cart possessed a computer console, which Eurydice had installed for her, and a monitor that assisted her in performing various functions: getting in or out of her cart and retrieving items from any distance up to twenty-five feet. With other controls, she operated the instruments of torture.

Now, as the Mistress spun toward Eurydice, she tapped a coded message on her keyboard. The bullwhip was being operated with astonishing facility from a mechanical arm extending out from the cart. At the Mistress's command, it stopped in mid-swing and lashed out instead toward Eurydice, who dodged out of the way.

A snarl curled the Mistress's mouth open to reveal blackened teeth. With gnarled fingers, tipped with brilliantly polished red nails, the Mistress entered more commands. The cart moved forward as all her instruments of punishment became concentrated on Eurydice. Homer was forgotten.

Eurydice was fast and agile, but she was no match for her pursuer. She dodged three of the bullwhip's lashes, but then the fourth caught her around the knees and yanked her off her feet. She fell hard on her back, the wind knocked out of her. Stunned, but still aware of the danger, she fought to get up, but even at peak efficiency, it would have been too late.

The electrified rod made contact with her hip. The pain lanced through her and she screamed.

"Haven't you been the feisty one, my dear!" The Mistress spoke into a mounted microphone on the cart. Her voice was mechanically amplified through a speaker, carrying over Eurydice's screams. "You defy me, disobey me and let Homer get drunk! I will not tolerate such insolence!"

The rod struck Eurydice again. Again she screamed

"I knew this was going to happen to you, Eurydice." The Mistress's voice had dropped to a sadistic purr. "As Museum curator, you were given too much power for your own good. You didn't know how to use it."

She struck Eurydice again and again with the rod. The young woman's screams diminished as she weakened.

"Then you allowed your passions to run away with you and you pursued the policeman like a bitch in heat. Of course I should have expected that, considering where you came from. Too many mistakes, Eurydice. Far too many mistakes!"

Eurydice had lost consciousness, but the Mistress was not through with her. Withdrawing the electric rod and the bullwhip, she activated a pair of metal grips that opened to form pincers padded with rubber linings. The Mistress lowered them to pick up Eurydice's unconscious body and then maneuvered the cart to the edge of the balcony. Eurydice was extended past the railing. The floor awaited fifty feet below.

Homer shouted, "Please stop!"

The Mistress spun around. Her watery dark eyes glared at him. "She's corrupt and she's trying to corrupt you! She must die!"

"No, Mistress, please." Homer was on his knees, his elongated arms extended in front of him. Tears streamed down his face. A single strand of saliva stretched from his lower lip to the gallery floor. "Please, Mistress," he begged. "I'll do anything you ask."

"I'm not worried about you, fool!"

He lowered his head in anguish.

A grin split the Mistress's face. She had always enjoyed torturing Homer.

"Before she came," the Mistress continued, "you did whatever I told you. But after she got here, you began questioning me. You, a moron with little more intelligence than a stray dog, questioning me!"

"Please, Mistress," he sobbed, "don't kill her."

"All right, Homer," she cackled gratingly. "But if she lives, you must swear that she'll obey me in all things, or I'll snuff out her life quicker than I would the flame of a flickering candle."

"I promise, Mistress." He kept his head lowered. Years ago she had killed a pet kitten he was keeping. Before she crushed the little animal's skull, she had taunted him as she was doing now, promising to spare the animal's life. But when Homer had jumped up too fast, she had smashed a hammer down on the poor kitty.

The Mistress spun the cart away from the railing and dropped Eurydice's body on the floor in front of Homer.

"She'll recover soon," the Mistress said, turning the cart around. "Then it will be up to you to make sure she does exactly as I say."

As the Mistress rolled away, Homer continued to hold the unconscious woman in his arms.

51

Barbara Zorin and Jamal Garth were the guest speakers at a half-day Contemporary Writers Workshop for graduate English Literature students at the University of Chicago. The lecture hall was packed to standing-room-only capacity as the scheduled activities came to a conclusion.

Jamal Garth stood at the speaker's podium. "I don't think many works of crime fiction over the past two decades have relied heavily on fact as a basis. The reason I say this is that crime as fact comes out so much stranger than it does in fiction. It's almost as if the truth is too fantastic to be taken seriously."

Laughter rumbled through the audience, which included Barbara Zorin and Professor Leonard Devlin.

"So, in closing, I say to those of you who plan to be fiction writers, continue to be fiction readers. Digest the routine police procedurals, private-eye tales and amateur-sleuth yarns to your heart's content. Remember, there are more bizarre stories in reality than any of us could imagine. Thank you."

The audience gave the two authors a standing ovation, with Professor Devlin joining in. Devlin, a University of Chicago professor, was the founder of the Contemporary Writers Workshop and he was particularly pleased that this session had gone so well.

Despite his academic accomplishments, Devlin looked like an aging pro-football middle linebacker. At sixty, his midsection was beginning to spread a bit, but his neck, shoulders and upper body bulged with muscle beneath his tweed suit coat.

As the professor and his guests crossed the university quadrangle, heading for the faculty dining room for lunch, Barbara said, "I understand you're on the board of directors over at the National Science and Space Museum."

"Have been for the past eleven years," Devlin said with pride.

"How many are on the board, Professor?" Garth asked.

"Actually five, but only two of us meet regularly with Dr. Fleisher, the Museum chairman."

"Would the other regular member be Dr. Jacqueline Loving from the history department here at the university?" Barbara questioned.

With a slight frown, Professor Devlin answered, "That's correct. Do you know Dr. Loving?"

"No," Barbara replied, "but I do know Eurydice Vaughn, the Museum curator. Miss Vaughn helped me with some research for a novel a couple of years ago. She's quite a brilliant young woman."

In the dining room, Devlin led the writers to a corner table overlooking the Midway Plaisance, which bisected the University of Chicago campus. Off in the distance, the green roof of the National Science and Space Museum was visible.

They were just starting on the main course when Garth asked, "Eurydice Vaughn was a student here, wasn't she, Professor?"

Devlin visibly stiffened. "I really don't recall, Mr. Garth. After all, a lot of students have passed through this place during the years I've been here."

"How many of those have you given personal recommendations to?"

Barbara reached for her shoulder bag. "I think I can explain what Jamal is talking about." She removed a folded xeroxed page from the purse and handed it to Garth.

He read it out loud and said, "This letter is a personal recommendation for Miss Vaughn from you."

"I know what it is, Mr. Garth. I wrote it. Do you mind telling me what this is all about?"

"You must excuse us," Barbara apologized. "But writing crime fiction sometimes makes us come on a bit too much with the third degree. We're doing some research about the Museum, and a couple of things came up that we found difficult to understand. Since we were coming over here for the seminar, we figured you could help us clear up our problems."

"I assumed from the recommendation you wrote that you remembered her when she was a student here," Garth elaborated.

"You must excuse what I said about not remembering her," Devlin replied. "In fact, I do. She was a brilliant student. One of the best minds I've ever encountered."

"Was she in many of your classes?" Barbara interjected.

"One or two, as I recall. It's been a few years since she graduated."

"She was also in some of Dr. Loving's classes?" Garth asked.

"I would think that as a graduate history major, Miss Vaughn would have taken a few of Dr. Loving's courses."

"You're right, Professor," Barbara said as she took a moment to butter a slice of bread. "Her degrees are in history. Both graduate and under-grad. But we have a problem with them."

Defensively, Devlin picked up his knife and fork. "And what would that be?"

Garth answered for her. "The university has no record of Miss Vaughn's attendance here, Professor."

Devlin managed a weak smile. "That's absurd. Why, you yourself just said she has two degrees from this institution."

"We went a bit further in our research than just looking up the degrees," Barbara said. "We asked to examine her transcripts. There were none."

"Undoubtedly a clerical error," Devlin said offhandedly. "Some clerk probably misfiled them."

"We thought of that too, Professor," Garth pressed. "But then, we're very thorough researchers. In a place like this, a student has to do a lot of things, like register for classes, check books out of the library, supply notifications of next of kin and leave a paper trail, so to speak." Garth stared straight across the table at Professor Devlin. "There is not a shred of information like that on Miss Vaughn. She has her degrees on file, yet she didn't attend any classes or participate in any campus activities. Not even those that are mandatory."

Devlin responded coolly, "All that means is that we have a very poor administrative operation here. No more, no less."

Barbara opened the letter of recommendation Devlin had written to the National Science and Space Museum's board of directors. She read directly from it; " 'Eurydice Vaughn is one of the most dedicated, brilliant and gifted students it has been my pleasure to instruct in all my years at this university.' Those are your words, aren't they, Professor?"

He merely nodded.

"And you still can't remember what classes 'the most dedicated, brilliant and gifted student' you ever encountered took?" Garth demanded.

Devlin slammed his fork down beside his plate and stood up. "I'm not going to sit here and be interrogated by you two like some common criminal!" Heads around the faculty dining room turned in the direction of their table. "If you have any questions about one of my students, I suggest you contact that student personally or the dean of students in writing! And if either of you dare approach me again, you'll have my lawyer to deal with." With that, Professor Leonard Devlin stormed away.

"I guess that means we won't be having dessert," Barbara said.

"I guess not," Garth conceded.

52

B lackie Silvestri knocked softly on Chief Govich's office door
before stepping inside.

"C'mon in, Blackie," Govich said with a smile. "How's it going?"

"Good, Chief."

Govich motioned the lieutenant to a chair. "Commander Cole
took off today or I'd assign him to this. As it is, I'm glad he's finally
taking it easy. Dr. Drake's been on my case about having him slow
down."

"I'm glad to see it too, Chief."

"Okay," Govich said, getting down to business. "This comes
straight from the fourth floor. Last night there was some kind of party
at the National Science and Space Museum. E. G. Luckett was there
along with his nephew and a young lady. It seems the nephew,
Eugene Luckett, age twenty-eight, got into some kind of fight with
a guy wearing a death costume. Seems that young Luckett got his
wrist broken in the scuffle, and his uncle's making a big deal out of
it. I want you to look into it and see if you can unruffle E. G.'s
feathers.

"Also, while you're at it, there was a guy hit by a car on Lake
Shore Drive this morning, who is supposed to have attended the same
party. The two incidents probably aren't related, but it wouldn't hurt
to look into it too."

Blackie wasn't crazy about the assignments, but then, you didn't
argue with Chief Govich.

"If it's all right with you, Chief, I'll take Manny with me."

"Good idea," Govich said as Blackie went out the door.

At St. Anne's Hospital, a retired police captain named Kelly was the security director. He and Blackie had worked out of the old Town Hall District nearly thirty years ago.

"Heard you hit the big time, Blackie," Kelly said. He was slender and athletic, nearly seventy, and ran in both the Chicago and Boston marathons every year. "Detective Division headquarters, aide to Govich and Cole. Rumor has it that someday they'll be the crown princes of the department."

"You got good sources, Kelly," Blackie said. "You always did, but now we'd like some info on a patient you've got here. Guy hit by a car on Lake Shore Drive this morning. I understand he was dressed in a costume."

Kelly's face split into a grin. "You're talking about Zorro. That's one for the books. You want to talk to him?"

Blackie shook his head. "Maybe later. We'd like to go about it a bit different. First find out why he was out there, if he was drunk, that sort of thing."

Kelly made three calls and hung up the phone. "Okay, this is the deal. Guy's name is Jonathan Gobey. He's an assistant curator at the National Science and Space Museum. Dressed in a Zorro costume, including a real sword. Guy who hit him's an immigrant who started babbling about Gobey trying to flag him down to rob him. The Traffic guys didn't let him take that too far, but they didn't charge the driver with anything, as it was obvious this guy Gobey was standing out in the road.

"From what I understand, there was some kind of party at the Museum last night and Gobey must have been very involved in it because he had a .47 blood-alcohol level. I talked to the nurse on duty in the emergency room when they brought him in. She said that while they were trying to get the Zorro costume off him, he was mumbling something about a giant in a death suit carrying him into hell."

"He say anything else?" Blackie asked, taking notes.

"Naw. He lost consciousness right after that. He's got a concussion, a broken leg and a couple of broken ribs. He's so full of booze they couldn't give him an anesthetic. They're watching him real close."

"Well, Manny," Blackie said, getting to his feet. "We won't be able to talk to this guy before tomorrow. I guess we'd better head downtown. Thanks, Kelly."

"So, you're saying this guy was nearly seven feet tall, Mr. Luckett?" Manny was conducting the interrogation this time, while Blackie looked on silently.

"The guy was huge, Sergeant," Cousin Gene said. "But the thing is, I don't think he grabbed me with his bare hand. It was just too big." He held up his uninjured arm for emphasis. "I got a twelve-inch wrist circumference. A guy would have to have a hand as big as your head to reach out and grab it like this guy did."

"Gene?" E. G. Luckett's voice came from the open door to his office. "Would you and the officers step in here please?"

Obediently, the injured man got to his feet.

As Luckett sank down into his specially reinforced chair, he said, "I was expecting Commander Cole to come out on this investigation." There was just the slightest note of disapproval in his voice.

"The commander's off today, sir," Manny said.

"He hasn't completely recovered from the injury he received a few weeks ago," Blackie added.

Manny turned to Gene. "So we got your assailant's height. What else can you tell us about him?"

"Not much at all." Gene shrugged. "He was in a costume. Had on this black, hooded robe with a skeleton mask over his face. He was supposed to be Death."

53

She was playing hide-and-seek in the *Glassware from Around the World* Hall. She would dart behind the stone bench and then run over to one of the display cases to hide. She looked around the edge of the case. She couldn't see anyone. She ducked back again. She would be found soon. What was the fun in hiding forever?

Something moved behind her. She turned around to look.

"Momma! Edna!" Eurydice screamed and jerked awake.

Eurydice was in the shower room with Homer. He had stripped off her Spandex suit and was supporting her naked body under the spray from one of the showers. The water was ice-cold.

Slowly, the pain from the bruises around her body left and the familiarity of this place brought her back to the present. Weak and exhausted, she moved away from him and slumped back against the shower wall. Her dream was forgotten. Homer did not move or speak.

When she finally spoke, her voice was hoarse. "How long was I unconscious?" It was a purely rhetorical question; although Homer could tell time, he had never worn a watch and there were few clocks down here.

"A long time, Eurydice," he said. "The Mistress was very mad. She said you're trying to corrupt me."

She looked at him. He had forgotten to take off his pants when he entered the shower and they were soaked. She shook her head from side to side. He was helpless.

She laughed. "What about what she's done to you?" She pointed to the welts across his arms and shoulders left by the Mistress's bullwhip.

"I was drunk. She had to punish me," he said without much conviction.

"You're an adult, Homer! You don't punish adults by beating them with whips and shocking them with cattle prods!"

"Shhh!" He held a finger to his lips as he scrambled across the shower room toward her.

He grabbed her and placed a massive hand over her mouth. She struggled, but this time he didn't let go.

"I promised the Mistress, Eurydice," he whispered in her ear. "I promised you'd obey her. You used to obey her before you went up there." He swung his eyes toward the ceiling.

Eurydice made one last vain attempt to free herself. Then she stared at him. The anger and hatred in her gaze were so intense, he was forced to look away.

In a near-tearful whisper, he said, "She was going to kill you."

It took some moments, but she finally relaxed and her eyes closed. Slowly, he removed the hand from her mouth. She didn't scream. He released his grip on her. She slipped from his grasp and leaned back against the wall of the shower.

They remained like that for a long time. Then he asked, "You are going to obey the Mistress now, aren't you?"

She didn't look at him as she answered, "Of course."

54

Edna and Cole walked slowly through the John G. Shedd Aquarium on the lakefront near downtown Chicago.

She held his arm. "Do you think the fish know they're trapped behind the glass?"

Cole thought about it for a moment. "They don't look like it. They've got plenty of room and they're probably fed very well. What would they be doing any different in their natural habitats?"

Her eyes looked terribly sad. "They'd be free, Larry."

"Hey, don't go all mushy on me over a couple of fish. Look, if you want, I'll break the case and let all of them out."

She recovered quickly. "I'm sorry. I have a bad habit of doing that. It's like I have this cloud of doom I carry around in my purse and yank out on unsuspecting people like a weapon."

"I can handle your cloud of doom," he said, squeezing her against him. "How about some lunch?"

They had spent a very quiet, relaxing day together so far. Cole had dozed off again after breakfast and slept soundly for two hours. Under the shower, he felt rested and free of tension for the first time in years.

He found Edna in the living room reading a Barbara Zorin novel. She was dressed in a sweater and blue jeans; her hair was combed back off her face. When she looked up at him and smiled, something deep inside him stirred.

It was a cool autumn day with a brilliant sun shining out of a cloudless sky. Now they were back in Cole's car driving north on Michigan Avenue. They were going to Houston's Restaurant, then to the Goodman Theater.

"Okay, I'm ready now," he said.

"Ready for what?" She looked quizzically at him.

"For your confession about last night."

"Only if you promise me in advance that you won't get mad."

"I promise."

She told him what she and Judy had done last night at the Museum, right down to her impersonation of Eurydice Vaughn in front of him and E. G. Luckett. She also told him about Death stalking him through darkened corridors, and about the giant's pursuit of them.

He was dumbfounded.

"You mean to tell me that was actually you I danced with?"

With her right hand, she crossed her heart.

They stopped for a red light at Wacker Drive. He turned to her. "Cover your eyes."

"Amazing," he said as he looked at the section of her face visible beneath her palm. It was the same as the masked Queen Azura's. It was also the same as the masked woman in the tavern-wench costume he had rescued from the Musketeers. He hadn't known who the real Eurydice Vaughn was last night, but he did now.

The light changed and Cole accelerated onto the Michigan Avenue Bridge over the Chicago River.

Finally, Edna spoke. "You've got this kind of funny look on your face, like you know something nobody else in the world knows."

Cole felt a flash of guilt. Lisa used to say the same thing to him. He realized what that stirring had been inside him earlier. He was falling in love with Edna.

He turned his attention back to his driving.

"Well? Are you going to tell me?"

Before she could say anything else, his beeper went off.

55

Dr. Jacqueline Loving was an extraordinarily tall woman, with silver hair hanging to her shoulders. She had striking features and eyes of such a startling blue as to seem almost artificial. At the Museum, Leonard Devlin was waiting for her in the main rotunda by the information desk. He was visibly upset.

"You want to tell me what's so urgent?" she asked.

He took her arm and led her away from a group of Japanese tourists. "We've got a problem. Barbara Zorin and Jamal Garth were asking a lot of questions about Eurydice Vaughn today."

The history professor blanched. "What kind of questions?"

"I haven't got time to go into all of that now, but they're onto something. They've been digging around in the university archives and it's obvious they're investigating this place."

Her hand went to her mouth. "I couldn't go through that again, Leonard."

He placed his arm around her shoulders. "There's no way they can find out about the baby. That was over forty years ago. That woman has got to be dead and long since buried by now."

She turned to look up at the galleries looming above them. It was in the *Glassware from Around the World* Hall that she had given her baby to the strange woman, as part of an arrangement she had made with the then curator, Dr. Andrew Weiner. An arrangement she had regretted every day of her life, even though the infant boy had been horribly deformed and illegitimate. Leonard Devlin had been the father.

"So what are we going to do now?" She was very close to tears.

"We're going upstairs to see Eurydice Vaughn and find out what the hell those writers are up to."

They took the elevator to the administrative level. A harried, flushed Janice Cotton was at her desk when Loving and Devlin came in.

"We need to talk to Miss Vaughn right away," Devlin demanded. "It's urgent."

"I'm sorry, Professor," Miss Cotton said, "but she's not in."

"Well, where is she?"

The secretary's face tensed at his sharp tone. "I don't know. She didn't come in or call today."

Loving stepped forward and touched Devlin's arm. "Maybe we should go and see Winston."

As he turned toward her, another voice called from the waiting area on the other side of the room. "Dr. Fleisher's not in either, Professor. We've already checked. We're also waiting for Miss Vaughn."

It was Barbara Zorin who had spoken. She and Jamal Garth were seated across the room.

Before Devlin could say anything, the door to the curator's private office opened and Eurydice Vaughn stepped out. Janice Cotton almost fainted. "How did you . . ."

Dressed in a tan business suit, black-silk blouse and heels, Eurydice coolly examined the four people waiting. "I see I have quite a few guests this afternoon, Janice. Who's first?"

56

Edna was seated alone at a table in the restaurant. At this hour of the day, between lunch and dinner, business was sparse. Larry had gone to use the telephone out in the hall beside the bar. The waitress had brought her a glass of iced tea and she planned to order the shrimp salad when he returned.

She looked around. Over in the far corner across the room, a couple was seated at a table, so close they had only to lean forward a bit for their heads to touch. They were holding hands and their eyes were locked as they whispered together. Despite the involvements of her past life, she had never been able to achieve that level of familiarity with anyone. However, Larry had become very important to her much faster than anyone else ever had. He had also managed to penetrate into levels of her soul where no one had been able to go before. This awareness frightened and fascinated her.

"Excuse me, ma'am?"

Edna turned to find the bartender standing beside the table.

"Yes?"

"How've you been? I haven't seen you since the night we had all the excitement in here."

"I beg your pardon?"

He squinted at her. The shadows of the late-fall afternoon were starting to lengthen. Against the glare of the setting sun, the draperies had been drawn, casting the area in shadow. But he was certain that this was the same woman who had been seated at the bar the night Dr. Sam Sykes disappeared.

"You drink grapefruit juice on the rocks, right?"

She shook her head. "I hate grapefruit juice. I have been known to try a wine spritzer from time to time."

He was about to say something else when Cole returned to the table.

"Good evening, sir." In a near panic, the bartender backed away. "Good to see you again, sir. Hope you enjoy your meal." He quickly retreated in the direction of the bar.

Amused and a little surprised, Cole asked Edna, "What was that all about?"

"He thought he recognized me. Asked if I drank grapefruit juice. Maybe your curator's been in here too? Then again, it could just be that he has bad eyes. He thought he recognized you also."

"But I've been in here before," Cole told her, then changed the subject.

"It was Govich who beeped me. He sent Blackie and Manny out on a couple of investigations for the superintendent. It looks like the two cases are not only related, but tie in to the Museum, the party last night and our friend in the Death costume."

Edna's brow furrowed. "I don't understand."

"I don't either, but Govich wants a full written report on his desk the first thing in the morning, because Luckett's interested."

Cole leaned toward her. They were nearly as close as the romantic couple across the room. Edna took his hand as he began to tell her the details.

57

The Mistress lived in quarters at the opposite end of the gallery from the shower room. A thick carpet, which produced clouds of dust, and overstuffed furniture cluttered the oblong, high-ceilinged room. It had originally been constructed as the operations center for the train station. On a canopied, raised bed surrounded by pillows, the Mistress sat in all her ancient, hideous splendor, Eurydice and Homer before her.

"Do you think you convinced the writers of your authenticity, Eurydice?" The voice was amplified through the same apparatus she had used on the cart.

Eurydice, still dressed in her business suit, stood rigidly erect and looked directly into the Mistress's face. Homer only hoped his friend wouldn't do anything to anger the Mistress.

"I showed them my diplomas, citations and awards along with my master's thesis with Professor Loving's comments. I also had some photographs of classmates."

"The ones I made up for you?" the Mistress asked.

"Yes." It took her a moment to add the "ma'am."

The Mistress reached down and picked up a book that had been lying beside her on the bed. Its title was *The Strange Case of Neil and Margo Dewitt*, by Barbara Zorin and Jamal Garth. "I have read this book and found that the two writers are not only fair stylists, but very thorough researchers. They won't take what they got from you at face value. After all, they went to the university first. They're looking for something."

"What can they discover?" Eurydice asked. "As long as I remain upstairs—"

"As long as I allow you to remain upstairs!" the Mistress corrected sharply.

Eurydice nodded solemnly. "As long as you allow me to remain upstairs, you will be protected in this place."

"Zorin and Garth are very good friends with your policeman, Eurydice. Of course you knew that from the research file you had made up on him, didn't you?"

For a brief instant, Eurydice's eyes flared, but she controlled herself quickly.

"I was aware that Cole had developed a close relationship with them. There are excerpts from their book in his file."

"And what about your look-alike detective, Edna Gray?"

"I don't know anything about her, Mistress." Eurydice's voice was strained.

"That's strange, my dear. The woman impersonated you to perfection at the Halloween ball. It was almost as if the two of you were related."

Eurydice's eyes glazed. "I have no family but you and Homer, Mistress."

"Don't forget that, Eurydice!" the Mistress snapped. "It will keep you from making any more mistakes."

"Yes, Mistress."

"We might have to do something about Zorin and Garth. In fact, your policeman and the female detective will have to go as well."

Eurydice didn't move a muscle or display any emotion at all.

"But first," the Mistress said softly, "we'll have to wait and see what they do next. Wouldn't want to tip our hands too soon."

"May I say something, Mistress?" Eurydice asked.

The Mistress nodded her approval.

"I don't understand why Professor Loving and Professor Devlin were so upset about the writers' questions. Nothing Zorin and Garth can uncover will affect them at the university."

The Mistress didn't respond for a time.

Finally, she nodded and her watery dark eyes swung to Homer. He quickly looked away.

58

The night nurse on the fifth floor of St. Anne's Hospital was approaching the end of her shift. A native of the Philippines, she was a petite woman with dark, pretty features and long black hair pinned up beneath her cap. She had studied long and hard to obtain her nursing degree and was engaged to an American doctor.

The corridor was empty and the floor silent as the wall clock above her desk swept methodically along. She had made her final rounds at five and no patients had rung for assistance since two. She smiled as she thought of the patient in 514. In his closet hung a Zorro costume, although the police had taken the sword for safekeeping. Americans, she mused, really took their holidays seriously. Of course Halloween was nothing like New Years or, the worse hospital holiday of all, St. Patrick's Day.

She began entering her final comments on the duty log when she felt a change in the air pressure. Someone had opened one of the stairwell doors. But all the doors were locked on the stairwell side.

She stepped into the corridor and looked down the dimly lit east wing. Most of the patients' doors were closed.

She turned to examine the west wing. That corridor was even darker than the other side. However, she was certain she saw something move between Rooms 514 and 516. But now there was nothing there.

She looked at the telephone and started toward it when there was a noise directly behind her. She opened her mouth to scream.

59

NOVEMBER 2, 1997
5:46 A.M.

Cole pulled his car into one of the spaces designated for police vehicles outside the emergency room of St. Anne's Hospital. He and Edna entered.

They found retired Captain Kelly, St. Anne's security chief, and Dr. Dean Drake, the CPD's medical director, waiting for them in the security office. Both men held steaming cups of coffee and were apparently old friends. The four of them left the security office and crossed a silent main lobby that smelled faintly of Lysol. Kelly used a special key to summon an elevator, as service from the lobby would not be available for another hour.

The doors opened behind the Filipino nurse, who spun toward them in stunned surprise. She would surely have screamed had she not recognized Kelly, her future father-in-law.

"What is it, Mary?" Kelly asked, moving quickly over to her.

Her voice trembled. "I thought I saw someone in the corridor outside Room Five-fourteen."

"Isn't that where Gobey is?" Cole asked Kelly.

The security director nodded.

"Do you think Death has come to visit, Commander?" Edna asked.

Reaching beneath his jacket, Cole pulled his gun. "If he did, he's in violation of hospital rules. No visitors before one p.m. We'd better go tell Mr. Death, Edna."

She removed a smaller version of Cole's 9-millimeter Beretta from her purse and flipped off the safety.

They flanked the door of Room 514, flattening their backs against the exterior wall. With hand motions, Cole indicated that he was going in first and that she was to follow.

The commander hit the door and dropped into a crouch on the other side. She came through a heartbeat behind him and had her automatic up and ready to fire as she braced against the far wall.

From their positions, they could see the shape of someone lying in the single bed. There was no one else in the room. They quickly checked the closet and the bathroom. Both were empty.

As Drake, Kelly and the nurse came through the door, they went over to check Gobey. His leg and one arm were in casts and his head was wrapped in a turban. There was an IV in his other arm. He was asleep.

"He's fine," the nurse said, checking him. "I guess I must have a case of early morning jitters."

"Nothing to be ashamed of," Edna said. "Where I used to work on the midnights, I'd get them all the time."

As the medical director moved behind the nurse and said softly, "Wake him up," Cole walked over to stand with Kelly. The security chief had closed the door to the outer corridor and now stood guard over it. Edna, pulling a chair up close to the bed, sat down and took out a notebook and pen.

The nurse turned a light on above the patient's bed and said gently, "Mr. Gobey. Wake up, Mr. Gobey."

Slowly, his eyes fluttered open. Agony was evident on his face. "Could you give me a shot?" he pleaded. "The pain is terrible."

"I've got something better than that for you, Mr. Gobey," Drake said with his most winning bedside manner. "We'll eliminate that pain and make you feel much better in the long run. All you've got to do is exactly what I tell you."

Then the medical director began to hypnotize the injured assistant curator from the National Science and Space Museum.

Across the hall from Room 514, the stairwell corridor door opened and a shadow appeared. It moved around briefly and then the door shut again.

60

B ill McElroy was working on plans for the Museum. However, his heart wasn't in it. He had the sinking feeling that this grandiose scheme of Seymour Winbush's would never pan out. With every day, the anger McElroy felt over his father's death receded. Actually, McElroy and his father had not gotten along all that well. Each possessed a marked inability to compromise. Now Bill no longer had to give in. That is, to anyone but Winbush.

McElroy was in his office on the forty-fifth floor of DeWitt Plaza. There was a knock on his door.

"What?" he called out.

Kyle Peters, his father's architect, stuck his head inside. "I'm sorry to bother you, Mr. McElroy, but Mr. Winbush needs to see you right away."

"The king summons his servant," McElroy sneered, following Peters from the room.

Seymour Winbush was re-reading Blackie Silvestri's report when McElroy and Peters entered. The only other person present was E. G. Luckett, who wore an expression of beatific self-satisfaction.

With a dramatic flare, Winbush quoted Gobey's words directly from the report. " 'I was walking along with Mays and Drew. We were angry and quite drunk after what Miss Vaughn had done to us. We were heading for the party.

" 'I don't remember exactly where we were in the Museum when Death grabbed me. It happened too fast. But I recognized him from Miss Vaughn's office and from other Museum Halloween parties over the years. Always the same giant in the same costume, and no one ever saw his face.

" 'Before I could say or do anything, he hit me. I lost consciousness. The next thing I knew, he was carrying me over his shoulder down a long, winding staircase. It was too dark for me to see, but I could reach out and touch the walls. They were of raw brick, and damp.

" 'We emerged into an enormous underground cavern. It was like something out of a horror or science-fiction movie. It looked like a train station, but one of those very old ones.

" 'He carried me into a room and laid me on a table. I tried to struggle, but he tied me down with ropes. Then Miss Vaughn came in. She was also masked and in costume, but I recognized her as the tavern wench. She had given us the cognac and then let the man in the Zorro costume rescue her from us.

" 'She came over to where I was and took one look at me before screaming, "It's not him, Homer! How could you have bungled this too?" She left briefly and returned with something in her hand. I think it was a pin like a brooch or something. She told Death to step back and then she held it in my face.

" 'I tried to get up, to struggle, but I quickly lost consciousness. The next thing I remember was the pain after the car hit me.' "

Winbush looked up. "You have definitely come through for me, E. G." He turned to McElroy. "This will be your passport to begin construction, William."

The young man managed to suppress his skepticism. "Sounded like a ghost story to me, Mr. Winbush."

Winbush's smile spread slowly. "Oh, it is a ghost story, William. A ghost story that's going to give Eurydice Vaughn nightmares."

61

NOVEMBER 2, 1997
10:00 P.M.

One of the local television stations, in which the DeWitt Corporation held the majority of the stock, broke the story as an "Exclusive" on its local six-o'clock news program. By ten o'clock, all the networks in the Chicago area carried it.

Cole sat in Edna's living room as the ten-o'clock news on CBS was about to begin. He'd put a new blank videotape in her VCR.

Edna came out of the kitchen a couple of minutes before ten.

"How did they get all the information that was in Blackie's report?" she asked.

Cole shot her a mirthless grin. "There's only one way to figure that, Edna. Luckett gave it to them."

She placed a hand on his forearm. "I know he's not very popular, but I don't think he would do something like that."

Cole's voice sounded hollow. "Do you remember yesterday when we talked about what happened at the party?"

She nodded. "It was in the restaurant after you told me what Blackie and Manny said about the man in the Death costume."

"When you danced with Luckett's nephew at the party, he mentioned that the DeWitt Corporation is continuing the work of the contractor who wanted to develop the land around the Museum."

"That's right. He made a point of mentioning it. In fact, I think he said it as kind of a warning. At least a warning to Eurydice Vaughn."

"How do you think Eugene Luckett found out what's going on over at the DeWitt Corporation?"

She shrugged. "I don't know. I guess being the nephew of the director of Public Safety puts him in a position to hear things."

"From what I hear, Luckett's looking to feather his political nest by doing favors for Seymour Winbush, the chairman of the board of the DeWitt Corporation. Me and Winbush are old friends, so to speak."

Edna required no further explanation. She had read *The Strange Case of Neil and Margo DeWitt*. In it, Seymour Winbush had been quoted as saying he felt that the Chicago Police Department, and specifically Larry Cole, had railroaded the DeWitts into early graves. It was obvious that Winbush hated Cole.

But now a craggy-faced commentator with gray hair appeared on the screen. *"Our top story tonight deals with the National Science and Space Museum. For years, one of the stellar attractions for visitors to our city, tonight the Museum is overshadowed by a cloud of suspicion and questions about strange and inexplicable occurrences that have recently taken place there."*

A black woman with a ponytail related the incidents that had occurred among the mysterious, costumed figure of Death, Jonathan Gobey and Eugene Luckett. Interviews with Gobey and Luckett followed. Although somewhat vague, they displayed their injuries on camera.

The female commentator came back on. *"The National Science and Space Museum has been the scene of many such bizarre events since its doors opened in nineteen-six. One such incident occurred just two months ago and involved one of the most highly respected officers in the Chicago Police Department, Commander Lawrence Cole."*

A taped segment of Cole outside police headquarters came on-screen. A caption with his rank and name appeared across his chest. Edna and Manny were standing behind him.

In Edna's living room, Cole wrote the numbers from the video-recorder timer on a pad.

On the screen, Cole said, *"What happened to me out on that island remains mysterious only because the facts surrounding it have not come to light. When they do, I'm sure there will be no more of a mystery surrounding what occurred than is the case with any other crime before it's solved."*

"Do you think the same thing will be true with what happened to Mr. Gobey and Mr. Luckett?" the reporter asked.

On-screen, Cole smiled. *"I'm sure of it."*

The scene switched back to the newsroom. The black reporter was saying, *"We reached the Museum's curator, Eurydice Vaughn, earlier today. She had this to say about the injuries suffered by the two guests attending the Museum's annual fund-raising masked ball."*

Cole made another time entry on his pad.

Looking cool and very much in command of the situation, the curator said, *"Mr. Gobey and Mr. Luckett, I believe, have both admitted to imbibing spirits prior to sustaining their injuries. Of course, others observed the person in the Death costume and the gentlemen drinking alcohol. I'm quite sure some of these other guests would be willing to come forward as witnesses if the Museum's reputation, as well as the safety of its guests, is further questioned."*

"Well said," Cole remarked. Edna gently pinched him.

As the newscast moved on to another topic, Cole stopped the videotape and muted the television's sound.

He turned to Edna. "Do you remember the other day when I asked you to cover your eyes with your hand?"

She nodded. "That was right before you got that kind of funny look on your face. The same look when the reporter was interviewing you."

"I think I'm on to something, Edna," he said, attempting to keep the excitement out of his voice. "Something that affects you."

She frowned. "Affects me how?"

Her VCR was equipped with an accessory that allowed the viewer to impose images from the same cartridge of a privately taped video recording onto the same frame. Now, as he tapped instructions into the remote, he said to her, "Watch."

First the frame with him talking to the reporter appeared. In it, Edna, standing behind him with Manny, was visible over Cole's right shoulder. He entered more coded instructions into the remote. A series of numbers appeared around the edge of the screen. Cole selected the appropriate numbers and tapped in more instructions. As

Edna looked on, her face expanded to take up the entire screen, then contracted, leaving the other half blank.

Now Eurydice Vaughn's face appeared beside hers. And Edna didn't like this. She didn't like it at all. She recalled that her last visit to the Museum had involved Eurydice Vaughn.

His machinations complete, Cole leaned back and asked with satisfaction, "What do you think?"

Edna recognized a familiar sense of dread, which usually accompanied her bouts of depression.

"I don't know what to think, Larry," she finally answered.

"Okay," he said. "I'm going to go out on a limb and make a few jumps. All I want you to do is listen to me and keep an open mind."

He was frightening her, but she kept her composure.

"We know what Gobey told us about some kind of subterranean chamber beneath the Museum. A week or so ago, you submitted a report detailing an interview you had with the caretaker of the Havenhurst Cemetery. A Luke something-or-other."

"Eddings. Luke Eddings," she volunteered.

"Right. Well, your Mr. Eddings mentioned an old underground railroad system Ezra Rotheimer tried to get going and the possibility of some tunnels still lying underground, beneath the Museum."

"I wouldn't put a lot of faith in what Mr. Eddings said, Larry. He isn't right in the head."

"But I'm not going to put him on a witness stand, Edna," Cole said. "All I want him to do is provide some corroboration that an underground chamber and tunnels are still down there."

"I don't understand what you're getting at. What do you think could be down there, anyway?"

"I'm going to tell you, but I need to let you know one more thing first."

She waited.

"There's something very odd about your curator."

"I'll agree with that," Edna said, attempting a smile.

"No, more than just an impression. There's a strong possibility that she's a fraud. Barbara and Jamal turned up some definite discrepancies in her records over at the U. of C. and a couple of very nervous tenured professors. Yet, Eurydice Vaughn was able to obtain one of the most prestigious cultural posts in this city and carry out her tasks with brilliance, from what everyone tells me."

Edna could no longer sit still. Standing up, she walked over to him. "I don't see where you're going with this. It seems very confusing to me."

All his humor and lightheartedness evaporated. Now he was very solemn as he reached out to grasp her arms. "It's not where I'm going with this. It's where Eurydice Vaughn came from."

Edna pulled away from him and looked into his face. She felt a sudden, uncontrollable fury building inside her. "What do you mean, where she 'came from'?"

He reached over and picked up the photo of Edna and Josie from the bookcase. He held it in front of the television, where the images of Edna Gray and Eurydice Vaughn were still caught in the "Pause" frame.

"I'm not sure of this," Cole was saying, "but it looks—"

"Get out," Edna said softly.

He heard her, but was hoping that he could possibly be wrong. "Edna, if only—"

"Commander!" She spoke very formally. "I want you to put my picture down, get your coat and leave my home."

When he was gone, Edna carried the photograph of herself and her sister over to the couch. There she sat throughout the night, looking from it to the images displayed on the television screen.

62

Homer was asleep in his room in the underground cavern. Over the past few days down here, things had returned to normal, more or less. The Mistress spent most of her time in her laboratory and Eurydice had remained in the Museum above. Since the night after the Halloween party, Eurydice had not slept down here, but instead in her apartment across the park.

The first couple of days, he was glad Eurydice was gone. That meant the Mistress couldn't attack her. But as the third day came and went, he began experiencing a growing loneliness. Eurydice was the only friend he'd ever had. And she treated him like a human being, not like a thing, or an animal, as the Mistress did.

The night before, at least he thought it was night, he had gone to sleep on the floor of the dark room. Just before he'd dozed off, he had softly called her name. "Eurydice?"

Now he was experiencing a rare nightmare. The Mistress was beating him with her bullwhip and calling him names. "Stupid!" "Moron!" "Imbecile!" He attempted to run away from her but she pursued him on her cart. He fell again and again. He felt the cart rumbling toward him. The electric rod was extended as the cart came closer, shaking the ground. When the rod made contact with his side, he screamed himself awake.

There was no pain from the ten-thousand-volt electric shock; however, the rumbling had not stopped. It continued and became more violent. The whole room was vibrating.

Alarmed, Homer jumped to his feet and raced for the door. Out on the gallery, he discovered, with ever increasing horror, that the entire cavern was shaking. Eurydice had once shown him a movie about an earthquake. Maybe this was one.

Or else it must be what the Mistress said would one day occur. That thing she had called the "End of the World."

"Homer!" The Mistress's voice roared through the cavern. "Homer, come here!"

As he raced off across the moving floor, he noticed that the Mistress's voice, despite the amplification from the loudspeaker, sounded different. In her chamber, he saw her aged face and recognized why: She was scared.

Accumulated dust from the ceiling was falling in clumps, making the old woman seem even more bizarre.

"I am here, Mistress," Homer said.

"What's happening?" she shrieked. "Why is everything shaking?"

"It is not an earthquake," he responded obediently. "So it must be the end of the world."

She glared at him through the dust haze. He expected her to hurl some damning insult at him, but instead, she looked at him with an all-encompassing terror. "No!" the thing in the bed screamed. "No, it can't end like this! It can't!"

Abruptly, the rumbling stopped and the place became still. Homer didn't know how the Mistress had done it, but he was glad that she had.

"Where is Eurydice?" the Mistress screamed. "She's got to come down here!"

As Homer looked on, the Mistress reached for her computer keyboard and began rapidly typing instructions into it.

63

Eurydice Vaughn's apartment was spacious, clean and sparsely furnished. In the small kitchen there was a Formica-topped table with a single chair and a microwave oven to complement the gas range and refrigerator. The living room held a twenty-seven-inch Sony television set and compatible VCR, a single easy chair and a sophisticated computer work station. A long hallway led to the lone bedroom. When Eurydice slept in the bedroom, the door was always securely closed.

The interior of the bedroom was in complete, impregnable darkness. Thick draperies and blinds blocked all light. A small makeup table with a theatrical mirror and a cushioned bench was against one wall, a chest of drawers against the opposite wall, and a queen-sized bed stood in the center. The only other object in the room was the twin of the living room's computer console.

The other wall was lined with floor-to-ceiling mirrors covering a sliding door for a large closet holding vast quantities of women's clothing and over a hundred fifty pairs of shoes. When Eurydice Vaughn had come to live in this apartment five years before, she had possessed no concept of how to dress. But within less than a month, with the right amount of money and the requisite eye for fashion and color, she had begun building a stunning wardrobe. A wardrobe that, had she been more of a social animal, would have put her on the *Chicago Times Herald*'s annual list of the "Ten Best-Dressed Women" in Chicago.

Now, at dawn, the curator slept soundly. Since she had started to work at the Museum, she had become an active dreamer. Some of her dreams were incoherent replays of her experiences, which kept her on an even psychological keel. A few were erotic, with the object of her nocturnal sexual fantasies being various versions of Jim Cross and Larry Cole. The remainder were nightmares, with the Mistress invariably her antagonist.

During this November night and early morning, Eurydice had experienced a lengthy dream period during which her erotic fantasies had intermingled with her normal dreams and her nightmares. In one segment, she was in the cavern library looking up at the painting of Jim Cross. Suddenly, the picture became animated. A cartoon figure leaped from the frame to land in front of her. As he reached for her, she laughed and dashed from the room. He pursued.

The gallery seemed to stretch before her for miles. As she ran, she was conscious of him gaining on her. However, she wanted to be caught. She rounded a corner and came face to face with the bungling Three Musketeers. All of them were wearing clown masks. With swords drawn, they rushed toward her. She screamed—a sound that held more joy than fear.

She attempted to retreat, but they were too fast. She stumbled and fell. As she tried to rise, a black-gloved hand reached down to help her. She looked up into the smiling face of Zorro. The Musketeers were forgotten as she tilted her head back to be kissed by the man in black. Suddenly, he vanished.

Then she found herself standing nude in the Mistress's bedchamber. From her raised bed, the Mistress's bullwhip whistled toward her. The blow landed across her back, and in the dream, she felt the pain.

"As long as I allow you to remain up there, Eurydice!" The Mistress cackled. "As long as I allow you to remain up there!" Then she struck her again and again with the bullwhip.

Eurydice forced herself awake. The coolness of the sheets and the clean smell of her apartment made her realize where she was. She sat up on the edge of the bed and let the dream recede back into her subconscious. Some parts she held on to, like the nearness of Zorro, a reminder of how close she had been to Larry Cole the other night. She touched her fingers to her lips in memory of the kiss she had shared with him.

She stood up and walked through the dark to her bathroom.

Turning on the light blinded her momentarily, but she recovered quickly. She splashed cold water on her cheeks and forehead and examined her face in the mirror. A couple of days ago, there had been faint circles under her eyes from the strain of her ordeal at the hands of the Mistress. Now they had faded.

Back in the bedroom, she turned on the overhead light. Only twice before in the five years she had lived in this apartment had she spent more than three consecutive nights in it. And on each of those occasions, she had hated it. But this time, after her last confrontation with the Mistress, she thought otherwise.

Eurydice crossed to the drapes and yanking them and the blinds open, she looked out on the first rays of the new dawn. Instantly, she noticed that there was something wrong.

She could see the Museum and its external exhibits. Everything there on the west side of Lake Shore Drive was fine. The east side, near the beach, was different.

One of the northbound lanes of the Drive had been blocked off. Also, four tractor-driven pieces of heavy equipment and a trailer had been parked on the beach directly across from the Museum. Already, men in hard hats were running around down there.

Slowly, Eurydice backed away from the window. She was momentarily too shocked to think. Finally, she spun toward the computer console in her bedroom. The instant the screen brightened, a message from the Mistress read:

"CAVERN VIBRATING VIOLENTLY. ROOF IN DANGER OF COLLAPSE. FLOODING IN LOWER LEVEL BECOMING SEVERE. TAKING AS MUCH AS A FOOT OF WATER AN HOUR. EXTREME DANGER FOR US! YOU MUST COME AT ONCE!"

It was signed "M."

The arguments and differences, even the attempt on her life, were forgotten as Eurydice raced to get dressed. After all, the Mistress and Homer were the only family she had ever had.

64

NOVEMBER 5, 1997
12:50 P.M.

Cole stepped out of the lawyer's office and with difficulty drank from the water fountain. He thought for a moment that he was going to upchuck, but somehow he managed to hold it down.

His lawyer joined him at the elevators. Tall and scholarly, with silver hair and an immaculately pressed gray suit, he said, "Now that wasn't so bad."

"Wasn't it?" Cole blurted angrily.

"Believe me, Commander," the attorney said, "it could have been a great deal worse for you. She's really not asking for much."

Cole's temples were pounding as he thought, *Just my son!*

At Detective Division headquarters, Blackie and Manny were waiting.

"Who's first?" Cole asked as he crossed to his office.

Blackie shot Manny a sharp glare. The sergeant wilted and said, "He is," pointing to the lieutenant.

Inside, Blackie asked the commander, "How'd it go?"

"She wants custody and what my lawyer calls 'minimal' child support."

"You don't like that, huh? Did you talk to Lisa?"

It took Cole a moment to answer. "I heard her voice over the speakerphone, but the lawyers did most of the talking. Everybody acted like they were doing me a fucking favor."

"Take is easy, Boss," Blackie said with compassion. "I know it's rough now, but this will pass."

Cole exhaled a long sigh. "You're right. The best thing for me to do is get back to work."

"That's the ticket. There *are* a couple of things we need to talk about."

Blackie perched on the edge of Cole's desk. "They had a problem over at the National Science and Space Museum this morning."

"Oh?"

"Seems the McElroy Lakefront Development Corporation has been issued a permit to do some work on the beach. I didn't get all of it, but they're going to be doing some blasting out there."

"You're kidding! Explosives on Lake Shore Drive?"

"Yeah, I thought it was crazy too, but somebody at City Hall issued this William McElroy a permit for heavy-duty demolition work."

Cole thought for a moment. "Seymour Winbush's moving through his puppet, E. G. Luckett, in this thing, Blackie."

"Yeah, well, Luckett is City Hall as far as we're concerned."

"He is right now," Cole said with an edge. "Is there anything else?"

For a moment, the heavyset lieutenant appeared uncomfortable. Then he said, "We're going to have to make a decision about Edna today, Larry. She hasn't been to work since last week. We can't keep carrying her."

Already deflated, Cole seemed to shrink a little more into himself. "I'll try and get in touch with her today. If she doesn't show up by tomorrow . . ."

Blackie completed the statement: "Then we carry her 'Absent Without Permission.' She'll be one young lady in a heckuva lot of trouble if she doesn't show up tomorrow morning."

Cole nodded slowly.

"You want to talk about it?"

"Maybe later," Cole said. "If there's nothing else, why don't you send Manny in?"

Blackie stood up and started for the door. "Why don't I have Manny wait and you call and see if you can get in touch with Edna?"

As Cole picked up the telephone, Blackie let himself out and closed the door.

65

The past three days had been the worst of Edna Gray's life. She had been unable to eat or sleep and had not responded to her doorbell or the telephone. After two days of sitting around staring at the old photograph of herself and Josie, she had left the apartment.

At a restaurant near her home, she forced down a bowl of soup and a cup of tea.

She had driven the streets for hours before going back to her old neighborhood. The buildings were now rundown, with panhandlers idling in front of taverns and liquor stores. The public playground she remembered taking Josie to had become nothing but a fenced-in lot inhabited by junkies.

Back on the Dan Ryan Expressway, she sped south. Exiting at 119th Street, she drove west to the Holy Sepulcher Cemetery.

Little white headstones in a row marked the places where both her parents and grandparents on her father's side were buried: Jane Margaret Gray, Joseph Thomas Gray, Ida Mae Gray and Ocie Gray. This was all she had left except—

"What are you afraid of, Edna?"

She spun around, but there was no one there.

"What are you afraid of, Edna?"

This time she had said the words herself.

Inside her car, she turned the heater up full-blast against the chill and drove away, exiting the expressway at Fifty-fifth Street. Getting out of her car in the parking lot of the National Science and Space Museum, she noticed the heavy equipment moving on the beach across Lake Shore Drive.

"I would like to see Eurydice Vaughn," she said to the guard at the information desk. Edna flashed her detective badge at him.

The guard made a call on the house phone, then said, "You can go on up to the curator's office. You know where it is, don't you?"

"I know," Edna said, walking toward the elevator.

66

Eurydice Vaughn stood at the window of her reception area, which provided an exterior view of the Museum, Lake Shore Drive and the beach. Her attention was focused particularly on the trailer with the sign, "McElroy Lakefront Development Corporation," across its side.

Accompanied by Dr. Fleisher and the Museum's attorney, Joseph Shapiro, she had confronted Bill McElroy there at nine o'clock that morning.

"You're endangering the structural integrity of the Museum with your equipment!" she had shouted at the big man. Yes, she could see his dead father in him. Including the inability to compromise.

"Then that joint ain't put together right," McElroy had sneered. "Millions of cars go down the Drive every year and they don't cause any problems over there."

"Those pieces of heavy equipment you've got out there weigh substantially more than any vehicle permitted on Lake Shore Drive!" Eurydice had countered. But it was obvious that she wasn't getting anywhere with him. She'd looked to their lawyer, Howard Shapiro.

"This area has been specifically zoned by the Chicago City Council for—" the attorney began in a nervously high-pitched voice.

McElroy had quickly cut him off. "Save the shyster bullshit for someone who might swallow it, pal." He reached over and removed a folded document from one of the compartments above his drafting table. He handed it to Shapiro.

Eurydice had only to glance over the lawyer's shoulder to see that it was a building permit.

Shapiro had turned helplessly to Eurydice. "This is all very proper, Miss Vaughn. There's really nothing we can do."

"There you are wrong, Mr. Shapiro," she'd said, barely managing to control her anger. "This project must be stopped before more damage is done. I assume that they taught you how to obtain an emergency injunction in law school?"

Then Winston Fleisher had said, "I was unaware there has been any damage sustained by the Museum, Eurydice."

"Yeah, Eurydice," McElroy said, flashing a mocking grin at her. "What damage?"

She'd looked directly at him. "I'm going to do whatever I have to do to stop you, Mr. McElroy. I'm not going to let you destroy this place." Or the Mistress, Homer and the cavern, she'd added silently.

Shapiro had failed to get the emergency injunction, which really didn't surprise her. However, for the time being, things in the cavern had stabilized. The water seepage from earlier in the day had stopped.

At noon, accompanied by Homer, she had donned scuba gear to dive beneath the seven feet of standing water that had flooded the lower level of the old station.

As she'd approached the place where the rising water and the staircase met, the Mistress had called to her, *"Daughter?"* The Mistress called her Eurydice only when she was displeased.

Automatically, Eurydice had turned toward the sound of the voice.

"Be careful." The amplified voice carried to her.

"Yes, ma'am," she'd said obediently.

Then she and Homer had dived beneath the filthy water.

The seepage came from the lake through a one-foot-diameter hole at the base of the hundred-thirty-year-old underground structure. Here time had weakened the bricks and mortar, but Eurydice was able to detect from the current that some of the water was flowing out again. This could mean that the flooding was only temporary, but McElroy had to be stopped.

After posting Homer to monitor the water level, she had met with the Mistress.

"And how do you plan to stop this McElroy?" the Mistress asked.

"He can't operate," Eurydice said, "if he doesn't have any equipment."

The Mistress thought for a moment. "That could be risky. Might actually cause more attention to be directed at us."

"Then, Mistress," Eurydice said with seeming sincerity, "you'd better learn how to swim."

For an instant, Eurydice had thought she had gone too far, as the malevolent glare the Mistress gave her was truly terrible. But then, on the ancient woman's face, Eurydice thought she detected resignation.

The Mistress had asked, "Tell me what you intend to do."

Now Eurydice stood alone by the window and waited for dark. After the rush hour, say about eight or nine that night, she and Homer were going to pay a visit to the McElroy Lakefront Development Corporation site.

Her secretary had gone home at five, but the telephone ringing distracted Eurydice from the mayhem she was planning. The guard at the information desk had to ask her twice for permission to send Edna Gray up. A few moments later, there was a knock on her outer office door.

"Come in," she called without turning from the window.

Eurydice still kept her back to the door. "Ghost-hunting, Detective Gray, or is there something else on your mind?"

"I have to talk to you," Edna said.

The strained voice forced Eurydice to turn around. The sight of the policewoman stunned her. Edna Gray looked haggard, with faint circles beneath her eyes exactly like those under Eurydice's own eyes a few days ago. The curator discovered that she was feeling compassion for the policewoman. A rare emotion for Eurydice Vaughn.

"Won't you sit down?" Eurydice prompted.

With slow, halting movements, Edna took a seat in one of the reception-area chairs.

"I'm not here officially," she began, speaking so softly that Eurydice could barely hear her. "In fact, I'm not sure if I currently have any official standing with the department at all."

A chilly smile froze Eurydice's features. "Then what do you

want? I don't have time to play stupid games with police officers, official or otherwise."

"I'd like to ask you some questions about yourself." Resolutely, Edna stood and faced the curator. "On August seventh, nineteen seventy-two, my sister Josie vanished inside the Museum in *Glassware from Around the World* Hall. For the past twenty-five years, I have been searching for her." Edna paused to gauge the reaction of her words, but Eurydice Vaughn made no reply.

"Larry . . . I mean Commander Cole," Edna forged on, "has this theory. You see, in my apartment, there's an old photograph of me and Josie. He saw it and—"

"The commander's been to your apartment?" The curator's words came out an accusation.

Edna merely nodded. "Miss Vaughn, a lot of people have been saying that we favor physically. That our eyes and features are very similar." Edna reached her hand up to touch her own face and then extended it to Eurydice, but the curator recoiled. "I don't necessarily agree with them, but then, the other night at the Halloween party—"

"I know all about that," Eurydice interrupted. "You had a lot of nerve impersonating me."

"I'm sorry, but no one ever challenged me. Even Dr. Fleisher thought I was you. There was this . . . man in a Death costume. He even called me 'Eurydice'."

The curator frowned. She looked away from the detective for a moment.

Edna slumped back into the chair. "I've been through twenty-five years of torture," she said in a very small voice.

Involuntarily, Eurydice's hand reached out to touch the detective's shoulder. She quickly caught herself and realized Edna hadn't noticed the gesture.

"So you think I'm your missing sister?" The curator vainly attempted a mocking tone.

Edna shook her head. "No. I don't think you're Josie. I would like you to be. Maybe it would help me and Larry get back together. But even though we favor, you're not my sister. You're not even close." Edna's voice was bitter.

"You loved her very much?" the curator asked.

"Yes," Edna answered as tears welled in her eyes. "I loved her like she was part of me. It hurt so bad after we lost her. Then Mama began blaming me, because I was supposed to have been watching Josie."

"Excuse me," Eurydice said, abruptly turning away from the sobbing woman and crossing to her private office. Once securely inside, with the door closed behind her, she nearly collapsed. *What is happening to me?* her mind screamed.

"Eurydice?"

Her head snapped up. Homer was standing over by the secret passageway leading from her office to the cavern below.

"What do you want?" She reached for a box of tissue.

He flinched at her sharp tone. "The Mistress wants you to come now."

"I'll be there in a minute. I have someone waiting in the outer office," she said, blowing her nose and taking deep breaths.

Homer's head bobbed up and down. "The Mistress told me to help you bring the policewoman. She wants her too."

67

November 5, 1997
8:14 p.m.

Bill McElroy was tired. His back ached, his head hurt and his eyes burned. He had been working since 5:00 A.M. But despite the long hours, lunch on the fly and the natural problems that come with any new construction job, McElroy was happy. For the first time in his life, he was positively, absolutely, in charge!

He straightened up from his worktable, feeling his tight back muscles spasm in protest. Stretching to his full six-foot-five-inch height caused his clenched fists to nearly touch the ceiling of the trailer. With a sigh, he shook his shoulders and said aloud, "I think we could say, this is Miller time."

McElroy was alone. The last employee, an old-timer named Sonny Filipiak—who had worked for his father for twenty-five years—had finally left at seven. And old Sonny had been surprised that "Billy," the younger McElroy, was capable of standing on his own two feet without old Harry around.

It was right after the people from the Museum had left that Sonny, a grizzled old construction worker with a mop of white hair and the strongest pair of hands McElroy had ever encountered, had popped into the trailer.

"What'd the suits want, Billy?"

Still irritated by Eurydice Vaughn's attitude, McElroy had spun on Sonny Filipiak. "That's none of your goddamned business, Sonny! And from now on when you address me, you'll call me Mr. McElroy!"

McElroy turned back to his drafting table. His face had been frozen in a scowl, as Sonny, head lowered in embarrassment, shuffled out of the trailer. But inside, McElroy was gloating. He had really put old Sonny in his place. He wished he could have done the same thing to his father!

The incident had charged Bill McElroy with energy. For the rest of the day, he had worked like a demon and driven his workers like a taskmaster from Hell. First, they were going to smooth down the sand on the beach and then push the waterline back about fifty yards. There were some boulders that had to be removed and some places where the landfill had to be built up. In a week or so, he'd be ready to start on the other side of the Drive. Then he'd see how smug that Vaughn chick would be.

When quitting time came, McElroy had decided to stick around. He had a small refrigerator full of cold cuts, potato salad and beer, and a new coffee maker with plenty of coffee. He could prepare for tomorrow's full work day.

Beer in hand, he returned to his worktable. He picked up a roll of yellowed blueprints Peters had found during his research for his father and spread them out on the table. And they were indeed old. The renderings were so detailed that they were actually works of art. In fact, he had drawings going all the way back to a time when the land on which the Museum now stood had been little more than a cow pasture. Like the one he was looking at now. Nothing, but. . . .

He stared. If he wasn't mistaken, this top drawing represented an upper level of something. He turned it around. Yes, it was the park. The pre-Museum park. He flipped to the next drawing. What he saw there stopped him.

Reaching for his beer, he said a whispered, "Well, I'll be damned."

The noise of an engine outside vibrated the trailer. He had heard this same noise so many times during the day that he paid little attention until he realized that no one should be out there to start up any of the equipment.

McElroy reached under his drafting table and picked up a Louisville Slugger. He'd had the bat since he was a kid. His father had given it to him.

As he headed for the trailer door, the lights inside went out. He was plunged into darkness so fast he stumbled over a wastebasket and banged his right shin on something hard. He cried out.

Now he heard a second engine start up outside. And he could swear the sound of the first one was receding.

He grabbed the bat and made it to the door. He leaped down the two steps to the sand on one leg and looked around.

To his horrified amazement, he saw one of his bulldozers plowing right into the lake. Behind it was a tractor-driven crane. No one was visible in either operator's seat.

As McElroy took a step toward his drowning equipment, he heard the third and fourth tractors fire up and follow their companions.

Then, as he stood on the beach with his Louisville Slugger raised, his trailer began to roll. He hopped back toward it, but he wasn't moving fast enough. The trailer was chained to the second bulldozer, which was now up to its tracks in water and going down fast.

Frustrated, McElroy wildly threw his bat. It landed half-submerged in the sand.

He stopped and glared at the trailer as it entered the water and began its slow slide beneath the waves. Somebody was going to pay for this, and pay dearly. Scowling, he started up the beach toward Lake Shore Drive, but stopped dead in his tracks. Standing directly in his path, less than twenty feet away, was a figure clad in some kind of gauzy, black material. It seemed to be floating in the air. McElroy took a step backward. The figure began moving toward him. Although there was nothing behind him but the lake, with a cry of fear, he fled. Bill McElroy ran headlong into the arms of Death.

68

The barbell, loaded with two hundred and fifty pounds, inched upward. Larry Cole, lying on the bench, strained to lift the weight to its highest point. A muscular young cop named Robin Allen was Cole's training partner and stood by ready to snatch the weight in case the commander faltered. Allen was concerned because Cole was working out like a man possessed.

Cole's elbows locked and Allen helped him place the bar back on the rack.

"Ten more pounds," Cole gasped.

Allen frowned. "Boss, I don't—"

"Ten more pounds!"

"Yes, sir."

Allen had to help Cole with the two-hundred-and-sixty-pound bench press, but not much. Then Cole left the weight room and jumped on one of the Airdyne bikes in the aerobics room. Allen watched him for a moment before hitting the showers. Thirty minutes later, when Allen came out of the locker room, Cole was still pedaling away. As the young cop headed for the door, he shook his head. He figured there had to be an easier way to kill yourself.

Cole got off the stationary bike feeling the stiffness in his thighs and buttocks. He picked up his towel and mopped his face and neck. His sweat shirt, with the CPD logo over the left breast, was soaked. Whether he liked it or not, he had done enough for one night. But the hollow ache was still inside him—not as bad as before, but still pronounced. Maybe it would always be there.

He stood under the shower for a long time. There was no one else in the shower room. In fact, the gym, which was usually crowded, had seemed unusually empty tonight. Cole was seldom here so late.

As he dressed, his mind kept drifting back to his son, now living in Detroit. Sure he and Butch would have one weekend a month, holidays and summer vacations, but not a father coming home every day.

An unwanted thought entered Cole's mind. He had found someone else in Edna. Maybe Lisa would find someone in Detroit as well. Then Butch would have a father, but it wouldn't be Larry Cole.

As he walked through the empty building, he felt a crushing loneliness descend on him. First he had lost Lisa and Butch, then Edna. He could always call Blackie or Manny, but that wouldn't be fair to them. They had their own lives to lead. Wet-nursing him through personal crises wasn't their responsibility.

He was saved by his beeper. Operations Command called only when he was wanted right away. As he headed for the gym office, Cole was smiling.

69

Edna came to slowly. A surge of alarm and fear ran through her. She was tied down!

She was restrained on a cushioned table by leather straps buckled tightly around her ankles and wrists. She was clad in a coarse green hospital gown. The table was directly beneath a single light bulb, which shone down on her with unmerciful brilliance.

"Help me! Help me, please!" she cried, but no one came.

She relaxed back against the cushions and futilely tried to break the restraints.

Suddenly, a woman stood a few feet away, looking down at her. Edna blinked, but the apparition remained.

"This must be a nightmare," she managed to say.

"No, my dear Detective Gray," the woman said in a mocking tone. "It is very real." She was Edna's exact duplicate.

Edna's head dropped back to the cushions once more. Then memory began coming back to her. Her visit to the cemetery, followed by the visit to the curator. Eurydice Vaughn had gone into her private office. The last thing Edna remembered was the curator calling to her from behind the partially open door to the office.

Edna's head snapped toward her double. "You're Eurydice Vaughn! You're even wearing my clothes!" Edna noticed the holstered nine-millimeter automatic, the extra bullet clips and the handcuffs—all of them strapped to her double's waist.

The double smiled. "You impersonated me at the ball; now I'm going to repay you. I always wondered if being a cop is as difficult as you people make it out to be."

Despite her predicament, Edna laughed. "You'll never get away with it."

Eurydice stepped close to the table and looked down into Edna's face. In an uncannily accurate imitation of Edna's voice, she repeated: " 'You'll never get away with it.' "

Employing a bravado she did not feel, Edna said, "It still won't work. It takes years to learn how to be a cop. You'll stick out like a sore thumb. The streets of Chicago are a lot different from a stupid museum."

The double moved away from the table. With a damning awareness, Edna realized that the woman's walk and every gesture were duplicates of her own. But the impostor couldn't copy what was in her mind.

As if reading the detective's thoughts, Eurydice turned and said, "I'll need you to tell me a thing or two, Edna. I'm sure you won't let me down."

Resisting, Edna shut her eyes, but opened them to find the giant in the Death costume from the Halloween party standing behind the impostor. "Are you sure you won't do this of your own free will?" Eurydice Vaughn asked.

"Go to hell!" Edna shouted.

Her double looked amused. "We're going to have to deal with that hostility, dear," she said, holding out her open palm to Death.

The most enormous hand Edna had ever seen appeared from beneath the robes and placed a small black case in the impostor's hand. As Edna looked on, Eurydice opened it and extracted a syringe.

"Now this won't hurt a bit, Edna," she said, advancing toward her captive. "Just a little something to get you in a more talkative mood. There are some things I really must know."

The double, with Death close on her heels, approached the trapped woman.

70

Manny Sherlock approached the marked Third District police car. It was parked on the sidewalk above the empty beach across from the National Science and Space Museum. In the back sat veteran construction worker Sonny Filipiak, a frightened look on his face.

Manny flashed his badge at Officers Warren and McGuire, who were baby-sitting Filipiak. The old man had come back to the beach construction site a short time before to check on McElroy and found everything, including his boss, gone.

"Chief Govich and Commander Cole would like to talk to this gentleman," Manny said to the uniformed cops.

"Sure thing, Sarge," McGuire said, opening the back door to let the construction worker out. "You want me to go along?"

Manny shook his head. "No, but you'd better stick around for a while."

Manny led Filipiak back to Govich's black command car. Govich and Cole were sitting in the front seat.

After making the introductions, Manny became silent and Cole took over. "You want to tell us exactly what happened, Mr. Filipiak?"

"Well, it was like this, Officers," the construction worker began. . . .

Forty-five minutes later, Lieutenant Commander Del Atkinson of the United States Coast Guard slid into the seat recently vacated by the frightened Sonny Filipiak.

"I tried to get a chopper up, gentlemen," said Atkinson, a muscular black man with a full beard. "It's just too rough tonight, though. But could you tell me something?"

"Shoot, Commander," Govich said.

"Why do you think this guy and all his equipment are in the drink?"

Cole answered, "We can't figure any other place they could be."

"Well, then I'd say you have a problem," the Coast Guard officer said.

"Such as?" Govich inquired.

"You say that stuff's damned heavy and I can believe it, but if it's out there," he hooked a thumb at the pitch blackness of Lake Michigan, "the current and the irregular seafloor around here are going to play havoc with us locating anything tomorrow. There are some places where the depth goes from four feet to fifteen or twenty feet with no warning at all. Plus, the bottom's soft. That stuff could be completely submerged under sand down there."

"That means we've got another one," Cole said with a sour expression.

"Another what?" Atkinson couldn't help but ask.

Govich answered this time. "Another 'Missing: Presumed Dead' case."

71

A s Cole headed home, it was approaching midnight. He had finally accomplished what he'd set out to do: exhaust himself. He pulled the police car into the driveway and cut the engine. The two-story house with the sloping lawn and two-car garage— he'd happily bought when Butch was a baby—now looked dark and forbidding, like a stranger's house.

Inside, he began turning on lights. He could live with the dust in the study and the dining room, but one look inside the kitchen told him what he had to do. He saw the stack of dirty dishes and smelled spoiled food.

Slipping off his tie and jacket, he rolled up his sleeves. For company, he turned on the living-room television; the 1971 movie *The French Connection* was playing, one of Cole's favorites.

As he began attacking the dishes, he could tell from the background music that Roy Scheider and Gene Hackman were in the club where they first spotted the drug dealer, played by Tony LoBianco.

"What do you say we stick around and give him a tail?" Hackman was saying.

Cole laughed. Only in the movies. Random surveillances without first establishing probable cause were a violation of First Amendment rights. A cop could get himself, or herself, in a world of trouble acting like the fictional Popeye and Cloudy.

Thinking about the department brought Edna Gray to mind. Tomorrow would be D day for her and there was nothing he could do about it. They called it "Job Abandonment," and even the police union shied away from defending officers who failed to show up for work. So it was quite possible that she could be summarily discharged tomorrow.

He finished the dishes and neatly stacked them on the drain board. Drying his hands, he opened the refrigerator to see what he could find for a late supper. He glanced at his watch. It was approaching 1:00 A.M. This would be a very late supper indeed.

He ended up with a ham-and-cheese sandwich on pumpernickel, a couple of slices of leftover pizza and a beer. As he settled in front of the television, Popeye Doyle was just being ordered off the case by a lieutenant played by Eddie Egan, a former real-life New York cop on whom the Popeye character was based. As Cole ate, Popeye commandeered a citizen's car and began a breakneck chase across Manhattan. Cole smiled. Only in the movies, Popeye. Only in the movies.

A sound outside drew Cole's attention from the television. The staccato clicking of a woman's heels could be heard coming up the sidewalk. Puzzled, Cole stood up and walked to the front door. As he looked through the Judas window, the doorbell rang.

There was a woman outside, but it was too dark to see her features. He switched on the porch light and caught a brief glimpse of Edna's face before she half-turned away.

His heart pounding, Cole opened the door. She still stood with her back to the light.

"Edna, where have you been?" He attempted to sound angry, but his concern was more evident. "We were about to start carrying you 'Absent Without Permission'."

"May I come in?"

"Of course," he said, moving back. As he closed the door behind her, she stepped into the living room and made a slow appraisal of what she could see of the house.

"Can I get you anything?" he asked awkwardly.

She looked back at him. "What do you have?"

"Beer," he said with a shrug. "And I think there might be some lemonade mix left."

"Yes, lemonade. That would be nice."

"Make yourself comfortable," he said, heading for the kitchen. As he began dumping ice cubes into a pitcher, he realized that

Edna was more relaxed than he had ever seen her before. In fact, she even seemed kind of laid back. Smiling, he went back to the living room with a pitcher of lemonade, a clean glass and another beer on a tray.

Edna was on the couch. She had removed her trench coat, suit jacket and gun belt and draped them neatly across a living-room chair. She had kicked off her shoes and folded her legs under her. As he set the lemonade on the cocktail table, he noticed that the two top buttons of her blouse were unfastened. He also noted the circular gold pin she wore above her left breast. The pin looked familiar, but he'd probably seen hundreds like it before.

He was surprised when she slid toward him and ran her hand across the back of his head and neck. He jumped.

"What's the matter?" she asked.

"Nothing," he said with a nervous laugh. "I guess I hadn't expected this reaction from you."

"What about this reaction?" She grabbed him by the back of the neck and pulled his head toward her. Her lips came down hard on his and for a moment, he was stunned. Edna had always been a tender, loving kisser. Now she exhibited a raw, unbridled passion.

When she permitted him to come up for air, he tasted blood where one of her incisors had nipped him. He looked questioningly at her. She stared back. He noticed a wildness about her and her feverish, near-hysterical eyes. It was Edna, but a much different Edna. He was actually beginning to wonder if she was on some drug.

"Now, are you going to answer my question?" His tone was insistent.

"Are you mad at me, Larry?" She leaned forward, attempting to bite his ear.

He pushed her away. "I think I deserve an explanation, Edna. I've been trying to get in touch with you for three days. I was even considering breaking into your place to see if you were all right. And I know that wouldn't have been the smart move after what you said last time."

Her brow creased slightly. Then she sipped her lemonade and adjusted the pin on her blouse.

"I'm sorry if I said or did anything to hurt you, Larry," she said matter of factly.

Cole felt a surge of anger. For just the briefest of instants, he fought an almost uncontrollable urge to hit her. His breathing became shallow and he could hear his blood racing through his head. The room, with only the single table lamp behind Edna for illumination, became remarkably brighter and the television blared with a deafening volume. He felt the irrepressible urge to do something violent. To attack, strike out, to . . .

Snatching the remote control from the cocktail table with such violence that he knocked over his beer can, he jammed the power button with his thumb until the screen blinked into blackness. He had a powerful urge to fling the device across the room. With a tremendous effort, he managed to place it back on the cocktail table.

"Take off your clothes, Larry."

"What!"

She had not moved from the couch. Now, as he looked at her, she had an expression of amusement mixed with curiosity. "You look terribly uncomfortable, honey," she was saying. "We're alone and, after all, we have no secrets from each other."

Her voice was all around him like the music played on a very expensive stereo system. And the sound was beautiful. It was as if she were singing to him.

"Come to me, Larry." She opened her arms to him. He couldn't resist her. The world around him exploded in a magenta haze. She had suddenly become the center of his universe. His total objective was to please her.

Cole's clothing seemed to fall away from him as he plunged into a world of intense hallucination. He was sixteen years old and in the backseat of a 1958 Mercury with Diane Brady. She was nineteen, a neighbor. She'd liked to call him her "little brother." But that night, he'd lost his virginity to her on leather seats that creaked with their every move.

For a short time, Cole was once more in that car with Diane. Then Diane became Edna.

His world boiled red again, and he was in a motel room in Iowa

City, Iowa. Her name was Kathyrn. Now he was nineteen. He didn't know she was sixteen. Their steamy, interracial union in the cheap room with the black-and-white television and the quarter-per-play radio would leave her pregnant and cause the University of Iowa to revoke Cole's football scholarship. As with the Diane fantasy, Kathryn again became Edna.

The world Cole inhabited boiled and steamed, scalded and scorched. He was in the arms of many women and at the same time, of only one woman.

There was Ursula, the landlady in the apartment house he lived in when he was a rookie cop. Millie, whose brother's mugging Cole had investigated as a detective. Cora, who had been in graduate school with Cole and had turned down his first marriage proposal. Finally, there was Lisa, his soon-to-be ex-wife.

In his mind, Cole spun through a kaleidoscope of memories fueled by fantasies. Every moment was exquisitely real and he relived each second of each encounter, whether it was one of love or lust. But each time, as the episode came to that brief, ecstatic moment of ultimate satisfaction, the body he had joined became Edna's. And when there was nothing left of his sexual history, she began creating a new one for him. A new one the likes of which Larry Cole had never dreamed of before.

72

Blackie Silvestri and Manny Sherlock sat in an unmarked police car on North Racine Avenue, across the street from the Tracy Starr dance studio. The dingy storefront was dark although the flaking gold-leaf letters on the door read: "Lessons Available Monday Thru Friday—9:00 A.M. to 9:00 P.M."

"What kind of dancing do they teach in there, Blackie?" Manny asked.

The lieutenant shrugged. "From what I hear, Tracy's diversified over the years. At the beginning, it was strictly tap and some modern dance. Lately, my sources tell me, she's into ballroom dancing as well. Fifteen years ago was probably her most prosperous period. That's when discos and the movie *Saturday Night Fever* were popular. From what I hear, back then she was charging fifty dollars per hour and had to beat students away from the door."

"And now?"

"It's like everything else, Manny. Fads run their course. That's why it's always good to have your pension waiting for you when the department finally puts you out to pasture."

Now a small woman with startling red hair and a very pale complexion was making her way toward the dance studio. As she approached, Manny noticed her springy, athletic stride and slender figure, although Blackie had told him she was over sixty.

"Shall we?" Manny asked.

"Give her a minute or two to get her morning tea started. Put her in a better frame of mind. She might even offer us a cup, if we're nice and polite."

Ten minutes later, the woman, who went by the professional

name of Tracy Starr, had her tea kettle going. As she waited for the water to boil, she was doing a back-and-thigh stretch, with her head almost touching the floor when the front door opened. She looked irritably through her spread legs at the two men who walked in. It had been a long time since she'd had any dealings with cops and she hadn't missed them one bit.

"Miss Starr," the heavyset one with the hard face said, "we'd like to ask you a couple of questions."

She straightened up and turned to face them. "Am I in any kind of trouble, boys?"

Her accent was pure Liverpool, England, although years of living in America had faded it considerably. Blackie knew her origins and that her husband had been a professional burglar named Tommy Bascomb, who had vanished in the National Science and Space Museum twelve years before.

The two cops smiled. "What would a nice lady like you be doing in trouble?" Manny asked.

Tracy Starr gave him a wicked grin. Looking up at his six-foot-four-inch height, she said, "You'd be surprised, Stretch. You'd be surprised."

73

NOVEMBER 6, 1997
9:22 A.M.

Barbara Zorin was putting the finishing touches on the data she and Jamal had accumulated about the National Science and Space Museum. She had already contacted the agent she and Jamal had shared when *The Strange Case of Neil and Margo Dewitt* had been published. After the success of last year's joint, non-fiction venture, the agent was clamoring for the new manuscript. Maybe in four but no more than six months, they would have the first draft ready. And as she scanned the monitor of her computer, Barbara had to comment that indeed, as Jamal had told the University of Chicago students attending the literature seminar, truth was stranger than fiction.

It began with the disappearance of Katherine Rotheimer and Jim Cross in 1902. Right after she bailed him out of jail, the two of them simply vanished. Through their research, Barbara and Jamal discovered that Rotheimer had hired a Cook County deputy sheriff named Oscar Cantrell to look for his daughter.

There were no written reports of what, if anything, Cantrell discovered about the missing Katherine Rotheimer, but the deputy sheriff had been found with his throat cut in a black neighborhood of Chicago known as the Levee District. Whether Katherine Rotheimer or Jim Cross had anything to do with Cantrell's death was unknown.

Next, Ezra Rotheimer had taken his family for a year's vacation in Europe from 1902 to 1903. After their return, as Jamal liked to say, "The paper trail gets wide, thick and deep."

The law firm of Sidney, Sidney and Olsen, one of the most

prestigious and influential in Chicago, was placed in charge of the search for Katherine Rotheimer. And this search was very thorough.

She was listed as a Missing Person with the Chicago Police Department, which at the time—January 17, 1904—had no established Missing Persons Section. Seven years later, on that same date in 1911, Katherine Rotheimer was reclassified from simply Missing to "Missing: Presumed Dead." She became the first such case connected with the National Science and Space Museum, which did not open its doors until two and a half years later.

But Sidney, Sidney and Olsen did not stop with the Chicago Police Department. Fliers were printed up and distributed nationwide. In her files, Barbara had a reproduction of each of the three fliers. One, which bore the photograph of both Katherine Rotheimer and Jim Cross, was mailed exclusively to police departments across the nation. Sidney, Sidney and Olsen had covered everything from the New York Police Department, which received a mailing of twenty-five thousand copies in November, 1904, to the Keokuk, Iowa P.D., which received ten.

Each of the police department-targeted fliers gave as much identifying information on the missing pair as possible. It also listed a reward of ten thousand dollars for information about either of them, with a substantial bonus to be paid if they were found together. There was also the admonition: "Do not apprehend, detain or interfere with either party in any way. THEY ARE NOT WANTED FOR ANY CRIME!"

There were two other fliers circulated. One of Katherine alone listed her as simply Missing. Other than vital statistics, the only additional information provided about her was: ". . . may be in the company of a tall, well-built Negro male who answers to the name Jim Cross. The Negro Jim talks like a white man." That flier was distributed in white areas. A similar flier was circulated about Jim Cross in the black enclaves across the United States. Aside from Jim Cross's physical description, it mentioned merely that he ". . . may be in the company of a white female answering to the name of Katherine or Kathy."

From all indications still available a near century later, hundreds of thousands, or possibly even millions, of these fliers were distributed. In 1908, an editorial in the *Chicago Tribune* criticizing accumulated rubbish on city streets commented: "Trash gathers in gutters, alleys and around street corners. Cigar butts, discarded newspapers, animal offal and, of course, soiled copies of the Katherine Rotheimer Missing Persons flier, pile up to make our City in a Garden resemble a stinking garbage heap."

And the fliers had gotten some results, which Barbara and Jamal gleaned from century-old archives. There were thousands of sightings of Kathy and Jim from as far south as Brazil and as far north as Alaska. There was a China sighting, a Russia sighting, two Mexico sightings, even a West Africa sighting. Numerous young women came forward claiming to be Katherine. More than a few muscular young black men showed up claiming they were Jim Cross. All were proven to be frauds.

Then, in the summer of 1910, a New York attorney appeared at the LaSalle Street offices of Sidney, Sidney and Olsen. Samuel Barry, Esq., a mustache-wearing man with fleshy jowls and a weak chin, claimed to represent a certain woman named Katherine and a gentleman of color with whom she had a personal acquaintance. Attorney Barry explained to Rotheimer's attorneys, and later to Rotheimer himself, that his clients wished the entire search affair to be dropped immediately. Barry further explained, again on behalf of his clients, that pressing the matter would result in litigation against all inquiring parties, which included Sidney, Sidney and Olsen, and their client, Ezra Rotheimer.

The National Science Museum, as it was then called, had been open for four years at the time. After his meetings with the attorneys and Rotheimer, a final meeting was scheduled between Rotheimer and Barry alone at the Museum, where the millionaire was serving as the first chairman of the board. There Barry disappeared.

Newspaper accounts at the time initially gave the story a great deal of attention, but later, when Attorney Samuel Barry, Esq., was discovered to be nothing more than a Bowery con man with a gift for lawyer impersonations, the story passed into oblivion. No one ever knew what actually occurred on that summer day in 1910. But it is known that Mr. Samuel Barry arrived at the Museum at approximately 1:00 P.M. A guide later testified that Barry set off toward the chairman's office. However, Barry never arrived at his destination, nor was he ever seen or heard from again.

Samuel Barry, Esq., phony lawyer and Bowery con man, became the second "Missing: Presumed Dead" case associated with the Museum.

That fall, following Barry's disappearance, the Rotheimers began to die. Ezra Rotheimer's second wife and the mother of seven of his nine children was the first. She caught fire while preparing Sunday dinner in the kitchen of the family home. Despite the Rotheimer family members seated in the dining room, the woman became completely engulfed by flames and burned to a blackened, charred corpse without uttering a sound. It was only after the millionaire smelled something burning that he'd ventured into the kitchen to investigate.

The death was ruled an accident. A terrible accident, but still, an accident.

Two weeks later, Ivan Rotheimer, age twenty-seven, Ezra's first-born child and Katherine's older brother, fell from his tenth-floor office in the Loop-located Rotheimer Building. Ivan was vice president of Ezra Rotheimer and Company. He was on his way out to lunch with some other employees when he found that his cigar case was empty. The police report stated that the young man walked back into the office and simply jumped out the window. No motive could be discovered, nor could suicide, accident or misadventure be ruled out.

A grief-stricken Ezra Rotheimer demanded further investigation, which revealed no more evidence. One inconsequential item that was discovered during the follow-up was a scribbled note on a writing tablet found lying on Ivan's desk. It read: "K. 1:00 P.M. Surprise!"

Between the years 1910 and 1912, the eight remaining Rotheimer children met with violent deaths or vanished without a trace. There were two drownings. One fell through thin ice as she skated across a pond on the family estate, and the other was found facedown in the indoor pool after a late-night swim. Three were traffic fatalities. Two of them were killed as they stood seemingly oblivious to danger in the middle of well-traveled thoroughfares. The second oldest daughter behind Katherine was killed when her two-seater roadster ran off the road, flipped over and caught fire. The remaining three children became "Missing: Presumed Dead" cases in their father's new museum.

Terrified over the prospect of losing his remaining innocents, Rotheimer withdrew from all commercial endeavors and concentrated on his Museum chairman duties. His surviving children were taken out of school and they, along with their governess and tutor, Mrs. Fitzwalters, spent their days inside the Museum with the millionaire. Then, two weeks before the first child vanished, Mrs. Fitzwalters suddenly quit the post she'd held for nearly twenty years, and in less than twenty-four hours, left Chicago. She was never seen or heard from again.

Despite bodyguards and all his money and influence, Rotheimer could not protect the children. The newspapers of pre–World War I Chicago made a game of the tragedy unfolding at the National Science Museum. Lurid headlines blared:

WILL REMAINING ROTHEIMERS SURVIVE?
ONE DOWN—TWO TO GO!
MILLIONAIRE NEAR EDGE OF HYSTERIA AS HE
BARRICADES HIMSELF WITH LAST CHILD

Her name was Estelle, a girl of seven, who was shown in old black-and-white newspaper photos as possessing a head of shining curls. She was with her father, four bodyguards, two of the city's toughest detectives and a *Chicago Herald* newspaper reporter in Rotheimer's second-level office. She had requested permission to use the washroom. As there were only men present, she was forced to go alone. But a bodyguard and one of the detectives stood right outside the closed bathroom door. When the little girl didn't come out, they broke the door down. The water closet was empty.

Overcome by grief, Ezra Rotheimer went into a rapid decline. Word spread, again through the local tabloids, that the reclusive millionaire planned to tear the Museum down, blow it up, or simply shutter the place forever as a monument to his dead family. Sometime during this period, encompassing the fall of 1912 and the spring of

1913, Rotheimer bequeathed his entire fortune to the Museum. It was also during this period that the millionaire went totally insane.

Rotheimer began wandering through the vacant halls of the Museum after closing time, mumbling to himself and at times shouting "Katherine!" On the day he died, the millionaire had summoned the Museum staff into his office, which was as disheveled and foul-smelling as its lone occupant. There Rotheimer had ordered these second-level rooms—where his last child had vanished, and the location of a bench carved out of stone taken from the side of a Himalayan mountain—turned into an exhibit hall. Holding up a priceless crystal goblet, whose origins he would not disclose, he decreed that this place would henceforth be known as the *Glassware from Around the World* Hall. Then, with wild-eyed fury, Rotheimer smashed the goblet on the floor and ordered the staff out with a scream.

Later that night, one of the Museum guards came upon the millionaire alone, kneeling on the floor outside his office. Standing out of sight, the guard listened to Rotheimer hold a lengthy one-sided conversation with someone he referred to as "the Mistress." The guard left the millionaire to his rambling monologue.

Rotheimer was found dead the next morning, still on his knees. The Cook County coroner issued a determination of "death as a result of natural causes." The papers eulogized the millionaire as having succumbed to ". . . a broken heart."

But Ezra Rotheimer was not cold in his grave before the ghost stories and tales of a haunted Seagull Island behind the Museum began circulating.

Barbara's eyes were tiring from reading the text. After she saved the data on a disk, she shut off the machine and went into her Lake Shore Drive apartment kitchen to fix a cup of tea. Still, her mind went back to events that took place after Rotheimer's death.

In the summer of 1915, the first ghost sightings were reported on Seagull Island. The only reports of them were in a cheap pulp magazine of the period called *Occult World*. Jamal had called this publication the 1915 version of the *National Enquirer*. The ghost was described as ". . . a young woman in a white gown, with skin as pale as the face of the moon and eyes that drip blood. Emitting an unearthly howl, she warns the living away from this unholy place."

Occult World devoted at least one story a month from July through December of 1915 to ghosts on Seagull Island. Now curious people ventured onto Haunted Island—as the magazine called it—in search of ghosts to invade their nightmares. Then in January 1916, the first disappearance from the island occurred—another "Missing: Presumed Dead" case.

The next four Museum curators following Rotheimer died in unusual ways on the anniversary of the founder's death in 1919, 1923, 1927 and 1931. Two were suicides and two were classified as accidents. After the last one was crushed when an airplane engine inexplicably fell from a ceiling exhibit in 1931, the chairman's post remained vacant for seventeen years.

By 1948, strange events in and around the Museum happened less frequently.

But as Barbara Zorin sipped her tea, she recalled one rumor Jamal had uncovered when he was researching his 1991 crime novel, *Shadow Man*. Its hero, a cat burglar, had the motto, "I don't do churches, synagogues or the National Science and Space Museum."

Jamal had remembered that the originator of the quote was Tracy Bascomb, who also went by the name Tracy Starr. Blackie was checking it out for them.

Barbara finished her tea just as the telephone rang.

"Hello?"

"Barb, Blackie. You're not going to believe what me and Manny came up with."

74

Eurydice watched Cole sleep. Over the years she had experimented with herself, so she had some idea of what a sexual experience would be like. But she was totally unprepared for the intensity of the actual event. It was as if her life had begun with that first orgasm she'd had on the living-room floor last night.

She even relished the soreness of that one most secret of all places, which he had repeatedly entered.

With childlike curiosity, she lifted the covers away from him. She studied his now-slack manhood, which she had watched throughout the night throb and swell to twice or even three times the size it was right now. The asexual Homer, despite his enormous physical dimensions, possessed nothing as formidable as this. But then, Eurydice thought, the male organ was the same as any other body part. It needed exercise to stay at peak efficiency. And she knew from the ramblings of Edna Gray under the influence of sodium pentothal that Cole'd had plenty of exercise lately.

But the thought of him being intimate with someone else caused an unbearable jealousy. When he'd slipped into an exhausted sleep an hour before dawn, he had even called the name "Edna."

Somehow she would have to figure a way to turn him from the policewoman to her. Eurydice was certain Edna Gray could never take him to the heights of sexual ecstasy she and Cole had shared last night—because only Eurydice possessed the aphrodisiac aromatic that drove Cole into a sexual frenzy.

Her eyes swung back to his face. She was awed with the striking resemblance between him and the Jim Cross portrait in the Mistress's library. Of course Cole was older; gray hairs dotted the black of his head and mustache, and faint fatigue lines etched his forehead and beneath his eyes. He was in his mid-forties. A sudden disturbing thought struck her. By the time she was thirty-five, he would be well over fifty. Now she noticed the photograph on the table beside Cole. Silently, she walked around the bed without disturbing his slumber.

The picture was of Cole with a pretty young woman with large, dark eyes and long, black hair, and a child who was the spitting image of Cole. Again she felt a stab of jealousy. She considered hurling the framed photo against the wall, but instead placed it facedown on the table.

She was about to get back into bed when the telephone, right next to the photo, rang. Cole came awake with a start and jerked upright. He glanced at her questioningly for a moment, as if he couldn't remember what she was doing there, before answering.

"Hello?"

Still standing beside the bed, she watched him grow suddenly tense.

"What has he got to do with it?" Cole asked into the phone.

A silence as he listened; then, finally, he glanced at his watch and said, "It's after nine now. I'll be there before eleven. Good. See you then."

After hanging up, he stared sightlessly at the far wall.

"Is something wrong?" An alarm went off in her head when she realized that she hadn't used her Edna Gray voice. The policewoman spoke slightly slower than Eurydice Vaughn and lacked her cultured inflections.

Cole didn't seem to notice.

"E. G. Luckett has called a meeting in Govich's office for eleven this morning. He's apparently on the warpath about what happened to McElroy."

"Why? People are reported missing in this town every day. Is he somehow special?"

Cole stood up and the sheet dropped away from his body. Now they were both nude, standing only a few feet apart. She felt a wave of passion rising within her.

"Like I told you the other night," he said, "McElroy is backed by the DeWitt Corporation, and E. G. Luckett's the puppet of Seymour Winbush."

"I see," she said. And the last piece of the puzzle fell into place. She had been striking at the tail of the snake with Harry McElroy and his son, whereas the serpent's head was down on Michigan Avenue in the penthouse at One DeWitt Plaza.

"I'm seeing a lot too," he said, stepping toward her.

75

When Cole and Govich entered the first deputy's office, Luckett was pacing the floor in front of Kennedy's desk. The superintendent was unavailable.

"Gentlemen," Luckett railed at them, "this situation is totally intolerable!"

"We're not security guards," Cole said quietly.

Meeting Luckett's glare with one of his own, Cole added, "The Chicago Police Department is not a security-guard company. We have the responsibility for protecting the three and a half million people who depend on us twenty-four hours a day. I'm sure McElroy and Seymour Winbush can afford to hire people to protect their assets.

"The Coast Guard's conducting a search of the lake area near where McElroy was working, and we're conducting an investigation from our end. We'll come up with something, Director Luckett."

"Dammit, that's not good enough," Luckett said as he started to wheeze and was having difficulty catching his breath. Snatching an inhaler from his jacket pocket, he sucked in the vapor, coughed noisily and sat down in a chair in front of Kennedy's desk. A resounding crash echoed through the office as the chair collapsed under Luckett's weight.

76

November 6, 1997
11:22 a.m.

Judy Daniels sat at her desk and stared at the monitor. She was supposed to be coordinating all available data on the disappearance of William McElroy into a comprehensive report for Chief Govich. She was waiting for a feed from the Coast Guard computer network's Navy Pier installation. One of their divers had discovered two of McElroy's cranes partially submerged in soft sand off the Fifty-seventh Street beach. The entire project wasn't really complicated and in fact, for Judy, it was fairly routine. But she was having a great deal of trouble just getting started today.

Rising, she poured a cup of coffee from the pot behind Edna Gray's desk. Now she glanced over Edna's shoulder.

Edna was correlating data on minor criminal incidents—muggings, auto thefts and purse snatchings—that had been reported over at the National Science and Space Museum since 1970. And from what Judy could see, she was nearly finished. Now Edna turned and smiled at the Mistress of Disguise/High Priestess of Mayhem.

Judy Daniels took the title Mistress of Disguise very seriously. A witty narcotics cop named Ahern had tacked on the "High Priestess of Mayhem" for her. She had first altered her appearance when she was still a probationary police officer, with less than six months on the force, for Operation Angel, an anti-street-prostitution campaign aimed at targeting johns. Judy'd been the best Operation Angel decoy in the city.

On the first night she was scheduled to work Operation Angel, Judy had sauntered into the squad room and come very close to being arrested by her fellow cops, who didn't recognize her.

Over the years, she had gotten better at working undercover

narcotics, and then she'd had the most dangerous role of her life. Disguised as a middle-aged Italian matron named Angelina Lupo, she had gone undercover inside the Oak Park mansion of vicious gangster Antonio "Tuxedo Tony" DeLisa.

To keep her hand in since she'd moved to Larry Cole's staff, she practiced her disguises on her co-workers. But now Judy had run into a problem. She believed Edna Gray was an impostor, and the Mistress of Disguise was an expert on impostors.

Back at her desk, Judy examined her misgivings about Edna. She'd been absent for the past three days, so when she waltzed in that morning a few minutes ahead of Cole, they'd been glad to see her. But the instant Judy set eyes on the policewoman, she knew that something wasn't right.

Physically, everything matched, although Edna seemed thinner. The voice, mannerisms and walk were unchanged. Edna even worked the same way on the report she'd started last week. She held her head and back the same when she typed.

Then what was it?

Judy would have related her fears to Blackie or Manny, or even to Cole himself, but there was some kind of flap on in the first deputy's office. Everybody had gotten tense and quiet after Cole and Govich had left to go to the meeting a few minutes before eleven. But even then she noticed that Edna was totally unconcerned that Cole could be in trouble. She worked lightheartedly—even happily— now. This was perhaps the most uncharacteristic thing of all.

Since she'd come to work in Detective Division headquarters with them, Edna had been very interested in everything connected with Larry Cole. She had treated Judy to lunch in exchange for information about their boss. She'd had so many questions, Judy could scarcely eat.

But now Judy was puzzled and exasperated when the chief of detectives and her commander returned to the office laughing so hard they were wiping tears from their eyes.

"Lunch later, Chief?" Cole finally asked, suppressing a chuckle.

"You bet, Larry. And we'll make Kennedy pay," Govich guffawed.

After Govich and Cole went into their offices, Blackie came in.

Even old Sourpuss Face, as Judy privately called him, looked like he was in on it.

"Blackie, could I see you for a minute?" she called to him.

"Later, Judy," he said, an enormous grin on his face. "As soon as I finish talking to the boss."

When Cole's door closed after Blackie, Judy became aware of someone standing behind her. Turning, she looked up into the face of Edna Gray.

"I wonder if I could ask you a favor, Judy."

"Sure."

"I need to go out for a while. I should be back in about an hour. Will you cover for me?"

"No sweat," Judy said. "You going to be on the radio?"

For only the shortest second, Edna hesitated. Then she said easily, "I'll be out of the car briefly, but like I said, I won't be long."

Judy decided to take a chance. "Edna, Blackie'll give me hell and a hangnail if you don't give me a destination. After all, you haven't been here in three days."

Turning, the detective said icily, "I'm going shopping down at DeWitt Plaza. Is there anything else you need to know?"

"No, ma'am," Judy said, scribbling the location on a memo pad.

The Mistress of Disguise/High Priestess of Mayhem watched her go. Whoever this woman was, she had blown it. Because all a detective had to do was to sign out on the log on Blackie's desk. On top of that, a veteran cop would never have made the excuse of "going shopping." The real Edna would have taken Judy into her confidence. So something was definitely very wrong with this woman.

Now it was up to Judy to convince Blackie and Cole. She headed for the commander's closed office door.

77

NOVEMBER 6, 1997
1:16 P.M.

Attorney George Doyle and Architect Kyle Peters were in a narrow, dimly lit bar off Michigan Avenue, around the corner from DeWitt Plaza. They both were on their second martinis.

The bartender could tell from just one glance that these guys weren't the martini-lunch type. They were too young and clean-cut. That and the fact that they looked scared shitless. They were either attempting to bolster their confidence or anesthetizing themselves.

They didn't talk for a few minutes. Then Peters whispered urgently, "I'm scared, Georgie. For all we know, we could be next. First the old man, now the kid! What in hell is going on down there at that Museum?!"

"Get hold of yourself, man!" Doyle was trying to maintain control. "All we've got is stupid coincidence."

"Where have you been, George?" Despite whispering, Peters' panicky tone carried to the bartender, who glanced in their direction. They waited for him to turn back to his television before they continued. Peters took two healthy swallows of his martini before saying, "Everyplace you go, somebody's talking about ghosts and that place. We don't know what happened to Harry and I'm still having nightmares about what we experienced."

"So what do you want to do, Kyle? Call in an exorcist?" Doyle sneered and took a short sip of his drink.

"No. I don't want an exorcist. I want out. I'm going to chuck the whole thing. The McElroy Lakefront Development Corporation, the DeWitt Corporation, Seymour Winbush, and everything connected with them. I'm even getting out of this damn town."

"Just like that? You'd walk away from a million-dollar deal and start all over again because of some bullshit ghost stories?"

Peters dropped a twenty-dollar bill on the bar and said, "You're right, George. Just like that. But when all is said and done, I'll still be breathing."

With that, the architect turned and headed for the door. Doyle called after him, but he kept going.

Out in the cold, crisp air, the alcohol hit Peters. But then the only thing he had to do was to return to DeWitt Plaza, collect his things and get out of Chicago.

He was crossing the Plaza lobby, heading toward the commercial elevators, when he became aware of someone walking beside him.

As he turned, he saw that the woman looked familiar, but he couldn't place her. When he lengthened his stride, she kept pace with him.

He boarded an elevator for his office on the forty-fifth floor. The woman got on the same car with seven other people.

The last passenger got off on forty-two, leaving him and the woman alone. When the doors shut, she stepped over to stand directly behind him. Now he was annoyed.

Without turning to face her, he asked, "You mind telling me what you want?"

"Take me to Seymour Winbush."

Now he turned. "Are you out of your mind?" Then he saw the gun.

The fear that ran through him erased the effects of the alcohol. He looked into her face. She resembled the curator at the Museum, the one who had behaved so strangely the day Harry McElroy died. And it was quite obvious that she was deadly earnest now.

Certain that he was going to lose control of his bladder, he faced the front of the car.

"Did you understand what I said?"

"Yes. You want me to take you to Mr. Winbush," Peters replied in a trembling voice. "We'll have to change elevators on forty-seven. Just promise you won't hurt me."

From behind him, she said a very calm, "I wouldn't dream of it."

78

Larry Cole skirted Michigan Avenue traffic by swinging over to Columbus Drive. In the car with him were Blackie, Manny and Judy, going to DeWitt Plaza in search of Detective Edna Gray, or rather, the woman impersonating Detective Gray.

Cole was numb. For the past twenty-four hours he had been on an emotional roller coaster. It had begun in the lawyer's office yesterday with a downer, swept him through a night of indescribable passion, plunged him back into a funk in the first deputy's office and then trapped him in the most hilarity he'd known in a long time.

Remembering that, Cole softly chuckled. They'd all been stunned after the chair collapsed under Luckett. The director of Public Safety had been lying there on his back, blowing like a beached whale and as immobile as a turned-over turtle. Cole, Govich and Kennedy had moved forward to help him. But before they could touch him, he started yelling.

"My back! I think I did something to my back! Oh, the pain! Get an ambulance! Oh, it hurts!"

A call on the police auxiliary phone to the Communications Center got an ambulance dispatched to the building in minutes. Kennedy had the foresight to get the First District to send up a few of their beefier police officers to help. A medic made a preliminary diagnosis that Luckett had sustained a strained back and possibly a dislocated sacroiliac.

As the paramedics took Luckett down in the elevator, Cole, Govich and Kennedy had headed for the stairs. It was just as they entered the stairwell that the usually straitlaced first deputy clutched his back and said in a fair imitation of Luckett, "Oh, the pain! It hurts! My back!"

That was it. Cole and Govich nearly collapsed on the stairs in hysterics. Blackie Silvestri was coming up from the fifth floor and encountered them. He stood by in shocked silence until Cole let him in on the joke. Then he laughed loudest of all.

But the emotional roller coaster had dipped again when Judy walked into his office a few minutes later. And Cole had been forced to agree that there was something wrong with Edna. He had noticed it this morning. In all honesty, something hadn't been right with her last night. What happened between them, despite the intensity of their lovemaking, hadn't been natural. The last time he'd experienced anything similar was on Halloween afternoon at the National Science and Space Museum, when he first met Eurydice Vaughn.

And that was what it all came down to. Cole was absolutely certain that the curator was Edna's long-missing sister, Josie, and that the woman he had made love to last night was also Eurydice Vaughn. That morning he had noticed the so-called Edna's voice change. Then she had known about McElroy's disappearance, which Cole hadn't mentioned previously. Finally, the bogus detective had told Judy that she was going to DeWitt Plaza. A DeWitt Plaza housing the headquarters of the DeWitt Corporation and its chairman of the board, Seymour Winbush—whom Cole had told her was behind the McElroy Lakefront Development Company.

"What's the game plan, Boss?" Blackie asked as Cole parked the car in front of the Plaza.

"I want the three of you to take a look through the stores and see if you spot her. I'm going upstairs and pay a courtesy call on my old friend, Seymour Winbush."

"Alone?" Judy asked. "With all due respect, Commander, that's crazy! Look, Boss, that chick's not our Edna," Judy continued heatedly. "She could be part of the same thing that almost got you killed out on that island. Hell, she might not even be human!"

"She's human," Cole said quietly.

"How do you know, Commander?" Judy pressed. "That disguise

is damned near perfect. She's the best I've ever seen. Nobody could make themselves up—"

"Judy!" At Cole's sharp tone, she became instantly silent. "If there is someone impersonating Edna, then I believe that person is the National Science and Space Museum curator, Eurydice Vaughn."

Judy looked about to explode, but Cole stopped her. "I'd be willing to bet my pension that the curator is Edna's sister, who was reported missing inside the Museum twenty-five years ago."

They stood on the busy sidewalk in stunned silence.

Cole unlocked the trunk and passed out small, single-frequency walkie-talkies. Taking one for himself, he followed them into the building.

The security officer who escorted Cole to the penthouse was the same one who had been arrested for obstructing justice a year and a half ago. Back then, despite a warrant, this guard had physically blocked entrance to the penthouse of Neil and Margo DeWitt. Now he was considerably more agreeable.

"Mr. Winbush has turned the penthouse into an office complex," he confided proudly. "Everything is very top-drawer. Only one or two other board members have offices there, but usually only Mr. Winbush and a secretary or two are around during the day."

The elevator doors opened on a corridor Cole recognized. As he recalled, the DeWitt Library was down on the left, the study on the right. The winding staircase led to what used to be Neil and Margo DeWitt's living quarters. The insane Margo's laboratory was up there as well—a bunker in the sky.

Despite what the guard said about Winbush's changes, the place still looked exactly the same to Cole. The guard proceeded to the study's double doors and knocked. There was no response from inside. He knocked again. Still no answer.

"Why don't you open it?" Cole asked.

The security officer stiffened. "Mr. Winbush wouldn't like that, sir. Unauthorized entries annoy him."

Cole jammed his hands in his overcoat pockets. "Does heat annoy him too?"

The security officer also noticed the chill. "I wonder if someone left the roof door open."

Cole remembered that Margo DeWitt had landed her helicopter on the roof. The same helicopter she'd left parked on second base at Wrigley Field the night she killed two members of Cole's Brain Trust.

"Why don't you go check and see?" Cole asked.

The guard eyed him suspiciously. "Okay," he finally said before starting for the winding staircase. "I'll be right back."

When the guard ascended to the forty-ninth floor, Cole opened the study door and stepped inside.

But Winbush wasn't there. A man was seated in a chair on one side. His back was to Cole. He appeared to be asleep.

Cautiously, Cole crossed the office and looked down at him. He didn't recognize architect Kyle Peters, but he did recognize the man's drugged stupor.

"Commander! Commander Cole!" the security officer called from the corridor. Cole found the guard on the staircase.

"It's Mr. Winbush!" the guard said, obviously terrified. "He's on the helipad near the edge of the roof. I think he's going to jump!"

Snatching the radio from his coat pocket, Cole ran for the stairs.

Seymour Winbush was getting a breath of fresh air. His offices down below were temperature-regulated and properly humidified, but there was simply no substitute for being outdoors. That wonderful young colored woman Kyle introduced to him had convinced him of the health benefits.

Winbush smiled. He knew they didn't like to be called "colored." Actually preferred "black" or "African-American" or some such nonsense. Of course Seymour had made sure he'd kept all of them out of the DeWitt Corporation, except in menial jobs like chauffeur, janitor or maid. Had actually made Margo angry when she'd found out, but then, what did a woman know about running a multinational corporation?

Still, the colored woman with Kyle did know what Seymour needed. He stopped, his feet less than a foot from the roof's edge.

"Would you like to fly, Seymour?" a voice whispered solicitously through his mind.

He looked around. There was no one up here but him. That was as it should be. To make the monumental decisions it took to run a conglomerate the size of the DeWitt Corporation required solitude in order to promote clarity of thought.

"Would you like to fly, Seymour?" The whisper came again.

Winbush smiled. "That would be nice."

"Then take a giant step forward," the voice instructed.

Winbush was preparing to comply when someone called to him, "Mr. Winbush! Over here, Mr. Winbush!"

The chairman of the board of the DeWitt Corporation turned in the direction of the new voice. When he saw Larry Cole, he frowned. Now this was one seriously annoying colored man, Winbush thought.

Cole could tell that Winbush was either drugged or in some type of trance. The wind on the roof of DeWitt Plaza was blowing fiercely, yet the chairman of the board looked as if he were strolling through a grassy meadow on a summer day.

It was Cole's original plan that he and the security officer would sneak up on Winbush from either side and grab him. But when Cole started out onto the roof, the security officer hung back. "I have vertigo," he said in a shaking voice.

Great! Cole thought. Just great!

So he was forced to do it alone. He had put out a call on his portable radio for Blackie, Manny and Judy, but he simply didn't have the time to wait.

Cole was thirty feet away when Winbush said, "That would be nice," and stepped to the very edge. With no other options available to him, Cole attempted to distract the potential suicide victim by calling out.

And it worked! At least temporarily. Winbush turned his pale, imperious, now expressionless face toward Cole and demanded, "What are you doing here?" The chairman of the board seemed displeased.

"I need some advice, Mr. Winbush," Cole said, easing slowly toward him.

"What kind of advice?" Winbush eyed the policeman suspiciously and took a step backward. When he stopped, his left heel was an inch over the edge.

Cole halted. "I was thinking about changing occupations and since—"

Winbush turned his head away from Cole and waved his hand in a gesture of dismissal. Cole exhaled slowly when he saw that Winbush's feet hadn't moved.

"I have no time to give advice, Cole. Why don't you see if someone from that organization all you people belong to could help you."

Cole took another step toward Winbush but was still fifteen feet away, too far to chance a leap.

"What organization is that, Mr. Winbush?" Cole was playing for time.

"Well, if you don't know the name of your own colored organization, then I'm certainly not going to waste my time trying to remember it for you. After all, I am busy."

Cole chanced two more steps. "Busy doing what, Mr. Winbush?"

The DeWitt Corporation chairman of the board turned his back to the policeman. "Questions, questions. You people are like children. Always asking questions. No wonder you're never able to get ahead. Well, it's none of your business what I'm doing! You wouldn't understand anyway."

Cole moved forward quickly, but halted briefly when Winbush looked back at him again. Only the chairman's head turned. The rest of his body had assumed the erect stance of a diver.

Cole was nearly an arm's length away now, but still too far to reach the man if he jumped. "I just want to know what you're doing. That's all."

"Very well then!" Winbush said angrily. "I'm about to do something you'll never be able to do."

"And what is that, Mr. Winbush?" Cole was in position now.

"Fly!" With that, Seymour Winbush bent at the knees and launched himself into space fifty floors above Michigan Avenue.

At that exact instant, Larry Cole grabbed for him and missed. Winbush was off the ground and starting his plunge when Cole grabbed again. The policeman managed to grasp an ankle, and Winbush dangled in midair, with only Cole's precarious grasp to keep him from plunging to his death.

Using both hands, Cole attempted to get a better grip. But now his shoulders were over the roof's edge. He realized with growing horror that Winbush, who didn't weigh more than one hundred and sixty pounds, was pulling him to his death inch by inch.

Frantically, Cole looked around the empty roof for help.

79

B lackie was outside "The Book Rack" bookstore on Level Six when Cole radioed for help from the roof. Elevators on the commercial floors only went up to Level Ten, so he had to return to the main floor and cross the lobby to get to the penthouse. Manny was already there.

"We have to change elevators on forty-seven to get up there," Manny said as he jumped on an empty car.

"Wait, Manny!" Blackie flashed his badge to keep an elderly woman from boarding the elevator. "Penthouse elevators require a special key. We need a security guard."

A curious crowd was starting to gather. Then Judy ran up to them.

"I told the boss this was going to be trouble! What are we waiting for?" she shouted.

Blackie looked around the lobby. Still no security people in sight.

"There's got to be another way to get up there!" Manny said, his voice quaking with anxiety.

"Hey, what're you guys doing?" A heavyset man with a bald head attempted to board the car. "This is a public elevator."

Judy flashed her badge under his nose. "Don't give us a problem, sir. We have an emergency in progress here."

The crowd dissipated.

"What do we do now?" Manny said. He was cut off by a loud, ear-piercing alarm.

Blackie stepped out of the elevator. "I pushed the 'Emergency' button. That should get somebody from security here on the double."

And it did.

80

The security officer, who had escorted Cole to the penthouse, stood at the entrance to the roof. Powerless, he watched the prone policeman attempting to keep Mr. Winbush from falling.

Twice since the policeman had gone to help Mr. Winbush, the security officer had tried to lend assistance. Each time the dizziness and anxiety had overcome him. He knew that if somehow he could overcome his height phobia, help the cop and rescue Mr. Winbush, he'd be able to write his own ticket with the corporation.

He was planning one final try when he became aware of movement behind him. He turned around. There was a woman on the staircase. A woman he had never seen before.

Cole was losing the battle. There was no way he could pull Winbush to safety without help. Now, as his wrists and upper arms screamed with fatigue, he realized he'd have to make a decision soon.

His chest was exposed above the asphalt and concrete hundreds of feet below. Cole could see past Winbush's dangling, inert form to the ant-sized people down on Michigan Avenue. He wondered how they would interpret what he was about to do. No matter how vehemently he denied it, there would always be allegations that he murdered Seymour Winbush. Against this damning speculation, Cole once more utilized every ounce of strength to pull Winbush up. But he had already exhausted himself.

The prospect of failure tormented Cole. That this was a man who had attempted to destroy him didn't matter. That Commander Larry Cole of the Chicago Police Department failed to save his life did matter! And as he sensed Winbush's ankle slipping from his sweaty palm, Cole felt tears burn his wind-blasted eyes.

"Damn you!" he muttered through clenched teeth. "Damn you, damn you, damn you!"

He held on for one last second and was about to open his fingers when he felt a presence at his side. Half-expecting to see Blackie or Manny, Larry Cole turned to look into the face of Edna Gray. An Edna Gray he knew was an impostor.

81

The security officer dispatched to handle the elevator alarm wasn't happy. But he figured that the three cops would have made him even more unhappy if he hadn't done exactly as they said. They were in the private elevator that operated from the subterranean garage direct to the penthouse. There were no other stops in between. Since they'd boarded the car, the female officer had been on her walkie-talkie trying to raise a "Commander Cole," without success.

Blackie led them to the helipad. At the entrance, they encountered a dazed security officer. Manny went past him onto the roof. Blackie and Judy gave the security officer a brief glance and followed.

Seated alone at the center of the helipad was Seymour Winbush. "Where's Commander Cole?" Blackie demanded.

Winbush looked up and graced the lieutenant with a stupid smile.

Blackie reached down and pulled Winbush up until the chairman's face was level with his own. "I said, where is Commander Cole?"

Winbush's expression didn't change one bit.

Blackie began to shout his question once more when Judy stopped him. "He doesn't hear you, Blackie. This guy's been drugged, like the guard."

With a groan of frustration, Blackie let Winbush go. Like a puppet whose strings had been cut, Winbush collapsed back to the helipad surface and resumed his cross-legged seat.

"All right," Blackie barked. "We're going to spread out and search this place. Judy, you get on City-Wide and get us some help. I want this building sealed off—"

"Excuse me." It was Seymour Winbush who had spoken. "As

you are summoning assistance, I wonder if you could get me an ambulance. I've injured my ankle."

They all noticed the way he was speaking. It was with a slow, dreamy quality, as if he were talking in his sleep.

"What happened to you, Mr. Winbush?" Judy asked.

"When Cole and that woman pulled me up, I heard something pop right here." He pointed to his black stretch sock, visible beneath a perfectly tailored pants cuff.

"Where did the commander and the woman go?" Blackie shouted.

Winbush raised his hands to the level of his shoulders. Making little flapping motions, he said, "They just flew away."

82

Edna Gray was learning to deal with her fear. Her subterranean prison was something out of a nightmare and her jailer could qualify for the lead in a horror movie. But she realized, after the confrontation with her double, that if she was going to get out of here, she would have to keep her wits about her.

After being drugged and questioned by Eurydice Vaughn, Edna had fallen into an exhausted sleep. Her dreams were filled with images of Larry Cole, Eurydice Vaughn, the figure of Death and even her sister Josie.

When she awoke, she understood what had happened to all those people who'd disappeared in the Museum. Somehow they were enticed or forced down here, and. . . . A chill went through her. *None* of them were even seen or heard from again!

A slight glimmer of hope shone through her despair. If Larry was correct, then Josie had survived. Survived to become Eurydice Vaughn.

Suddenly the light above her head snapped on, nearly blinding her.

Blinking, she saw the tall figure in the Death costume looming over her. Beside him was a large dog, partially hidden in shadow.

Death began undoing her bonds. She considered attempting an escape but realized she was weak and still groggy from the injection. She also realized there was no way she could challenge him physically—but just maybe she could outsmart him.

When she was free, he turned and walked away, the animal following. Edna sat up. She experienced a brief wave of dizziness—

probably, she thought, this was why the dog seemed to have six legs and a horn between its eyes. When her vision cleared, the animal was gone, but Death had returned. He beckoned to her.

She didn't move.

He beckoned again.

Edna saw no choice. If she was going to attempt an escape, she'd better find out as much about this place and her captor as she could. Still clad in the green hospital gown, she followed.

She stepped out onto a gallery and looked around at the inside of a very old, high-ceilinged building. Perhaps some official structure . . . yes, a train station. Like Grand Central Station, only this place was much larger and older.

She was still studying the cavernous room when Death spoke. "You can shower and change in here. Then you can eat."

He had spoken slowly and very precisely, but she was still able to detect the speech impediment. Somehow this made him seem less menacing.

Following his directions, she walked down the gallery and through an open door into a huge shower room with eight shower heads going at once. Her escort slammed the door behind her. Frightened, she opened it again. He was standing out on the gallery. It dawned on her that he had closed the door to give her privacy.

"Thank you," Edna said and shut the door.

She found soap and clean towels. There was also a black Spandex body suit along with thick socks and soft-soled black running shoes on a chair in one corner. After her shower, she put on the new clothing and emerged. Death hadn't moved.

Her fear nearly gone, Edna walked over to him. "You said something about eating."

He didn't answer. He also didn't move. She could feel his eyes, beneath the mask, studying her for a full minute. Finally, he turned away and led her back down the gallery.

Although she had never formally studied architecture, she could tell this place was old. In fact, older even than the Museum. And well preserved.

Now Edna felt sure this was Rotheimer's underground train station Luke Eddings had told her about. So maybe there were tunnels leading from this place toward the cemetery, which was right across the street from the Third District police station.

She followed Death to another room. This one had no iron door. It was a kitchen. A very old, but exceptionally well-equipped kitchen. There were three stoves—electric, gas and woodburning; a freezer, a refrigerator and an antique icebox with a bulky motor on top; two sinks—one with a faucet and the other with an old-style water pump; and an enormous kitchen table that could seat ten. There were hand-carved wooden cabinets around the walls.

Death pointed to the head of the table, where a single place had been set with a bowl, bread plate, glass, white linen napkin, and silverware. Edna sat down, noticing that the napkin and silver bore the engraved initial "R."

From a cabinet he removed an individual serving package of raisin-bran cereal, set it in front of her with an unopened quart carton of milk, a block of cream cheese and a freshly baked loaf of bread. Edna speculated that the food came from one of the restaurants serving the Museum, or from the *Baking Through the Ages* Exhibit, which was actually a fully functional, walk-through bakery.

She was famished, but before she took a bite, she looked up at her guard. "Aren't you going to join me?"

He made pantomiming motions, indicating his mask and the difficulty he would have eating with it on.

"Why don't you take it off?" she asked.

He shook his head vigorously.

She got up and walked over to him. He turned his back on her. She reached out and touched his arm through the cloth.

"Please," she said softly. "I don't like to eat alone."

"I can't," he said, making a spluttering sound under the mask.

"Yes, you can."

"You'll be scared!" he sobbed.

She refused to move. "No, I won't. I promise."

Slowly, he turned to face her and pulled down the black hood to reveal his blond crew-cut head. Then, after hesitating a heartbeat, he removed the mask.

Edna stared up into his face. He couldn't meet her gaze. After a moment, she took one of his enormous hands. "Come on, sit down."

Reluctantly, he sat beside her.

"What kind of cereal do you like?" she asked, going to the cabinet from which he had removed the raisin bran.

He pointed to her box on the table. She removed another one, and searching around in the other cabinets, she came up with a bowl, silverware and a napkin. "What's your name?" she asked.

He still wouldn't look at her as he mumbled, "Homer."

"Hello, Homer," she said. "My name is Edna."

"Hello," he managed.

"Eat, Homer." She pointed to his bowl.

Tentatively, he opened his cereal package and poured its contents into the bowl. Adding milk, he looked up at her, as if he expected to catch her staring at him. She was spreading cream cheese on a slice of bread, which she gave to him.

For a time, they ate in silence. Finally, he got up the courage to speak. "Edna?"

"Yes, Homer."

"You look a lot like Eurydice."

"I know."

"Why?"

"Because I think . . ." She stopped and started again. "Because she's my sister."

The rumbling of the Mistress's cart could be heard coming from the gallery. Frightened, Homer leaped to his feet and fumbled to put on his mask. But the Mistress was rolling through the door.

Edna slowly stood up. Whereas she'd felt pity at the sight of Homer, she experienced only revulsion, horror and very real fear at seeing this old woman.

The Mistress looked from Homer to Edna.

"You are the inquisitive, meddling little bitch, aren't you, Detective Gray?" The Mistress purred as her bullwhip whistled through the air toward them.

83

Cole was driving south on Lake Shore Drive from the Loop. Beside him sat Eurydice Vaughn. By agreement, she had dropped all pretense of impersonating Edna Gray.

After the rescue of Seymour Winbush, she had reached for her brooch, but Cole was quicker. He'd held her wrist firmly as he unpinned the ornament. "You won't be needing this for me." He slipped it in his pocket.

"Now what, Commander?" Her confidence had been unflappable.

"Where is Edna?"

She smiled at him. "I'm Edna."

"No, you're not!"

Her smile remained in place a moment longer. Then she'd reached up and removed five small strips of latex from beneath her eyes, above her cheekbones and under her mouth. Standing on the roof of DeWitt Plaza, Eurydice Vaughn had looked back at him, her face clouding with anger. "I'll show you where your precious Edna Gray is, Larry. But you've got to come with me."

They'd walked down to the first level of the penthouse on the forty-eighth floor. They entered the study just as Blackie, Judy and Manny rushed in. While the police officers were on the roof, Cole and Eurydice had taken the penthouse elevator back to forty-seven and a commercial elevator to the lobby.

"How did you become part of this?" Cole asked as they passed McCormick Place at Twenty-third Street.

"You'll find out soon enough." But she seemed a bit apprehensive now.

"You know Edna's your sister."

"That's ridiculous," she said.

"I don't think so. Whoever or whatever is responsible for what's going on at the Museum kidnapped you in August, nineteen seventy-two, Josie."

"Don't call me that!" She spun on him and bared her teeth. "My name is Eurydice! An epic figure from Greek mythology, not some tart's name given out by a ghetto babymaker!"

"Who renamed you?" Cole's voice remained calm.

She spun back to face front. "I was never renamed. It has always been Eurydice."

"Then who named you?"

The smile she displayed came hard. At this moment, Cole realized that the two women—possibly sisters—were as opposite as they could be. A yin and yang; a top versus a bottom; even good versus evil.

"You're going to find out very soon, Larry. And I don't think you'll like it."

"So you don't believe that Edna's your sister," Cole pressed.

"I know she's not my sister." Eurydice suddenly sounded tired.

"Then who were your mother and father?"

"I didn't have a mother and father in the sense you're talking about." Her answer was mechanical, as if she'd memorized it. "Look, I'll answer all your questions at the Museum. The Mistress will—" She stopped suddenly.

"Who's the Mistress?"

"Soon, Commander. You'll find out very soon."

As Cole turned into the park, he said, "I guess Judy was right."

"Judy?" Eurydice frowned. "Oh, yes. Detective Daniels, the disguise artist."

"She's also known as a Mistress. She said that you weren't human."

Eurydice bristled. "I was human enough for you last night! As human as Edna Gray!"

Cole shook his head. "Edna and I didn't use drugs. What we did was natural. Edna and I have a lot more going between us than you and I ever could."

"As long as she lives, Commander," Eurydice said. "As long as she lives."

Cole had just turned into the Museum parking lot nearest the Constellation space shuttle. Even at this distance, a block from the Museum, they could see the squadron of police cars, with Mars lights flashing, parked in front.

"What now?" Cole asked matter of factly.

"Turn around!"

With a shrug, he complied. He was starting to head back for Lake Shore Drive when she said, "Not that way. Drive around in back of the Museum. It's time for you to pay a return visit to Haunted Island, Commander."

84

NOVEMBER 6, 1997
4:05 P.M.

DeWitt Plaza had been sealed and secured by a combination of DeWitt Plaza security personnel and Chicago police officers. When Chief Jack Govich entered, Sherlock escorted him to the penthouse. They did not discuss the case on the way up in the elevator.

In the library, they found Blackie, Detective Judy Daniels, Barbara Zorin and Jamal Garth.

Blackie gave a very thorough account of what had occurred. The bottom line was that Larry Cole was missing, and he had possibly been kidnapped by a woman impersonating Detective Edna Gray.

Blackie concluded with, "We've got to figure it this way, Chief. Larry's been taken to the National Science and Space Museum."

Govich frowned. "Last night McElroy; now Larry Cole. That place is turning into a real house of horrors. But why?"

"I think Mrs. Zorin and Mr. Garth can explain, Chief," Blackie said.

Garth stood up and began. "Since its doors opened in nineteen-six, Chief Govich, someone or something has been responsible for a number of strange things that have happened at the Museum.

"When we looked back over the years, we found that two separate patterns emerge in relation to the events. Up until around nineteen-seventy, the general pattern implies vengeance. From Rotheimer's death, and the deaths of his family members, down to the deaths of the first four Museum curators and the strange disappearances, everything could be categorized as a premeditated act of violence. It was as if the entity, or whatever is responsible, wanted to scare people away. But after nineteen-seventy, the pattern changes. Events become more reactive, as if protecting the Museum is the paramount consideration. Including now, with what happened last night to McElroy and his equipment."

Govich interrupted. "If what Larry and I found out last night is correct, McElroy, with the DeWitt Corporation's backing, was going to excavate everything around the Museum and turn the area into some type of urban architectural nightmare."

"It may sound strange," Barbara put in, "but it all points to one person being responsible; Katherine Rotheimer."

Even Jack Govich snorted. "Oh, c'mon, Barb! That would mean she would have to be what, over a hundred and ten years old?"

"One hundred and fifteen on her birthday this past March," Garth volunteered.

Blackie shook his head. "No one-hundred-plus-year-old woman could be physically capable of carrying out the stuff that's been going on over there, Jamal. I don't care how well preserved she is."

"But she's got help, Blackie," Garth countered. "Eurydice Vaughn, the curator, who has no verifiable past. There's a distinct possibility the curator could be Edna Gray's sister, who as a child vanished inside the Museum. According to Judy, there's some kind of monstrous giant in a Death costume running around in there as well. We have no idea of who else she's got with her, but I do know that Barbara and I made a couple of University of Chicago professors very nervous when talking about Eurydice Vaughn."

"I don't think 'who' she's got in there is as much a problem as 'what' she has," Barbara said. "If Katherine Rotheimer has been able to manipulate events up to this point without apparent detection, then she and her minions are very dangerous people."

"I don't follow you," Govich said.

She explained. "Every major scientific advance, from simple propulsion systems to atomic power, has been available for her to study. When she was younger, she possessed an aptitude for science, although her biological experiments tended toward the bizarre. And for decades, she's been able to make people die or simply vanish without leaving a trace. I'd say she has mastered a great deal of scientific knowledge and is capable of using it for whatever reason she chooses."

"Then we're going to search that place from top to bottom until we find this Katherine Rotheimer, Eurydice Vaughn and Larry Cole!" Govich said angrily.

"I talked to the Third District commander before you arrived, Chief," Blackie said. "He's started an evacuation of all the civilians. Right now that museum should be sealed up tighter than a drum."

Barbara pulled a folder from her attaché case. "I think the maps and blueprints we've got will help with the search, Chief."

She was spreading the maps on the large mahogany desk when Govich ventured a final question: "But what do they want with Cole?"

85

A t that exact moment, Larry Cole was asking himself the same question. Autumn twilight was descending over the city as he followed Eurydice Vaughn through the deserted park area south of the Museum and Haunted Island. The sky was darkening, but the old bridge at the south end of the island was still visible. Cole halted.

Eurydice turned to look at him and waited.

The memory of that night nearly two months ago came back to him with startling clarity. The scar on his back was healing rapidly, but he felt a renewed pain as he relived the incident. Even the sounds were the same as they were that night, from the remote murmur of Lake Shore Drive traffic to the gurgling of a stream.

"Nothing will hurt you now, Larry," Eurydice said. "The Lullaby won't sing until we've passed."

"And then?"

She walked over and took his arm. He tensed at her touch. "I'm not going to hurt you," she said.

"Then let me go," he told her coldly.

She dropped his arm and stepped away, her mask of fury once more in place. After a second's hesitation, Cole followed her across the bridge.

Eurydice walked along rapidly down the very old cement path at the center of the island. Cole had no difficulty keeping up, but he kept looking around for signs of danger.

They stopped in a dark grotto totally surrounded by trees and bushes. She turned to face him.

"I'll have to take your gun before we go any farther."

"I think I'd better hold on to it," Cole told her.

"I expected this kind of obstinacy from you," she said. "So I prepared for it."

It happened so suddenly that Cole had no time to react. The ground beneath him was simply no longer there and he fell through empty space. An empty space cloaked in inky darkness.

86

The rush hour was in full swing. Lake Shore Drive at Fifty-seventh Street was the point of origin of a huge traffic backup to the Loop, seven miles away. It was a gaper's block. Curious motorists were watching two enormous Coast Guard helicopters attempt to lift a submerged crane that rested in the lake some fifty yards from shore.

In the cockpit of one helicopter, Lieutenant Commander Del Atkinson barked orders into the headset of his crash helmet.

Glancing out the starboard window, he could see the headlights of slow-moving cars stretching to the horizon.

"Awright, let's pull this big bastard out of there!" his voice snapped over the ship-to-ship radio. "When it's clear of the water, we're going to put it down on the beach!"

The operation commenced.

But the effort had severely weakened one of the steel cables attached to the crane's housing.

The yellow vehicle cleared the water, spewing streams back into the lake, and as if propelled from a fountain, it hung in the air for a moment before the helicopters began a slow flight toward the beach. Traffic on Lake Shore Drive had now come to a complete halt as drivers watched the airborne salvage operation.

Then the cables on the other helicopter snapped consecutively within a span of twenty seconds. Without the requisite support, one side of the crane dropped, increasing the strain on the remaining cables. Before they too could snap, Atkinson ordered them released.

Fifteen yards from shore, the crane plunged downward. Gravity increased its force as it fell through shallow water, a few feet of sand and then impacted a hard surface.

Ezra Rotheimer's underground train station had sprung leaks. Very serious leaks.

87

NOVEMBER 6, 1997
5:15 P.M.

In the cavern, the vibration drove Larry Cole back to consciousness. As he attempted to focus his vision, he remembered the fall through the dark and being slammed unconscious.

He sat up. The wind had been knocked out of him, and he was lightheaded but otherwise unhurt. He was in a brick-walled room with a stone floor; a naked light bulb shone down on him from high up in the ceiling. He had been stripped to the waist and his arms manacled with a pair of sturdy handcuffs. The chain between the two steel bracelets was nearly a foot in length. Nothing like that had been used by law-enforcement authorities for decades.

Cole got to his feet and leaned against the wall until his head stopped spinning. Although Eurydice Vaughn had left him with his belt, his Beretta, holster, extra bullet clips and handcuffs were gone. He took a couple of tentative steps.

There was a steel door on the other side of the room. Cole crossed to it and tried the knob. It was locked, as he had expected. He turned back to study the room. There was a cushioned table at its center, but nothing else.

Cole sat down on the table. As he did so, he caught a whiff of a familiar scent. He lowered his head closer to the cushioned surface. It was the same perfume Edna wore and the one Eurydice Vaughn had on last night. He noticed the restraints attached to the table's sides. So whoever was in league with the Museum curator had held Edna here. He only hoped that she was okay.

"You'd better worry about what's going to happen to *you*, pal," he told himself out loud.

As if the sound of his voice had triggered it, the door opened and

Eurydice Vaughn came in. She had changed into a skin-tight black suit with a hood and belt. Her face was flushed.

"Been awake long, Larry?" she asked cheerfully.

When Cole glared at her, her face froze into a cruel smile. "You're going to have to learn to be more polite for us to get along, Commander. After all, you are going to be with us for a very long time."

"Don't bet on it," Cole said.

He heard the whistle of the bullwhip through the air an instant before the blow landed on his back. From the sting, he knew his healing wound had reopened. He leaped off the table just as the whip snaked again, this time wrapping around his throat, and he was jerked across the room toward his torturer.

Through his anger and pain, he fought to think. She'd made a mistake pulling him toward her. Already he could feel his fingers caress that lovely neck before he squeezed the life out of her.

Then, a few feet away from her, he charged. But she was prepared.

A metal rod appeared in her other hand. She jabbed it at him, and as ten thousand volts of electricity raced through his body, Cole screamed.

Deftly, Eurydice stepped away from him, uncurling the bullwhip from his neck.

Cole braced himself against the wall for a moment before charging again, but she was waiting with her weapons.

She repeatedly shocked him with the rod and beat him with the whip, without fear of retaliation. A few times during the attack, Cole managed to catch a glimpse of her face—intensely excited and twisted with pleasure.

After fifteen minutes, Cole's blood was smeared across the floor. They were both breathing heavily as they jockeyed for position. Still, she was landing all of her blows below neck level. It was as if she were making a conscious effort not to scar his face.

Cole knew he was nearing the end when she wrapped the whip around his knees and yanked him to the floor. Electric rod raised, she walked toward him.

He looked up into her face as she approached and he could see the madness and cruelty there—primitive, unchecked, and terrifying.

She feinted at him with the rod and when he jerked, she laughed, spittle flying. "You'll learn to be very nice to me in any way I want. And if you don't . . ." She raised the rod again.

"*Eurydice!*"

The amplified voice froze Cole's tormenter, but she never took her eyes off him.

"*You don't know what you're doing! You'll damage him permanently if you continue! Bring him to me!*"

For a moment, she hesitated. Then she stepped away.

"Get up, Larry," she purred seductively. "It's show time!"

88

The exterior of the National Science and Space Museum had taken on the appearance of a fortress under siege. Police cars' strobe-flashing lights surrounded the buildings, while police officers ran back and forth between the vehicles and the Museum. The command post inside had been taken over by the first deputy, with Jack Govich directing the search operations.

The Museum had been evacuated. Security personnel were assigned to noncritical posts, but the only other civilians allowed inside were Barbara Zorin, Jamal Garth and Museum Chairman Winston Fleisher.

As Zorin and Garth examined architectural drawings in the command post, Govich and Blackie paid a visit to Fleisher. Two uniformed officers were stationed in the chairman's outer office. Inside, Fleisher sat behind his desk, a glass of sherry in his hand and a look of despair on his face.

The chief smiled warmly. "How are you this evening, Doctor? My name is Jack Govich. This is Blackie Silvestri." Then his smile faded. "Now before we begin—you don't mind if I call you Winston?"

Bleakly, Fleisher shook his head.

"Good," Govich continued. "So, Winston, I think you should know right up front that he's the good cop." He pointed at Blackie. "And I'm the bad cop."

Fleisher closed his eyes, as if in pain. When he reopened them, Govich and Blackie were still there.

89

NOVEMBER 6, 1997
6:00 P.M.

Like a huntress with her captured prey, Eurydice Vaughn paraded Cole down the gallery toward the Mistress's chamber. Her bullwhip was loosely wrapped around his throat. His upper body gleamed with sweat and blood. His hands remained shackled. His face was a mask of intense anger.

"You'll find that it's not so bad down here, Larry," she said conversationally. "In fact, the air and water, even the food we eat, are far superior to anything on the surface. Up there, everything is polluted. Chemicals, carbon emissions, radiation. I'm actually surprised that the human race has managed to survive so long."

Cole didn't answer. He was making his mind come up with a plan.

When she abruptly stopped talking, Cole followed the direction of her eyes. The door to one of the rooms had opened and now the robed, masked figure of Death stepped out, with someone right behind him. Cole's heart leaped when he saw Edna Gray.

Edna made a soft noise and ran toward him. Snatching her bullwhip from around Cole's neck, Eurydice raced to intercept her, snapping the whip behind her to lash at the policewoman. This gave Cole the chance he'd been looking for. Leaping forward, he grabbed the tail of the whip. As she swung it, he held on, ripping the handle from her grasp.

With a snarl of fury, she swung toward him just as Edna reached him and placed her arms protectively around his bloodied shoulders. Together, they turned to face the curator. Death stepped up beside her.

Brandishing the electric rod, Eurydice advanced on them. Weakly,

Cole hefted the bullwhip, but Edna took the weapon and stepped in front of him. Less than ten feet apart, the two women faced each other.

"I enjoyed what I did to your friend," Eurydice said, "but I really don't have the time to play games with *you.*"

The curator advanced.

"You can't take her, Edna." Cole seized Edna's arm and backed down the gallery.

"Eurydice?" The giant in the Death costume spoke. "Don't hurt Edna. The Mistress wanted to hurt Edna, but I wouldn't let her."

Lowering the electric rod, Eurydice turned to Homer and took off his mask and hood. When she saw his newly scarred face, she cried out in fury and anguish.

Cole stared at the giant as Edna said, "That thing you call the Mistress was trying to get at me, but Homer wouldn't let her. He shielded me with his body. I thought she was going to kill him."

Eurydice undid Homer's robe, revealing injuries like Cole's. But Homer's crisscrossed nearly every visible inch of flesh.

The curator jerked violently back toward Cole and Edna. "This is your fault!" she screamed at the policewoman. "You did something to make her angry! The Mistress would never have beaten him like this. You did something!"

She raised the rod again.

"No, Eurydice," Homer said. "Don't hurt Edna. She's your sister."

"Shut up!" Eurydice screamed. "She's not!"

The sound of amplified clapping echoed through the chamber. Then the Mistress's voice carried to them. *"Very melodramatic. Better than imbecilic soap operas. But then, enough of this. For your information, Officers, Eurydice and Homer are my children. Not children of my body, but children wrought by my genius. What you guests will become has yet to be determined, but I assure you that whatever I decide for you, it will make medical history. Bring them!"*

As if they had rehearsed the scene, Eurydice and Homer parted. Still holding the whip, now a pathetic, useless weapon, Edna walked beside Cole down the gallery.

90

"The final air duct for the train station was constructed right here. It has got to be still in place near this stand of trees." Garth stabbed his finger at a diagram on the blueprint.

Terry Kennedy, with Barbara Zorin looking on, stared at the spot. "That's out on Seagull Island, Mr. Garth," he said.

"What difference does that make?" Barbara responded crossly.

Kennedy released a sigh. "Okay, I'll send some people to take a look, but only if they're wearing vests and carrying armored shields."

"Shields," Garth said, nodding. "Good idea. Tell them to pretend they're walking across a mine field."

Kennedy realized that Garth was deadly earnest.

91

The Mistress's laboratory took up the largest amount of space in the cavern. Situated at the far end of the gallery, it was originally constructed as a wing of an upper-level corridor, to provide spectators a view of the activities below. An enormous clock, visible from anywhere in the station, was mounted high on the back wall. This wall was built of five-foot-thick reinforced cement; its exterior was buried under Lake Michigan sand. Now it was threatened by the falling crane.

The clock had not worked since the spring of 1937, and the hands, on a face circled by Roman numerals, had stopped at 8:19. Now a narrow stream of water ran across the minute hand, pushing it slowly forward.

A short distance away, the Mistress, astride her cart, was examining slides under a microscope with a twelve-inch-square viewer to accommodate her ancient eyes. As she heard the others coming down the gallery behind her, she flipped a switch on her computer console and turned her cart around to face them.

Yes, the policeman did resemble Jim. The chest and arms of the two men were identical, with well-defined, sinewy muscles. The long-ago memory of passion, shared with Jim Cross on a summer day in a room not very far from where she now sat, came back to her.

She studied Cole more closely. There was something different about the man she had loved and the policeman. It was in the face and the carriage. Jim Cross had exuded brute strength whereas Cole exhibited a combination of character and intelligence. The Mistress, once Katherine Rotheimer, recalled Jim's intellect: purely practical—

involving mechanics, applications of basic physics and hard work. Katherine had been frustrated that he possessed no appreciation for literature, art or music, other than for the banal tunes of the Levee District.

It was in the Levee District that they had been forced to hide from her father during those early years. There, in a filthy alley, Katherine had seen Jim cut a white man's throat. A white man named Oscar Cantrell, who had been following them and whom, they discovered, was a deputy sheriff. Cantrell's death forced them to flee the Levee. With no place else to go, they'd escaped to the building in the park behind the Museum that had housed her lab and Jim's workroom.

The abandoned structure was in disrepair, but Katherine had remembered the underground station and the tunnels below the surface. A place where they could hide from her father and the authorities. A place in which she would remain for nearly a century.

"Mistress?"

She came out of her reverie slowly. Eurydice had spoken to her. Yes, Eurydice had been a good daughter and was very much like herself. She had enjoyed viewing Eurydice's chastisement of the policeman. In her time, she had given out many such thrashings of her own. Bogus attorney Samuel Barry. A muscular Museum security guard who had intercepted her in one of the corridors on Christmas Day in 1927. Even her little sister, Estelle. These were a few who came to mind. And she'd beaten many of her victims to death intentionally, except for Estelle. The child, whom she had planned to make the first female Museum curator when she reached adulthood, had simply caught the Mistress on a bad day. A blow or two too many and. . . . Poor thing.

"Mistress?"

It was Eurydice again. Now her daughter was annoying her. "I heard you the first time!"

Eurydice recoiled.

The Mistress examined the policewoman. Indeed, there was a remarkable resemblance between Edna Gray and her Eurydice. As the Mistress recalled, she had instructed the moronic Homer to kidnap the *older* girl on that long-ago day. If only he had followed instructions!

Oh, well, the Mistress thought, *there's no use crying over spilt milk.*

"Remove his manacles," she said to Eurydice before turning back to Cole and Edna. "Since you've been so interested in what we do, Commander Cole and Detective Gray, I think it's time we gave you a closer look."

After Eurydice removed Cole's handcuffs and Homer took the bullwhip from Edna Gray, the Mistress turned her cart around to lead them on a tour of her lab.

The Mistress's laboratory looked like a zoo of the macabre. In both the glass and the wire-mesh cages lining the walls, Cole and Edna looked at insects with oversized eyes, the six-legged dog Edna had seen before, a lamb with canine teeth, and scores of other mutated specimens. And as she conducted this tour of the damned, the Mistress, whom they now realized was Katherine Rotheimer, was visibly pleased with her creations.

"So what do you think?" she asked.

Cole replied, "We're speechless."

The Mistress stared at him before her hideous face twisted into what could have been a smile. "I know what you're thinking, and you're right. It's all crap. I spent nearly a century alone, working night and day trying to accomplish something different. Something significant. None of those things ever came out right."

"Why would you want to tamper with nature?" Edna asked.

"Tamper with or improve, Detective Gray?" the Mistress snapped. "There is always room for improvement in anything." She eyed her captives. "Even you two."

"Perhaps I could venture a question," Cole said.

"Go ahead," the Mistress allowed.

"What happened to Jim Cross?"

Despite its ugliness, Edna and Cole noticed the old woman's face soften. When she spoke, her voice, even with the amplification, was distant, as if the body as well as the heart had traveled back in time. "He couldn't live down here. He said it was too confining. I could understand that. He loved freedom. Working in the light. He said that being forced to live down here was like being in prison."

"So he left?" Cole asked.

The Mistress turned icy as her ancient eyes locked with his. "He tried. But I didn't bring you down here to ask me stupid questions. I wanted to show you what I've been doing that *is* of relevance to the world."

She touched a key on her console, and the curtain behind her slid back to reveal a cushioned table with restraints, a duplicate of the one in the room where Edna and Cole had been held. Strapped to the table was a heavyset man whom Cole and Edna had never seen before.

The Mistress identified him. "The young Mr. McElroy, like his father before him, had such grandiose, but destructive, plans for my Museum and the land around it. Land that rightfully belongs to me. After all, I am Ezra Rotheimer's sole surviving heir."

Cole could tell there was something wrong with McElroy. The construction boss looked critically ill. His eyes were sunken and his skin was ashen.

"And what do your sharp little detectives' eyes tell you two?" the Mistress questioned.

"Something's wrong with him," Cole said.

"He looks like he has a virus," Edna said before adding, "You did something to him!"

"A virus?" The Mistress cackled. "That's very good, Detective Gray, but you're only partially right. Viruses can be deadly, but diseases like cancer and leukemia are even more devastating. Our friend here—"

The cavern shuttered violently.

The Mistress's head jerked toward Eurydice. "I thought you said there would be no more of that! That's the second time in less than an hour. It sounds as if the roof is caving in on us!"

For the first time in several minutes, Eurydice looked alert. "It's from the salvage operation. They should be almost finished by now. If my calculations are correct, the walls should be able to withstand the pressure as long as nothing unusual happens."

"And if you're wrong?" The Mistress's balding head, with shriveled chin, jutted toward the young woman.

"Then we will all die, Mistress."

Briefly, Cole and Edna thought that the curator was being

sarcastic. But then they realized she was simply reciting an honest response, as she'd been trained to do. Cole saw what had turned a happy child named Josie Gray into the cold, inhuman Eurydice Vaughn. Brainwashing!

The Mistress's voice diverted him. "Getting back to young Mr. McElroy. I have favored him with a place of immortality in the medical advances of history, as he is going to survive an advanced state of leukemia to lead a perfectly normal life, free of the disease."

"There is no cure for leukemia," Edna said.

"Now there is," the old woman responded. "I have created it, and he—" she pointed a gnarled index finger with a crimson-red nail "—is my proof."

"So what you're saying," Cole interjected, "is that McElroy had leukemia before he was kidnapped."

The Mistress smiled and shook her head.

"Then you exposed him to it."

Her head bobbed up and down. The smug, black-toothed smile did not alter.

"Is this the first time you've tried your vaccine on a human?" Edna asked.

After hesitating, the Mistress answered, "Yes."

"So you have no idea whether it will work or not," Edna said.

"It will work!" the Mistress screamed.

Another rumble shook the cavern.

Cole looked down. The floor was suddenly wet.

Edna was still arguing. "What about side effects? Chemotherapy has been used as a cancer cure, but it can wreak havoc on the body."

"Eurydice!" the Mistress snapped.

The curator stepped forward, her electric rod raised. Cole moved to intercept her, but Homer was suddenly behind him, pinning the policeman's arms to his sides.

"Give Mr. McElroy the injection," the Mistress ordered Eurydice. "Then we'll see what kind of side effects he has."

Obediently, Eurydice went to a table behind the Mistress and picked up a syringe. She began filling it.

"If my estimates are correct, he will begin to recover from the blood disease within hours," the Mistress said.

Edna was about to speak but Cole, still held by Homer, said, "This is a tremendous development, Miss Rotheimer. You will be hailed as a great scientist."

"Please, Commander, don't insult my intelligence with flattery," she spat. "You think I'm some gullible schoolgirl?"

"But surely," Cole pressed, "a cure for leukemia is a monumental advance."

"The Rotheimer Vaccine is not only a cure for leukemia, Commander, but for all forms of cancer. In fact, I'm very interested to see how quickly the vaccine works on lung and ovarian cancer strains."

As the Mistress said "lung," she looked at Cole. When she said "ovarian," her eyes swung to Edna. It was obvious that she intended to use them as guinea pigs.

Eurydice injected McElroy and returned to stand guard over Edna. The Mistress said, "Everything has been prepared for you. The cancer cells will be implanted into your bodies and given a catalyst to enable them to grow rapidly and spread. Then, at your darkest hour, I and my vaccine will be there to save you."

As Cole's eyes met Edna's, they knew that now was the time to fight. At that moment, the final rumble shook the cavern. The wall behind the clock imploded and thousands of gallons of water began rushing into the underground station.

92

It's got to be somewhere in here," Barbara Zorin said as she led the group into *Glassware from Around the World* Hall. Standing behind her were Govich, Kennedy, Garth, Blackie, Lieutenant Commander Atkinson—still clad in his flight suit—and Deputy Chief Doug Collins of the Chicago Fire Department.

"Dr. Fleisher told us that a number of the disappearances occurred right from this room," Govich said.

"Edna's sister vanished in here," Blackie added.

The group stopped at the Himalayan stone bench.

"Everything looks pretty solid to me," the fireman said, patting the sturdy bench as he looked around.

Barbara studied the cases also. Each of them was immense, full of exhibits, and appeared to have been stationary for a long time. "There's got to be a secret passageway or some other kind of hidden access point in here."

"But how are we going to find it?" Terry Kennedy asked with building frustration.

Fire Department Deputy Chief Collins stepped forward. "You authorize it, First Deputy, and I'll find your secret passage for you." Collins paused to take another look around the room. "Of course some of this stuff might get damaged."

Kennedy glared at him. "Two of my officers' lives are at stake! If you have to tear this joint to pieces, do it!"

Fire Chief Collins ran off to summon a squadron of ax-wielding fire fighters to, if necessary, demolish *Glassware from Around the World* Hall.

93

The cascading waters obliterated most of the Mistress's lab. Equipment, furniture and the Mistress's bogus specimens were swept over the railing into the lower levels of the station, fifty feet below. The relentless rush of water, pouring through the break in the wall where the clock had been, smashed into the gallery. The floor buckled and then began to give way.

In a panic, the Mistress, on her cart, raced away from the flood's origin. Obediently, Eurydice and Homer ran after her. Cole and Edna, along with the leukemia-infected Bill McElroy, were forgotten.

"What are we going to do now?" Edna shouted over the roaring water.

Cole squinted up at the spreading cracks in the wall. He could tell that the entire place was in danger of imminent collapse.

"C'mon," he said, grabbing Edna's hand.

"What about him?" Edna pointed at McElroy, who was still strapped to the table.

They rushed to help him, but before they could undo the straps binding McElroy's arms, the lake water smashed a second hole in the ceiling of the ancient structure. Water washed down onto the gallery to sweep Cole, Edna and McElroy, the latter still on the table he was strapped to, into the station below.

They dropped into waters swirling up from earlier leaks. Cole fought a fierce undertow to reach the surface of the swelling flood. Head barely above water, he was swept along as if caught in the rapids of a raging river.

"Larry!"

He attempted to swim toward Edna's voice, but he was dragged down again. With a tremendous effort, he surfaced. This time, he saw her.

She had called to him from McElroy's table. It was afloat. McElroy was still strapped on top, and Edna hung precariously to one side.

As the freezing waters raced and swirled around him, Cole swam. He was dragged down a half-dozen times. Finally, he reached the makeshift raft and clung to the side opposite Edna.

"We're being pulled to the other side of the station!" she called to him. "That's where the unfinished train tunnels are!"

Tired and battered, Cole forced himself to reconsider their position. If they were swept down into one of the tunnels, they would surely drown. If they managed to stay inside the main chamber, their odds of survival were only slightly better, as it was rapidly filling up.

"We've got to get back on the gallery!" he yelled to her. "From there, we might be able to find a way out of here!"

Using the table for flotation, they began paddling toward the gallery railing.

"We need to get him off this thing when we get there!" Edna shouted, pointing at McElroy. "Undo the straps on your side."

Fighting to keep from swallowing water and going under, Cole struggled to undo McElroy's bonds. Although the construction boss's eyes opened periodically, he seemed unaware of his surroundings.

Finally, they floated beneath the gallery. The rising waters reduced their headroom rapidly, but they managed to get McElroy off the table and into the water. Instantly, he went under, but bobbed up again. Then their floating table drifted away. At last Cole got a firm grip on the railing.

As Cole and Edna, with their burden, attempted to climb back onto the gallery, they were certain they were going to die. McElroy became a curse, and separately each almost decided to let the surging underwater currents take him. But somehow they managed to carry him to the gallery. There, with McElroy between them, they collapsed.

But then the rapidly rising water forced them to their feet. They struggled to lift McElroy.

"Which way?" Edna gasped.

Cole, draping one of McElroy's arms over his shoulders, looked around. Eurydice had brought him from that direction. Somewhere down there, there had to be a way up to the surface.

All he could do was to point. Edna grabbed McElroy's other arm and they struggled through the water.

"Eurydice!"

The Mistress's voice echoed through the cavern.

"Eurydice, help us!"

The lights in the cavern went out and Edna, Cole and McElroy plunged into a pitch-black hell, with water swirling and continuing to rise.

"Larry?" Edna cried.

All Cole could say was, "Good-bye."

They were still holding on to McElroy when they heard a loud, cracking noise above, and then a blinding light engulfed them.

"Commander! Commander Cole!"

Dazed, they looked up, but could see nothing for an instant. Then ropes were dropped and three Coast Guard frogmen leaped into the water beside them.

"Eurydice!" The Mistress's wail echoed through the darkness.

Another spotlight swung above the flooding cavern. As the frogmen rigged a hoist for McElroy, Cole and Edna looked across the chamber. The spotlight framed the Mistress, who sat in her cart on the gallery opposite them, Homer standing beside her. They were too far away to be rescued before the waters would rise over their heads.

"Jesus H. Christ!" one of the frogmen said when he spied the Mistress and Homer. "What in hell are they made up for?"

"Larry!" Edna screamed. She pointed to the rising waters at the center of the cavern. There Eurydice Vaughn swam against the current toward the only family she had ever known.

Without hesitation, Edna jumped into the water. She vanished below the surface, then came up struggling to swim toward her sister. As Cole and the frogmen watched, she went under again. Then Cole dived in after her.

When McElroy was secured and lifted, the frogmen followed the two police officers into the water. Meanwhile, across the cavern, the waters continued to rise around the Mistress and Homer.

EPILOGUE

S pring came early that year. The park surrounding the Museum had turned a lush green due to unusually warm temperatures, mild weather and a moderate winter. For the next eighteen months, the beach across Lake Shore Drive would remain closed for repairs to the irregular seafloor.

The National Science and Space Museum was open. That past November, for the first time in its long history, the Museum had remained closed for three consecutive days. A press release, issued jointly by the Chicago Police Department and the Museum, with Jack Govich acting as spokesperson, gave a brief explanation of the reasons. The Museum had been endangered by an underground flood of unknown origin. A valiant rescue effort had been carried out by Larry Cole and Edna Gray of the CPD. The rescued: then Museum Curator Eurydice Vaughn, and William McElroy of the McElroy Lakefront Development Corporation.

The press release was vague as to the circumstances of the rescue. Questions were raised by the media as to McElroy's presence there. Govich's response was simply that the construction boss had been located and saved simultaneously by Cole and Gray. Then, with an exit worthy of an American President under fire, Govich adroitly terminated the press conference held in the Museum's rotunda.

A triple homicide involving a well-known movie celebrity in Los Angeles pushed the three-day-old story off the front page and left irate reporters' questions on the floors of their editors' offices. The National Science and Space Museum had again succeeded in keeping its secrets.

On this spring morning, the unmarked black sedan with the buggy-whip antenna pulled into the main parking lot in front of the Museum. As Cole and Blackie got out, uniformed Police Officer Dane McGuire, on duty in the parking lot, approached them. McGuire remembered Cole from that night on Seagull Island that past September.

After exchanging greetings, McGuire told Cole, "Dr. Fleisher and Mr. Gobey are expecting you. They'll be waiting outside the new exhibit."

Cole looked past the officer and up at the gray stone facade of the Museum. He hadn't been back inside since that night five months ago and he had no desire to ever go in there again. However, now duty required it.

A guard at *Glassware from Around the World* Hall stepped back and unlocked a door at the center of the floor-to-ceiling partition.

The area beyond was still under repair. A substantial layer of plaster dust covered every surface. The majority of the glass-cased exhibits were intact. The glass case with the crystal platter as its centerpiece had been damaged when Chicago firemen smashed through it to get to the hidden passageway concealed behind it. The Himalayan bench had been destroyed when Coast Guard rescuers used it to anchor their hoists. The remnants of both had been removed.

Behind the former location of the exhibit case was a large hole in the wall and a lighted staircase leading down. Cole and Blackie crossed to it.

"Wait, Boss," Blackie said as Cole was about to descend. "The guy outside said Fleisher and Gobey were supposed to be here to meet us."

On cue, the sounds of footsteps ascending the staircase carried to the policemen. Rounding a corner of the winding staircase, Winston Fleisher and Jonathan Gobey came into view. Gobey walked with a cane.

"Gentlemen," Dr. Fleisher said with obvious excitement. "Thank you for being so prompt."

"You said it was urgent," Cole said.

"And it is!" Fleisher turned to his companion. "Jonathan, would you show the officers what our workmen discovered?"

"You're not coming with us?" Gobey asked with a raised eyebrow.

"No," the chairman replied nervously. He walked rapidly past Blackie and Cole. "I've got a million things to do before lunch. Nice seeing you gentlemen again." With that, he was gone.

"You must excuse Dr. Fleisher," Gobey said. "He doesn't have a very strong stomach."

They followed Gobey down the staircase. Here the Fire Department had smashed a hole in the wall to get into the underground chamber during the flood. The breech, through which the survivors had been lifted to safety, had been enlarged to accommodate workmen and equipment. To facilitate restoration and repair activities from above, a platform elevator had been installed in the chamber. Gobey ushered Cole and Blackie into it and they descended into the cavern.

It all came back to Cole. The beating at the hands of Eurydice Vaughn, the Mistress and her bizarre experiments, the deformed Homer, how Cole and Edna almost drowned, and finally their rescue.

Now noisy workmen were scattered throughout the underground train station. Construction lights lined the water-stained walls. There was a constant din from the generators serving to pump still-standing water from the lowest level of the station and provide light for the workmen. The flood had shorted out all of the makeshift electrical circuits installed over the years by the Mistress and Eurydice.

The workmen, under Gobey's supervision as acting curator, were restoring the train station to its original state. The Museum was currently negotiating to purchase a couple of nineteenth-century locomotives, along with coal and passenger cars, from a West Coast museum. In a year or two, the *Transportation of Yesteryear* Exhibit would be ready for public viewing. No one ever said that the National Science and Space Museum was an institution that failed to take advantage of opportunities.

The elevator came to rest at the bottom of the station. Admonishing them to watch where they stepped, Gobey led Cole and Blackie onto a series of wooden walkways crisscrossing the station floor. The boards were necessitated by the six-inch accumulation of sand and garbage left behind by the flood.

Hopping along on his cane, Gobey said over his shoulder, "We uncovered this room about an hour ago. It looks to have been constructed originally as some type of storeroom."

They came to a pair of sliding doors set into the wall. Another Museum guard stood outside.

"These gentlemen are from the Chicago Police Department," Gobey said to the guard. "They've come to take a look at what we've found." Nodding solemnly, the guard turned and pulled open the doors.

Inside the room, the gray stone walls were faced with shelves for baggage storage. At first the police officers thought all the shelves were empty. But one was not.

Lying side by side, surrounded by bouquets of wilting flowers, were the Mistress and a black man who bore a startling resemblance to Cole. At last, the Mistress looked peaceful. Her hands, with the lacquered, bright-red nails, were folded across her chest and she wore a simple, old-fashioned black dress with a strand of cultured pearls around her neck.

The man, whose black skin had turned gray, was dressed in a brown, five-button wool suit with a stiff white collar. A dark brown cravat ornamented with a diamond stickpin was at his throat.

His striking resemblance to Cole made the police officer think he was seeing his own corpse.

Cole reached down and touched one of the icy hands. Oddly, neither corpse had an odor of decomposing flesh.

Reading Cole's thoughts, Blackie asked, "What'd they do, Boss, embalm them?"

Cole looked around the otherwise empty room. "This is better than any embalming job I ever heard of. I'd say they'd been mummified."

The Cook County medical examiner's wagon and the Chicago Police Department's mobile crime laboratory van pulled away from the front of the Museum, carrying the perfectly preserved bodies of Katherine Rotheimer and Jim Cross.

"How do you think they got there?" Gobey asked, a slight tremble in his voice.

"I guess," Cole said, "they were entombed."

"You don't think that giant guy who grabbed me before is still alive inside the Museum, do you?" There was panic in the acting curator's voice.

Cole turned to look back at the Museum. For just a brief instant, he had the feeling they were being watched. Still, he tried to reassure Gobey. "I wouldn't worry about Homer, Jonathan. After all, he only comes out on Halloween."

Blackie suppressed a chuckle as he and Cole headed for their squad car.

"Oh, by the way," Gobey called after them. "I forgot to congratulate you," he said to Cole. "I read in the papers that you were promoted to chief of detectives after Govich replaced the other superintendent."

"Thank you," Cole said with a smile. "I'll be in touch."

As he turned around, Cole considered the irony of it all. The civilian superintendent had resigned from his post in Chicago to go to work for the Smithsonian Institution in Washington, D.C. They had made him director of security for Artifacts and Antiquities. E. G. Luckett had retired from his post as director of Public Safety due to health reasons. The political grapevine had it that the mayor had no intention of filling Luckett's old post soon.

On January 3, Seymour Winbush was found dead at his desk in the penthouse at One DeWitt Plaza; he had passed away peacefully from a heart attack. Bill McElroy seemed to have made a complete recovery from his illness. Medical experts at University Hospital, however, where McElroy had been treated back in November, would make no comment. He was reportedly still under study.

Back in the car, Blackie asked, "You want to head over to headquarters?"

Cole glanced at his watch. "Yeah. I'm taking off early. Tonight I'm preparing steak à la Cole for Edna at my place."

* * *

The walls were painted a soft beige; the chairs and sofas were a medium brown, and the lamps, blinds and carpeting a burnt orange. It was a comfortable room. A room to encourage relaxation and peace.

Edna and Eurydice sat in overstuffed chairs six feet apart, facing each other. They were dressed almost identically in white, open-necked blouses, dark skirts and black heels. Eurydice wore a gold teddy-bear-shaped pin over her left breast. Edna wore a heart-shaped, diamond-studded pendant on a gold chain and a small, square-cased gold wristwatch on her left arm. They both wore their hair in a similar fashion. Their builds—as Eurydice had put on a pound or two over the past few months—were the same, and their features were exactly alike, but arranged in a slightly different configuration.

Few were capable of telling them apart without the jewelry. Larry Cole was one. Judy Daniels, after ample study, another. Then there was Dr. Mitchell Vargas, Eurydice's psychiatrist.

The two sisters were seated in one of the patient lounges of the minimum-security wing of the Dillon Psychiatric Treatment Center of University Hospital. Eurydice was a patient there. A prize patient, as she had made tremendous progress since her admission to the maximum-security ward, which was exclusively for criminally violent patients.

Edna was permitted to visit her sister for forty-five minutes three times a week. They had progressed from talking over telephones with a Plexiglas partition between them to sitting quietly together in the lounge. However, despite Eurydice's remarkable progress, the two women were kept under constant surveillance via closed-circuit television cameras.

Dr. Vargas, a dark-haired man with a winning smile, was cautious about the prognosis for his most valuable patient. Eurydice had gotten over her dependence on the unusual, mind-altering substances she had been exposed to for most of her life, and had also conquered her paranoid delusions. But Vargas knew that she was far from cured.

She was perhaps the most intelligent woman the psychiatrist had ever treated. However, that only served to complicate the therapy.

He knew she was smart enough to fool them if they weren't careful. She could also put up formidable physical resistance if given the opportunity.

Eurydice Vaughn, or, as she was listed on the hospital admittance form, "Josie Gray," was the most unusual case of schizophrenia Mitchell Vargas had ever encountered. Kidnapped at the age of four, tormented with chemical, physical and psychological tortures until she became malleable, and then brutally channeled toward a specific goal, she had become the curator of one of the most renowned historical and scientific research facilities in the country, while at the same time serving as a nocturnal assassin of terrifying competence. In Vargas's estimation, a remarkable achievement of mental engineering. But then, people were not machines. What might have worked on a robot, or as his children now called them, "androids," had left the attractive young woman with scars. Very severe psychological scars from which she might never recover.

Still, Dr. Vargas allowed the sister, Edna, to visit with Eurydice. But Vargas would continue to make sure that they were constantly and carefully monitored.

"But don't you see, Edna," Eurydice was saying, "there is really no truly adequate tome in existence that provides clear-cut guidelines on how to maintain a museum that mixes exhibits from the past, present and future with the same skill as we do over at the National Science and Space Museum."

Eurydice was into her lecturing mode. This was a normal occurrence. At least once every time Edna visited, her sister would preach to her authoritatively about one thing or another. At times, these discourses sounded patronizing and insulting.

But Edna was used to this. Usually, during these forty-five-minute visits, Eurydice's moods swung through a whole gamut of emotions. She invariably began with the same snotty traits she'd displayed as museum curator. However, as time passed, she softened and became reflective. When this occurred, Edna would begin encouraging her sister to talk.

"Now the Mistress could run a museum," Eurydice was saying. "Of course she virtually developed National Science and Space from the embryonic stage into what it is today."

Edna leaned toward her. "Tell me about the Mistress."

A sadness dropped over Eurydice, who suddenly looked away. Edna persisted. More softly, she repeated, "Eurydice, tell me about the Mistress."

Eurydice shrugged and sighed. "She was a very brilliant woman. She set up everything down there. The electrical wiring; the monitor system, which enabled her to view anything in the museum she wanted to see; and even the passageways. You see, she was inside all the time they were doing the original construction. When Jim Cross was alive, he helped her, but then . . . things didn't work out between them."

"What happened to him?" Edna asked quietly.

"She never told us, but he's buried down there. Somewhere."

"How did you feel about the Mistress?"

Eurydice looked up at Edna. There was confusion on her face. "What do you mean, how did I feel about her?"

"Did you love her?"

Eurydice shook her head violently.

"Did you hate her?"

Eurydice thought about this for a moment. "No. I didn't hate her. I guess you could say that I respected her." She suddenly became animated. "You know the ghost? The thing Larry saw out on the island?"

"I understand that was you," Edna volunteered.

"It was, but Larry had a gun. Suppose he had shot me?"

Edna didn't understand, but she played along anyway. "Well, that would have been very dangerous."

"Not really," Eurydice said smugly. "The Mistress had it all figured out. You see, it really wasn't me in front of him. I was actually behind him. What he was seeing was a holographic projection, which even seemed to float in the air. When I decided to save him from the Lullaby, I ran toward him. That made it seem like the ghost was rushing him. I pushed him out of the way, but he was stronger than I thought he was and the blade clipped his shoulder."

Edna nodded her understanding. "Why did you save him?"

A shy smile played at the corners of her mouth. "I love him," she admitted.

Edna became uncomfortable, but she forged on. "Eurydice, do you love Larry Cole or the picture of Jim Cross in the Mistress's library?"

She didn't respond right away. Then, "You know Larry made love to me."

Edna nodded slowly. "Do you think Larry loves you?"

She shook her head in the negative again. "He loves you." She pointed at Edna. "I tricked him into thinking I was you."

Now Eurydice was reverting into Josie, the child Katherine Rotheimer had stolen. Even her speech and gestures were becoming childlike. The key, Dr. Vargas had explained to Edna, was to find a place where the two personalities could merge. Vargas didn't know how long this would take.

"Edna?" It was now Josie Gray talking. "Is Larry mad at me for what I did?"

"No, honey. He understands."

"I didn't mean to hurt him or those other people." Her voice trembled.

Edna got up and walked over to place her arms around her sister's shoulders. Josie buried her head in her sister's bosom for a long time and cried—a woman whose mind swung on a pendulum between the maturity of a twenty-eight-year-old and that of a four-year-old child. And as Eurydice wept, she reached up to finger the teddy-bear-shaped pin on her blouse.

Larry Cole was busy in his kitchen preparing dinner. His special repast would consist of tenderly broiled rib eye-steaks with baked potatoes, broccoli with hollandaise sauce and hot buttered rolls, to be preceded by a tossed salad with blue-cheese dressing and a special turtle soup he had purchased from a Loop restaurant. A dessert of cherries jubilee would follow. A light blush wine would be served before and during the meal. Amaretto would be served after dinner. Cole took his time to make sure everything would be just right. Now all he had to do was wait for his guest to appear.

He was placing a romantic music disc in the CD player when he heard Edna's heels clicking on the sidewalk outside. This was the first time she had visited his home. She had refused to come here until after his divorce was final in March. But then, as he turned to go to the door, the smile on his face froze. He stopped. He could still hear the staccato clicking of her heels, which seemed to develop a resounding echo the closer she came. It was exactly like the night Eurydice . . .

He reached for the knob and again halted. He looked through the Judas window. She had stopped outside and was reaching for the door bell. Her face was in shadow.

As the chimes rang through the house, he flicked the switch to turn on the porch light. Nothing happened. Probably the bulb was burned out, he assured himself as he opened the door.

Edna walked into the house and kissed him.

He came out of the kitchen with two glasses of wine and stopped dead in his tracks.

Edna had removed her jacket, gun belt and shoes. She was sitting on the couch with her legs folded beneath her in the exact same pose as Eurydice on that long-ago night.

"What's the matter, Larry?" she asked with a confused frown.

He laughed. "Nothing. I thought I'd forgotten the Amaretto, but it's right there." He pointed at a tray on the table behind her.

She turned around to look. "So it is."

Dinner went off without a hitch. They had returned to the living room and were seated on the couch with their snifters when she asked, "Larry, are you mad at me?"

The words were the exact ones Eurydice had used that night.

"What's the matter? You look as if you've just seen a ghost!" she said, reaching for him.

He caught himself before he pulled away from her touch. This was crazy! he thought. Eurydice Vaughn was in the hospital. Although cleared of all criminal charges because of the bizarre influence of Katherine Rotheimer, Josie Gray would be incarcerated for a long time to come. This was Edna Gray here with him now. His Edna.

"I'm sorry, honey," he said awkwardly. "I guess I'm having some kind of weird flashback."

"You've been working much too hard," she scolded. "You need to relax. That's my department."

As he watched, she reached up to adjust the gold pin in the shape of a teddy bear, which was pinned over her left breast.

"Edna, where did you get that?"

She smiled at him. "I've had it since I was a little girl, Larry."